A NOTE FROM LEXXIE

The Tasmanian tiger, or *thylacine*, was a beautiful carnivorous marsupial living in Australia over five millennia ago. It was similar in appearance to a large dog and earned its name thanks to its sandy yellow-brown fur and distinct fifteen to twenty black stripes across its back from shoulder to tail.

While the thylacine was almost nonexistent on the mainland of the country, by the time of European colonisation, it did live in large numbers on the small island state of Tasmania. However, the Tasmanian tiger was deemed a threat to sheep and chicken farmers—an unlikely scenario—and a large bounty was placed on its head. As a sad consequence, the thylacine was hunted to extinction, and a beautiful creature was lost to the world forever.

The last thylacine died in a Tasmanian zoo in September, 1936, alone and pacing its concrete and metal cage, no doubt longing for its freedom.

There have been numerous unconfirmed sightings of Tasmanian tigers in Tasmania to this day. However, most believe these sightings are fake or attempts to gain personal notoriety. The thylacine is still considered extinct by all official agencies and government bodies.

Of course, official agencies and government bodies don't know everything...

SAVAGE
TRANSFORMATION
SAVAGE AUSTRALIS, BOOK 2

LEXXIE
COUPER

The characters and events portrayed in this book are fictitious. Any similarity to real persons, living or dead, is purely coincidental and not intended by the author.

Savage Transformation
Copyright © 2020 by Lexxie Couper
Editing by Heidi Shoham

DEDICATION

For my daughters, my little Australian animals.

And my editor, Heidi—took me forever, but I finally did it. Thank you for being wonderfully patient and wonderfully wonderful.

PROLOGUE

New York, New York.
Four months ago.

The woman stared at Marshall Rourke, her expression both guarded and menacing. *Don't try it,* her clear amber eyes said. *Don't even think about it.* What "it" was, Marshall didn't know, but he'd bet his left testicle it'd be fun finding out. Fun and dangerous. Probably painful too. A grin pulled at the corner of his mouth. He didn't mind danger. And when it came down to it, a little bit of pain wasn't too bad either. A certain type of pain, that was.

He studied the still image on his laptop, his grin stretching wider. This one would bite. Of that, he had little doubt. In both the metaphorical and literal sense of the word. Frozen in millions of vivid coloured pixels on his computer's screen, the woman stared back at him, those striking light brown eyes of hers sharp and piercing despite the fuzziness of the photograph and the distance from which it was taken.

She stood in a busy city street, surrounded by pedestrians dressed in an array of business suits, jeans and short summer dresses. She could be standing in any big city in the world, but the short note accompanying the image told him she was in Sydney, Australia.

Marshall raised his eyebrows. That was not where he expected her to be.

He ran a slow inspection over the distance-blurred image, noting the confident straightness of her shoulders, the slim but athletic frame, the confident way she held the Glock 9mm in her hand.

She wouldn't be easy to capture. He didn't need to read the short dossier attached to know that.

He dragged his cursor over the image, zooming in on her face. Something about her eyes intrigued him. They were intelligent, almost arrogant, but somehow haunted as well. Like she'd witnessed events more than one lone female should, and had made her judgment.

He thought of the Glock, held so loosely in her long, slender fingers, of the menacing expression on her face. Of the coiled tension in her slim frame. What type of judgment had she cast to cause her to become what she let the world see?

Flicking his gaze to the printout beside his laptop, he scanned the dossier he'd already committed to memory. Family. Foster family she no longer had contact with. Relationships. None of any significance. There was one close girlfriend living in the small island state of Tasmania and one ex-lover living on the opposite side of Australia in Perth, but that was it. There was no one she was close to in Sydney. No real weakness to exploit.

Marshall rubbed his jaw, a distant part of his mind noting the stubble there. He'd have to shave before the hunt began, otherwise he'd look like an animal by the time it was done.

The absurdity of the thought struck him and he chuckled, returning his attention to his laptop's screen and the woman on it.

How long would it take for Einar to hunt her down?

Marshall narrowed his eyes. It would be fast. The bastard

never wasted time when hunting prey. The question was, would Marshall be able to find her faster?

He let his gaze move over her, noting the subtle feminine curves beneath the utilitarian suit, the glossy softness of her chestnut-brown hair, the fullness of her bottom lip. What would that lip feel like against his own? Between his teeth?

Something tightened in the pit of his gut and he scowled. He had to stay focused on the task, no matter how appealing her petite little package. Scowl growing deeper, he closed his laptop and stood, picking up his own Glock as he crossed his private suite to stare out the large window overlooking Central Park West. He knew what she looked like and he knew where she was. That was all he needed. Now he just had to get to her.

First.

CHAPTER ONE

L aunceston, Tasmania. *The bottom of Australia.*
    Sydney Detective, Jackie Huddart stood motionless in the swarming, laughing, shouting, jostling airport-terminal crowd and cursed her best friend. She wished she had her gun. Not that she wanted to shoot someone, although the creep with the wandering hands and bad body odor walking behind her as she'd disembarked from the plane would have been her first choice. No, she wanted her gun because it kept her temper under control. And right at this very moment, her temper was well and truly on its way to snapping. Why the hell had she let Delanie organise her flight home? Delanie couldn't organise a booze-up in a brewery.

Maybe your bad temper has nothing to do with Del? Maybe what you really wanted to do was stay in Sydney and track down who killed Detective Vischka?

A sudden image of the murdered detective flashed through Jackie's head, followed just as quickly by an image of Vischka's hulking bear of a partner, Detective Peter Thomas.

She released a sigh and hitched her bag higher up her shoulder. Detective Peter Thomas would find Vischka's killer, of that Jackie had no doubt. Not just because that's what the homicide detective did—his arrest rate was phenomenal—but because he and Vischka had been more than just partners on the force. When you killed a cop's lover, you could start counting down your days.

Besides, if she started poking her nose around in a homicide case, she'd have to start dodging questions she wasn't willing to answer.

Fixing her sights on the closest car rental kiosk, she began shoving her five-foot-three, one-hundred-and-fourteen-pound, wringing-wet frame through the horde of arriving and departing passengers and their grinning, hugging associates. She'd hire a compact and get out of Dodge, or in this case, Launceston, immediately. She didn't have anything against the city, but when she'd agreed to come home—home. Such a dangerous concept—she hadn't expected to be stood-up by her best friend.

Casting a quick look around the busy airport terminal, she shook her head. God alone knew where Delanie was. Probably buying another pair of shoes. Or getting her bikini line waxed. The life of a test consumer/shopper was not, if anything, boring.

Finally reaching the rental desk, Jackie crossed her arms on the counter and blew at her fringe. "I'll take whatever you have that's cheap and will get me to Pyengana without breaking down."

The clerk raised her overly plucked eyebrows. "Pyengana? Why would anyone want to go to Pyengana?"

Jackie ground her teeth. Even in Tasmania the small coastal town of three hundred souls was derided. It was known in the state for its historic cheese factory. It was known on the mainland for one thing only: the last possible sighting of the very extinct thylacine. The Tasmanian tiger, an animal of ancient beauty and mystery, now just a symbol of Australia's barbaric past.

As if the clerk read Jackie's mind, she pursed her lips in a condescending smirk. "Going hunting, are we?"

Jackie bit back a low growl. Damn. It was a good thing she didn't have her gun. "No," she stated calmly. "Going home actually. To a funeral."

Bright red heat flooded the clerk's face. She stared at Jackie, mouth opening and closing like a drowning fish for a few moments, before she dropped her head and focused her entire attention on her computer terminal. "I have a Mazda convertible that I can do for the same fee as a compact. GPS unit and premium insurance free of charge." She darted Jackie a quick, furtive look. "Special offer today."

Jackie smiled, letting the woman see her teeth. "That would be lovely, thank you."

It would take an hour and forty minutes to drive to Pyengana from here. One hour and forty minutes through some of the most lush and beautiful terrain on the planet. As tempting as it was however, she couldn't risk putting the top down. That level of concentrated sensory exposure would call to the very spirit within her. The one she'd spent the last twenty years trying to suppress. She couldn't risk that. It was too dangerous. Too—

"Heya, Huddart!" A loud but somehow husky voice called behind her. "What the bloody hell are you doing renting a car?"

Jackie chuckled. Rolling her eyes, she turned away from the clerk to watch a tall, willowy redhead weave her way through the crowd still amassed in the airport terminal. Well, weave probably wasn't the correct word. The crowd seemed to melt away from the redhead's path, the men gazing at her as she passed by, the women scanning her five-foot-nine frame for any sign of cellulite the snug denim short shorts and an even snugger white T-shirt she wore may reveal. Of which, there was none. Delanie McKenzie was every inch perfect.

She was also every inch the perfect pain in the arse, and

Jackie's best friend since they were little girls with scraped knees and snotty noses.

"What the bloody hell am I doing renting a car?" Jackie cocked an eyebrow at her friend and folded her arms across her chest. "Maybe it has something to do with the fact my ride left me in the lurch."

Delanie laughed, the sound full and throaty and completely contagious. "Not in the lurch. I'm here, aren't I?"

Jackie hitched her bag farther up her shoulder and gave her friend a pointed look before going up onto tip-toe to kiss her cheek. "Two hours late."

Delanie kissed her cheek back before straightening. "And you expected differently?"

With a snort, Jackie shook her head. "I should have known better."

Delanie grinned, her wide mouth stretching wider to reveal white, perfectly even teeth. "Yes, you should have. But I'm here now. Ready to hit the road?"

"Only if I'm driving."

Delanie laughed. "Of course you're driving. I've just had my nails done and I so very much miss your blatant disregard of the posted speed limit."

Jackie laughed. "I do not speed."

Delanie chortled. "*No.* Of course not. That's why you came first in your driving skills component at the police academy, correct?" She nodded at the clerk behind Jackie. "Sorry. We won't be needing you." Giving Jackie a quick grin, she threaded her bag over her shoulder. "I'll go get the car. Grab us a latte each from the cafe, will you? I need a caffeine hit before we get on the road."

She turned on her heel and made her way back into the fray, once again parting the crowd like Moses parting the Red Sea. Jackie watched her go for a while, realizing how much she'd missed her friend since moving to Sydney. Delanie was a perfect example of ADD, and so extroverted she made a puppy

Fox Terrier look calm, but she was honest and loyal and knew all of Jackie's secrets. All of them.

Which made Delanie McKenzie the only living human in Australia to know exactly what Jackie really was.

Turning back to the clerk, Jackie gave her a cool smile. "Thank you for the 'special offer'."

The woman gave her a wobbly smile in return, her cheeks still flushed with embarrassed consternation. "I'm very so—"

"That's quite okay," Jackie cut her short.

With a sympathetic smile, she turned away from the counter and headed for the airport terminal's cafe. One hour and forty minutes of winding roads and Delanie McKenzie. She better order a double expresso instead. Otherwise she'd have no hope of keeping up.

The waiting line extended beyond the store's entry and Jackie bit back a curse. She hated standing in line. Especially for coffee in cardboard.

Suppressing an irritated growl, she scanned the crowd around her. Eighty percent of it was tourists—bright-eyed and eager at the beginning of their holidays. Shoulders still straight, suitcases and backpacks packed neatly, lacking the tell-tale bumps and bulges of luggage packed at the end of a trip, parents still patient with young children, teenagers still civil to their elders. In amongst them all, like blemishes of reality, stood the odd local, regarding the holidaymakers with wry amusement. Locals whose attire was suited to the cool evening awaiting them outside.

Jackie chuckled softly to herself. The rest of the country tended to forget Tasmania was not hot, hotter, hottest all year round, let alone international visitors. The summer days may be warm, but the nights still required a light jacket.

Unless you were Delanie McKenzie, of course. To this day, Jackie had never seen her best friend in anything more concealing than a long-sleeve T-shirt and jeans.

Thinking of Del turned Jackie's thoughts back to the coffee

line and her position in it. Damn it. She was no closer. Delanie would be sitting in the waiting bay, engine gunning before she even made it to the counter at this rate.

She huffed into her fringe, turning her gaze back to the crowd. She was on extended leave from work, called home to attend her foster father's funeral, but that didn't mean her cop's instincts went on leave.

Nor her.

A tall man with shortly cropped blonde hair near check-in caught her attention, killing the unwanted thought. He was looking at her.

The second Jackie's eyes made contact with his he looked away.

Jackie frowned, studying his profile. *Are you sure you're not imagining it?*

Her frowned deepened. Maybe he was just a typical bloke? See a woman alone in the crowd, check her out. After all, she wasn't that uneasy on the eye. In a short, look-at-me-sideways-and-I'll-kick-your-arse kind of way.

She sighed and turned back to the line. It had been too long since she'd had any kind of intimacy with anyone apart from her hand, and to make matters worse, she suspected she was coming on heat.

"What would you like?"

Jackie started, staring at the barely pubescent teenager looking at her with wary expectation from behind the counter. Heat flooded her cheeks. "Latte. Large. Two sugars. Double espresso. Short."

She spat the order out like bullets, for some reason on edge. Twisting at the waist, she searched the crowd behind her for the blonde man, but there was no sign of him.

What did you expect?

Scowling, she turned back to the counter. Back in her home state for two hours and she was already jumping at shadows.

This is why you moved to Sydney, you know. Less history to rattle your cage. Less skeletons in the proverbial closet.

True, but since Declan O'Connell had killed Nathan Epoc, Sydney had more weres to take into account.

Yes, but how many werewolves can detect a thylacine? How many werewolves even know what a thylacine is?

Apart from Declan himself, none that Jackie knew of. Well, Yolanda Vischka, but the murdered detective wasn't talking to anyone anymore.

Picking up the coffees from the end counter, Jackie made her way to the terminal's exit, weaving through the crowd with a scowl.

It was a mistake coming back. Even with Delanie's infectious craziness, she should have stayed away. The moment she saw her dead foster father in the ground she was on the plane and headed back to Sydney. It was safer that way.

Forty minutes later, her espresso long gone and Delanie's latte now ice cold, Jackie pulled her mobile phone from her hip pocket—again—and flipped it open.

She was worried.

More than worried.

Del hadn't come back from getting the car and her mobile was going immediately to her message bank. Still.

Growling silently, Jackie snapped her phone shut.

Her cop instincts were itching.

Just your cop instincts, Jackie? What about your—

She cut the thought dead. She had suppressed those instincts for many, many years. She didn't need the instincts of an animal to tell her now something wasn't right.

"Jesus, Delanie," she muttered, throwing the cold latte into the rubbish bin. "What the hell is going on?"

She wriggled her fingers, a nervous tick she'd thought she'd gained control of when she was a teenager. The urge to shift, to transform into her true form had never been stronger. Delanie's scent would be much easier to follow in her other form. She'd be able to track her trail without any problems, hopefully finding her friend well and safe and chatting up some hunky bloke in complete ignorance of how much time had passed since she'd told Jackie to get them both a coffee.

That's not going to happen, Jackie, and you know it.

A ripple shivered up her spine and her blood grew thin. The transformation called her animal closer to the surface than it'd been since she was twenty-one.

Find her. Track her. Hunt her.

Jackie sucked in a sharp breath, grinding her teeth and digging her nails into her palms. She couldn't change. She wouldn't. She wasn't that person anymore. She'd denied that part of her existence over a decade ago and she wouldn't let it return.

But what about Delanie? What if she's in trouble?

"I'm a bloody cop, for fuck's sake," Jackie stormed back into the terminal, "I don't need to change into a bloody Tasmanian tiger to find a missing person."

Besides, the last time she'd shifted she'd almost been captured on film, and she couldn't risk that again, even for Delanie. The Tasmanian tiger was considered extinct to the world, and she needed to keep that misconception as it was. Stripping off her clothes, shifting in an airport toilet cubicle and sprinting through the crowd on all fours was not the way to stay out of the public eye.

Wishing more than ever she had her gun, Jackie approached the information desk, giving the man behind it a worried, harried look. She'd spoken to him three times in the last sixty minutes and she could tell he was beginning to tire of her. "She still hasn't turned up," she said, hoping he saw the worry in her eyes. "Can you make the announcement again, please?"

With a disdainful sigh, the man—David Lee, according to the name badge pinned to his shirt—snatched a mic from the desk before him and punched a button. "If Delanie McKenzie is in the terminal—" his voice boomed around the cavernous space, each word amplifying his irritation, "—will she please come to the information desk. Your friend is waiting for you."

He removed his finger from the mic with a pointed flick and fixed Jackie with a patronizing look.

"Drop the attitude, David," she snarled, before she could stop herself. "Or I'll reach over this counter and give you something to have an attitude about."

He blinked, a sudden flash of startled apprehension destroying the condescending expression on his face. "S-sorry, ma'am."

Jackie suppressed a sharp sigh. She felt her canines lengthen in her gums, felt her blood run thin and hot again. Fuck. This was why she never came home anymore. Being too close to her natural environment lessened her control of the animal in her blood. Even the air in Tasmania was dangerous to her.

"Damnit, Del." She forced her hands into fists to stop her fingers from wiggling and searched the faces in the crowd for her best friend's. "Where are you?"

Twenty minutes later, and Delanie still hadn't appeared. The information-desk attendant gave Jackie a nervous smile. "I suppose you want me to page her again?"

Jackie scowled at him. "No. But thank you for your concern." Hitching her bag higher onto her shoulder, she pushed her way through the thinning crowd, heading for the exit. She didn't know what was going on, but she knew she needed to try and find Delanie's scent. If nothing else, to see if her best friend made it to her car.

The automatic doors parted as she approached them, the cool crisp air of a typical Tasmania summer assaulting her before she crossed the threshold. Her inner animal growled and flexed, hungry for release. Jackie shoved the powerful urge aside, focusing instead on the air. She pulled in a deep breath as she stepped outside the terminal onto the sidewalk, hunting for Delanie's scent. Her senses weren't as strong while in human form, but they were still hyper enough to hopefully find a trace of her friend.

She filled her lungs with air, tasting the breath as it streamed past her olfactory nerves. Melaleuca, eucalypt, gasoline, tar, spent cigarette butts, rotting refuse from a nearby rubbish bin, bad BO still lingering on her clothes from her annoying companion in the terminal, bird shit baking on the row of rental cars to her left and—

"Sorry!" Delanie's cry came from behind, full with apologetic mirth. "Sorry!"

Jackie spun, glaring at her best friend running toward her across the car park. "What have you been doing? I was just about to—"

What? Shift?

"I've locked the keys in the car." Delanie pulled an embarrassed face, coming to a halt before Jackie. "And I tried to find someone to help me get them out." She grinned. Sheepishly. "Obviously, I didn't."

Jackie raised her eyebrows, doing everything she could to stay calm. The soft tingle in her belly told her just how close she'd come to transforming. She hadn't been that close for many, many years.

That's it. You need to get out of here ASAP.

"How could you lock your keys in your car? Don't tell me you still drive Bernie?"

Delanie's sheepish grin turned to one of pride. "Okay, I won't. Just close your eyes when you sit in him and pretend you're in a Ferrari."

Jackie rolled her eyes. "Okay, a Ferrari it is. Although I can't imagine you'd lock your keys in a Ferrari."

Delanie grinned wider. "Probably not, but where's the romance in a Ferrari? At least Bernie has history."

With a laugh, Jackie hitched her bag farther up her shoulder. "A history is right. In and out of the mechanics more time than on the road. I'm convinced the only reason you keep him is so you have a legitimate excuse for seeing that mechanic you rave on about."

"Mmm, Shaun Whitmore. Now there's a six-pack I could lap up."

"That's it." Jackie shook her head. "I'm going back to the rental desk. Maybe I can get that convertible after all."

"No, no, no." Delanie draped her arm around Jackie's shoulder. "We're good. I've called roadside service. They'll be here in ten minutes or so."

"Called? With what? I've been ringing your phone for the last forty minutes."

A pink tinge painted Delanie's cheeks. "Ummm, my phone's flat."

Jackie pressed her hand to her face. "Damn, I'd forgotten what it's like."

"What what's like?"

"Being your best friend."

Delanie grinned. "It's wonderful, isn't it?"

A warm glow flooded through Jackie and she smiled. It was wonderful. Frustrating, irritating and down-right exasperating, but wonderful as well. Delanie reminded her to laugh. Delanie reminded her there was goodness in the world. Delanie reminded her she had someone real to turn to. That she wasn't alone in her secret.

"Anyways, enough of this idle chit-chat." Her best friend tugged her into a rough hug. "Let's get our sexy, desirable arses back to Bernie so we can ogle the roadside assistance's butt."

Jackie laughed and shook her head. And then stopped. The tall, blonde man from the terminal stood beside a low, black Audi about ten yards to her left. Looking at her.

She blinked, and in the space it took for her eyelids to open, he dropped into the sports car and slammed the door.

Jackie frowned, staring at the vehicle as its engine kicked over.

"Jackie?"

The windows were dark. Too dark for her to make out the man behind the wheel, but she could feel his gaze on her. Her nipples pinched tight.

"Jack? What's up?"

The Audi sat motionless in the car space, engine idling like a sleeping beast. Jackie studied it, a tingle growing in the pit of her belly. Current model S5. Tasmanian registration plates RRF 042. Small sticker on the top right corner of the windshield: Luxury Rentals.

"Earth to Jackie. Come in Jackie."

With a soft growl of its engine, the car moved, rolling forward before turning right and smoothly purring away from her.

"What's up?"

She tuned out Delanie's voice. Her throat felt tight. Twice in the space of one hour?

Now you're being paranoid, Jackie. It's an airport. People come and go all the time.

"Jack?"

True. But do they move as quick as this guy?

Do their eyes seem to bury into you, even from a distance? And are they as sexy?

The last thought turned Jackie's frown into a scowl and she clenched her fists. Damn it. If she'd known she was coming on heat she never would have come back, regardless of her foster father's funeral. Marsupials didn't have mating cycles but, thanks to the combination of her dual existence, whenever she drew close to her human menstrual cycle, the urge to mate grew to a fever pitch. She'd suppressed that urge for the last eighteen years; the big-city air and taste of Sydney acted like an antidote to her primal needs. Being in her home environment however, with its sweet unpolluted air, its rich, fertile soil…

She stared at the taillights of the distant Audi and her sex constricted.

Bad timing. Damn it, bad timing.

"Jacqueline Huddart, if you don't tell me what's going on this very second, I'm calling animal control."

The worry in Delanie's sardonic statement snapped Jackie's stare from the Audi. She turned to her friend, forcing down the unexpected surge of animal agitation. "I'm sorry, Del." She smiled, the action feeling brittle. "I'm a bit off at the moment."

Delanie fixed her with an intent look. "I get that. I didn't expect coming back to be easy."

Jackie's wry chuckle caught her by surprise. "Easy is not the word I'd go for right now, no."

With another closer inspection, Delanie nodded her head. "Well then, let's get this farce of a funeral over and done with then, shall we. I want to make your brief time home enjoyable. Maybe I can find a ball and we can play fetch."

Jackie gave her a sideways glare, her lips twitching into a grin. "Maybe I can bite you on the butt and ruin that perfect backside of yours."

Delanie laughed. "Ooh, now that would be interesting in a kinky, paranormal male-fantasy kinda way." She began walking, smiling broadly even as she squeezed Jackie closer to her side in a tight embrace, as if she worried Jackie was going to run off.

A deep, ancient longing stirred in Jackie's gut at the thought of running away.

Run off, run wild, run free, run, run, run.

Jackie slid her arm around her best friend's waist, shutting the enticing, dangerous notion down. Damn, she wished she had her gun.

The hunter studied the two women walking through the car park—one tall and animated, one petite and radiating controlled savagery. Jacqueline Huddart. A creature of forgotten myth. A creature of primordial magnificence and ancient spirituality.

A shape-shifting thylacine. Part-human, part-Tasmanian tiger.

And he'd found her.

A small thrill shot through him, clenching a cold fist in his chest. To discover a living Tasmanian tiger in itself was something considered impossible. Hunted to extinction in the nineteen thirties, the animal now only existed in the dreams of scientists deluded enough to believe they could resurrect the species through DNA cloning.

To discover the existence of a shape-shifting thylacine...

The thrill in his chest spread to the pit of his belly, his groin.

The moment he'd learnt of her existence, he'd flown to Australia. He'd hunted more deadly game before, he'd tracked more unpredictable, but Jacqueline Huddart had proved the most difficult to find.

With no name for his quarry, he'd only had a location to start with, a last known sighting: Pyengana, a tiny town with barely more than one hundred and twenty people living there.

Moving about the small town unnoticed was not hard. Trying to decipher whom of the one-twenty was his target proved a bit trickier. Two months spent tracking each one, following their every move, studying their behaviour, their garbage, their interaction with the other townsfolk finally revealed what he'd begun to suspect on his second day of observation. The shifter was not there.

Another month and he had located the whereabouts of every person once living in Pyengana. A month after that, he narrowed his target down to two: a female in Far North Queensland and Jacqueline Huddart.

All it had taken was one precise act of violence—the brutal murder of a werewolf bitch in Sydney—to draw her out. He'd found her.

And then she left Sydney.

Just as he was about to begin the true hunt.

Which brought him back here. Tasmania. An island state at the bottom of a country older than time.

Shifting his weight slightly, he watched her move across the bitumen, the deepening shadows of dusk folding around her.

She moved with animalistic grace. Fluid. Smooth.

He felt himself smile. It was a thing of perverse beauty to observe. He doubted any man would not find her walk hypnotic. A steady, purposeful stride. Hips swaying, spine straight, shoulders square. An ancient energy radiated from her. He could feel it even from this distance, some fifty-five yards away. Like the trapped fires of a dormant volcano simmered through her veins.

She would not succumb easily.

Nor would she be easy prey. That was evident in the way she surveyed everything around her. To a casual observer, she would appear calm and composed and confident. To a trained eye however, an eye specializing in the behaviour of such creatures, Jacqueline Huddart was in a constant state of heightened anticipation. Alert. Ready.

Just the way Daeved Einar wanted his quarry to be.

He smiled, sliding his stare over the shifter's petite form.

"So begins the hunt."

CHAPTER TWO

Jackie stood motionless, watching the coffin lower into the ground. She knew she should feel something. She knew she should shed at least one tear, feel a lump in her throat, anything, but she didn't. Her foster father had meant little to her besides a hard fist, a swift kick and a contemptuous meal twice a day.

She looked at the spray of peace lilies adorning the coffin's deeply polished lid, a white blanket of beauty hiding the lies and violence. If only those sobbing around her knew the truth.

About what? Richard Smith? Do you really think they'd care? Or do you mean the truth about you? About why you became a child of the state? About why you stayed one?

Removing her gaze from the wooden box, she studied the handful of mourners standing beside the open grave. Dairy farmers and cheese makers. All dressed in their rarely worn Sunday bests, suits pulled from the back of the cupboard, moth balls withdrawn from pockets, replaced with handkerchiefs and eulogies printed at the Photo-Copi-To-Go in nearby St. Helens. All standing there with red-rimmed eyes, not wanting to look at her, not wanting to see the lack of misery in her face.

She sighed, wriggling her fingers by her side. The black,

tailored trousers and shirt she wore prickled her skin, the material of each sucking up the sun's rays like a thirsty child, turning her clothes into a pliable oven she longed to be rid of.

God, she didn't want to be here.

A soft hand threaded through her fingers and she turned to look at Delanie.

You're growling, her best friend mouthed.

The silent words stabbed into Jackie's chest and she sucked in a hiss, earning more than one furtive glance from those beside the grave.

She looked back at the rectangle hole on the ground, before studying the artificial grass spread out around its edges. Growling?

Run, run, run wild, free run, run.

The latent urge to run away snaked through her, an insistent itch she wished she could scratch. The delicate scent of melaleuca threaded through her breath, the damp earthiness of freshly turned soil teasing her taste buds, feeding the primitive longing to transform. Jackie closed her eyes, her pulse rapid.

Shift, run, hunt, kill, mate.

Wild impulses assaulted her. Potent and all too compelling. Her stomach knotted. Her chest tightened. She felt her muscles begin to tingle. A blistering cold heat—fire on ice—rushed over her flesh.

God, no!

She turned away from her foster father's grave. "I have to go," she muttered. The words sounded strange. Her mouth felt full, like her tongue was battling too many teeth. Wicked, sharp teeth designed with one purpose only, to kill. Teeth evolved to tear and rip and rend raw flesh asunder.

"What?" Delanie's surprised whisper scratched at Jackie's senses, but she ignored it. She had to get away. Before she lost control of her animal.

She pushed through the silent mourners, head down, shoulders bunched. The sweet Pyengana air streamed into her nostrils, fire to dry tinder. Another tingle rippled through her muscles and she bit back a curse.

Not a curse, Jack. A growl.

"Damn it."

The sound of disgusted grumblings rumbled behind her, like thunder on distant clouds, her foster father's friends following her rapid escape with disapproving glares. She could feel their contempt stabbing into her back. Her skin prickled.

Run, shift, kill, mate.

"No!"

She shouted the denial, breaking into a sprint. The heels of her shoes sank into the soft soil, releasing the rich scent of earth to the air. It threaded into her breath and a surge of icy heat blossomed in her belly. The transformation was beginning. She couldn't stop it.

Oh, God, no. No, no, no, no, no, no.

She vaulted a headstone, stare locked on the dense grove of melaleuca and eucalypts edging the cemetery. Cover. Concealment.

Territory.

Her palms itched. Her pulse roared. She ran, wind-whipped hair tugging at her temples, beads of sweat popping out on her forehead. She ran.

Until she saw the man from the airport.

Her feet stumbled beneath her. She scrambled for balance, her gaze locked on his tall, lean frame.

He stood under a large snow gum on the cemetery's perimeter, the ancient tree's branches shrouding him in deep shadows, muting the golden streaks in his short hair, turning the dark sunglasses on his face to a black mask. Yet even from this distance, she felt his stare drilling into her. Hard. Unrelenting.

Inescapable.

Exciting.

Her sex constricted and she pulled in a sharp breath, forcing her feet to stop. What did she do?

Run, mate, fuck.

Jackie clenched her jaw, shutting out the primitive suggestion. She wriggled her fingers, her hand moving toward her torso before she realized she was reaching for her gun.

Why? Are you going to shoot him, or fuck him?

Her forehead pulled into a scowl. Neither.

Fixing him with a steady stare, she began to walk in his direction, ignoring the pulse between her thighs and the hammer in her chest. Just a question. That's all she wanted to ask. Just one question: who are you?

She quickened her pace, feeling his gaze move over her body, a slow inspection that turned the beat in her sex to a damp tightness.

One question, Jackie. Just one.

Will you fuck me?

"Jack?"

Delanie's shout—high and stretched with worry—snapped at her focus. She blinked, shooting her best friend an impatient frown over her shoulder.

Not now, Del. Later. Later. After I've run. After I've mated. After I've—

Jackie froze, her throat squeezing shut at the wild notion thrumming through her consciousness. She swallowed. *God, what am I doing?* A tingle racing up her spine, she turned back to the man.

Gone.

Rooted to the spot, she searched the tree line, her mouth dry, her sex heavy.

Nothing. Just ancient eucalypts, blossom-heavy wattle and callistemons.

Jackie reached to snatch her gun from its holster before she remembered it wasn't there. What the hell was going on?

"Are you okay?"

Delanie's husky, breathless question made Jackie start. She jerked her stare from the shadows beneath the snow gum up to her friend's face. Jesus, what had she been about to do?

"Jack? Are you okay? What's up?"

Jackie studied the tree line, searching for any hint of the man. She pulled in a deep breath, straining to detect an unusual scent.

"Jack?" Delanie's voice grew taut with worry. "This is the second time you've done this to me since coming home. Answer me. Are you okay?"

Nothing. It was as if the man never existed.

Are you sure he did? Three times in the last twenty-four hours? And seriously, in Pyengana?

She released a sigh, turning back to the hovering Delanie. "I'm okay, Del, honest." She gave her a small smile. "Just having difficulty keeping my calm."

Delanie raised her exquisitely shaped eyebrows. "Yeah, I'd say sprinting away from an open grave and jumping over a gravestone constitutes as not keeping your calm. You know you almost knocked over Mr. Carmichael."

Jackie pulled a face, dragging her fingers through her hair. "Did I?"

"This is not like you, Jack. Even when you were living here you were the epitome of control." Delanie's forehead puckered into a frown. "Is there something you want to tell me?"

I'm about to go into heat, I keep seeing a mystery man who may or may not be real and something about him makes me horny?

Jackie shook her head. "No."

Delanie didn't look convinced. "Hmm."

"I'm fine. Honest." Jackie smiled, just to show how fine she was. The action felt forced. She wasn't fine. She was on edge. Not just because she was home, not just because she felt her inner animal clawing its way to freedom, not just because of her now-you-see-me-now-you-don't, maybe-maybe-not stalker, but because things felt...wrong. Like the way the air thrummed just before an electrical storm—angry and charged with sleeping violence.

The same uneasy sensation had twisted through her the second she'd learnt of Detective Yolanda Vischka's brutal murder. Who was capable of murdering a werewolf? Especially one as old as Vischka? One as unassailable? Or more to the point, who was capable of hacking a werewolf to pieces until little remained but a few body parts?

Swallowing the sudden bile in her throat, Jackie smiled at her friend again. "I'm fine." She curled her arm through Delanie's. "Except I need coffee."

"You need to say hello to your mother."

The smoke-course voice behind her turned the bile in Jackie's throat hot. She turned, fixing her foster mother with a flat stare. "I would, if she was alive."

Rhonda Smith didn't react to the blunt statement. She stood in the late afternoon sunshine, hair the colour of rust, lips and nails shining with equally abrasive colour. Blue eyes flinty and cold, she ran a slow look over Jackie. "I am surprised you deigned it necessary to come back." She pulled a cigarette from her handbag, placed it between her lips and lit it with a dime-store lighter. "Or are you here to take pleasure in my grief?"

Jackie drew a deep breath in through her nostrils. "I'm not here to fight, Rhonda. I came, now I'm going. My sympathies for your loss."

Rhonda laughed, the sound low and humourless. "Your sympathies? I half expected you to break into song and dance beside Richard's grave."

"Mrs. Smith," Delanie began, sliding her arm around Jackie's waist.

A small smile pulled at the corners of Jackie's mouth. Just like Del to feel she needed to protect her.

"I see you're still the upstart little know-it-all you were as a child, Delanie McKenzie," Rhonda snapped, flicking Delanie a savage look through the rising tendril of smoke leaking from her mouth. "Things haven't changed much. Shut up. This is not your concern."

"You're right, Rhonda." Jackie lifted her chin. "Things don't change. You're still the same rude, bitter woman you were when I was a teenager." She turned away from her foster mother, her gaze falling to the ancient snow gum on the cemetery's perimeter. "The funeral is over. There's no reason for me to be in Pyengana."

"There was no reason for you to come back," Rhonda snarled. "We were done with you the day the government stopped paying us the foster-family allowance."

Jackie closed her eyes, her palm itching for her gun.

No, it wasn't her gun her skin itched for. It was the shift. The transformation. The carnal urge to sink teeth, long and sharp, into Rhonda's neck and tear it wide. Tear it open until the woman's blood flowed, staining the grass around her still, lifeless corpse the colour of her hair. Tainting the sweet air with the scent of raw flesh and sustenance.

Jackie opened her eyes, staring at the snow gum. Forcing the potent hunger down, she turned her head, giving her foster mother an empty smile. Rhonda's words didn't cut her to the core, didn't tear her apart. They just made her angry. Angry that such a woman had abused the system for so long. And in that anger, Jackie realized she didn't care what her foster mother thought anymore. "No, Rhonda, you were done with me long before that. I just kept hoping you weren't, stupid, naïve kid that I was." She cocked her head to the side a little. "I've often wondered what closure felt like. Now I know. Good bye, Rhonda. Be kind to yourself."

From the corner of her eye, she watched Delanie give the woman a broad grin. She let out a silent sigh and began walking away. From the cemetery. From the snow gum. From the man who may be lurking in the tree's shadows.

No. He's not there. Not now. You can't feel him studying you.

She swallowed at the stubborn lump in her throat and ignored Rhonda's blustering shout. Closure, did indeed feel good. As cutting and hurtful as it was. Throwing Delanie a quick look, she headed for the car park. "Did I already mention I need coffee?"

Delanie nodded. "I believe you did."

"Does the Healey Cheese Factory still make those delicious lamingtons?"

Her friend's laugh was answer enough.

Jackie smiled. "Okay. Caffeine and cake first, then it's goodbye Tasmania."

Delanie stopped walking. "Really?" Her bottom lip protruded in a comical pout, but Jackie could see the disappointment in her striking green eyes.

"I can't stay, Del." She shook her head, flicking her gaze toward the distant tree line and the ancient snow gum. "You know why. The air is getting to me. The smell of this place is intoxicating. I'm fighting the transformation every second of every minute." She dragged her fingers through her hair. "I need to get back to Sydney where all I can smell and taste is saltwater, smog, sweat and eucalypts. I need to get the animal back under control before I surrender to the pull and lose myself."

"I'll keep you safe," Delanie offered. "You can run amuck in my apartment. My neighbours aren't going to care. The noises they hear coming from my place most nights must—"

"I can't, Del," Jackie interrupted. She took a step forward, smoothing her palms up her best friend's arms. "You know I love you. I don't have to tell you that, and I miss you like hell every single day, but if I don't leave soon I'm gone."

Delanie sighed, turning her stare to the few remaining mourners hovering by Richard Smith's grave. Jackie gave them a disinterested glance, wishing she could take away Delanie's despair. For all her extroverted bravado, Delanie

McKenzie was a small-town girl who missed her one true friend.

Perhaps you could stay a few days...

The thought came from deep within the lonely shadows of her mind. Alluring and enticing. And dangerous. She couldn't stay. She had to go. Delanie would just have to understand. It wasn't just for Jackie's sanity. It was for her safety as well. If she transformed here, in Tasmania's lush, unspoiled beauty, she may never transform back.

Threading her fingers through Delanie's, she gave her friend's hands a gentle tug. "I'll make you a deal—coffee and cake at Healy's, my shout. Then we'll drive to St. Helens for a movie, crash at the most expensive hotel we can find for the night and, after a ridiculously indulgent breakfast, we'll drive back to Launceston where I'll let you shout me copious amounts of coffee before my flight back to Sydney."

Delanie didn't take her stare from the mourners.

"I'll even let you steal the hotel robes without pitching a fit. How does that sound?"

The sides of her friend's lips twitched. "Throw in a bottle of champagne at dinner and it's done." She swung her gaze back to Jackie, giving her a wide grin. "We have to at least celebrate the last conversation you'll ever have with the Wicked Witch of the arse-end of Australia."

A warm glow spread through Jackie's chest and she squeezed Delanie's fingers. "Deal."

Okay. This is getting ridiculous.

Jackie turned on the spot, studying the car park around her. A few cars stood silent and still in the hotel's parking bay, the late afternoon sun bouncing off their windshields in glinting spears of white-orange light.

She frowned, turning back to the hotel they'd only just checked into. The Tasmanian Gardens' entryway doors stayed shut, the glass panels revealing an empty check-in foyer. No sign of Delanie there either. "Where are you, Del?"

Swallowing an uncomfortable sense of foreboding, she crossed the car park, heading for Delanie's beloved Volkswagen Beetle. Bernie stood between a black convertible BMW and a silver Toyota 4x4, jarring and smug in his eye-stinging bright green paintwork, dented hubcaps and hot-pink windscreen wipers. Nothing looked out of place. All the doors were locked.

Jackie circled the car, fingers wriggling. She narrowed her eyes, studying the ground, car park, surrounding buildings and trees. After checking-in, Delanie had returned to Bernie to retrieve their overnight bags while Jackie found their room. Ten minutes later, the mini-bar, bathroom and balcony over-looking the pool thoroughly inspected, Jackie had perched herself on the foot of the softest bed in the room and waited for Delanie to arrive.

Eleven minutes after that, she'd begun to gnaw on her lip. Two minutes later, she'd begun to clench her fists to keep her fingers still. Another minute and she was out of the room, doing everything she could to stop herself sprinting through the hotel's hallway on her way to the car park.

The second she'd pushed through the foyer's main doors the pre-dusk air assaulted her, as if waiting for her to step into its intoxicating sweetness. Her thylacine growled, surging though her being with rapid ease. Snatching back control had been hard. She'd shoved the need to transform down into the pit of her existence and half-walked, half-ran down the hotel's stairs into the car park, scanning the area for any sign of Delanie.

And now here she was, walking around her best friend's car, breathing shallow for fear of losing herself to her inner animal when she knew she should be breathing deep to detect any hint of Delanie's location.

Then stop being a chicken shit and do it.

Coming to a standstill, wishing—again—she had her gun, Jackie closed her eyes and pulled in a long, slow breath.

There! Delanie.

Faint, almost dispersed to nothing, but there. To her right. Delanie's scent tinged with…

She turned, lifting her head slightly and pulling in another breath.

Her heart clenched. Fear. Delanie's scent was tinged with fear. The acrid kind of a sudden fright.

God, what is going on?

Following the scent, the thylacine inside her itching for release, she moved through the car park. Clapped-out combi-vans stood beside shiny hybrids. Dented station wagons shared the asphalt with lovingly looked-after sedans. Each waited for their owners to return, the setting sun casting their paintwork in a fiery orange glow.

Jackie pulled in another breath, tasting the air. Del had been here.

She narrowed her eyes, approaching a low red convertible. Heat rolled from it in unpleasant waves, the stench of burning motor oil almost choking her. Reaching out, she placed her right palm on the car's hood. Hot. Hot enough to tell her the engine had only recently been running.

She took another breath, separating the car's fumes from the delicate scent of her best friend. Delanie's scent grew stronger here. More concentrated.

Jackie's chest squeezed tight. It wasn't just Del's scent that was more potent here. Her fear tainted the air like a thick mist.

Damnit, Del. What's going on?

She took another breath. There was more on the air than Delanie's fear-laced scent. There was something else, something she couldn't put her finger on. A scent that wasn't a scent.

That doesn't make sense, Huddart.

No, it didn't, but she didn't know how else to explain it. There was a void to the air, as if something had erased the particles of which it was comprised. Removed them from existence.

Her pulse quickened. Removing something from a crime scene—and worryingly, this is exactly what this seemed to be—meant Delanie wasn't just missing. She was…

"Taken," she whispered.

Her stomach rolled and she ran her stare over the red convertible. She could do one of two things. She could call the local police force and report Delanie as missing, and aid them in finding her by following standard police procedure. Or she could track Del herself. Alone.

She straightened, removing her hand from the car and turning into the gentle breeze at her back.

It blew against her face, barely strong enough to move the strands of her hair. Closing her eyes, she drew in another breath, through her mouth as well this time, tasting Delanie on the air. No, it wasn't just on the air. It was on the ground as well. Whoever had taken Del had left a scent trail on the road.

On purpose?

The question slipped through Jackie's mind, making her already fast pulse thump faster. Who would do that? Who would take her best friend and leave a scent trail?

She ground her teeth. No one. She was being dramatic. Ridiculous. She had to stop standing here wasting time with stupid notions of malevolent intentions and find Delanie. Find her and then teach the bastard who took her what happens to those who mess with a cop's best friend.

Heart racing, she began running, nose into the breeze, Del's scent flowing into her body.

Four blocks passed. Five. Six. The houses flanking her became light industrial buildings and warehouses. And still, Delanie's scent pulled her forward. Faster. Her inner animal ached for release. Hungered to track, to run…

She ran, her blood roaring in her ears, and skidded to a halt, heels digging into the now gravel road when a man stepped toward her from behind a big black van. A tall man with impossibly broad shoulders and narrow lean hips.

The very man she'd caught looking at her inside the airport terminal yesterday. The same man who'd driven away from the airport car park in a black Audi an hour later.

The same man she'd seen standing under a snow gum at Pyengana's cemetery.

Cold fury ripped through her. "You've been following me." She bunched her fists by her side and took a step closer to him, fixing him with an unwavering glare. "What the hell have you done with Delanie?"

A tiny dimple creased his left cheek beside lips curled into a small grin, giving Jackie the impression he knew a secret he found entirely humourous. Dark honey-blonde hair fell over his forehead in a tousled mess, brushing straight eyebrows a shade darker. "I have, Detective Huddart. But I'm afraid I haven't taken your friend."

He studied her from behind impenetrable black sunglasses, the intensity of his unseen but wholly felt inspection making Jackie want to shiver.

And smash her fist against his far too square jaw.

"I've seen you three times in the last twenty four hours and now my best friend is missing." Her heart thumped hard in her throat. "That's not coincidence. Who are you and how the hell do you know who I am?"

She could hear her control cracking, hear the violence of her animal's soul cutting each word she said, but she didn't care. He—whoever he was—had the advantage over her. She didn't like that. Not as a cop. Not as an animal. She didn't like it at all.

He however, seemed unaffected by her obvious aggression. His lips curled into a broader grin. "Marshall Rourke, at your service."

Jackie didn't return his smile. "You're American?"

Long, straight fingers came up to tip an imaginary hat. "Texan, actually, but it's pretty much the same thing."

"Enough of the charm, Mr. Rourke." Jackie snapped. Damn, she wished she had her gun. And her badge. She'd wipe that far-too-sexy grin from his face in two seconds flat. "Time to tell me why you're following me, how you know who I am and where the hell Del—"

Her best friend's name slipped from her lips before she could stop it and she bit back a sharp curse. Damn it, cop law 101—don't give away information not already revealed. She clenched her fists, glaring at Marshall Rourke.

"I know you have no reason to trust me." He removed his dark sunglasses, and Jackie's chest squeezed. His eyes were stunning. Piercing light blue the colour of Antarctic ice. "But if you want to see Delanie McKenzie alive again, I recommend you come with me."

Delanie lifted her head from the cold, dirty floor. At least, she thought it was dirty. What felt like grit ground into her right cheek and jaw, like tiny stabs from an even tinier blade, but the room was too dark to make out exactly what scattered the floor. If in fact it was a room.

Pressing her palms to the cold surface, she pushed herself partially upright, wincing at the sharp pain stabbing through her head and down across her shoulders. Damn it, she'd just finished a bout of chiropractic sessions. Now, she'd have to start all over again.

Start all over again? Is that what you're worried about? Someone you still haven't seen knocked you out, you wake up in a dark bloody room on a cold bloody floor and you're worried about more sessions with Dr. Templeton?

Biting back a groan of agony and a growl of exasperation, she pushed herself farther into a sitting position and peered about. Dark. Very dark. Looming shadows in the darkness that may or may not be boxes, a window high off the floor to her right, boarded up from the outside by the look of it, weak slivers of red light spearing through the miniscule cracks. Cold floor. Cold, gritty floor.

Which you've already established, Del. Focus. You're in serious trouble here.

Ignoring the uneasy knot trying to tighten in the pit of her belly, Delanie shifted onto her knees and sniffed. A musky, slightly rotten odor threaded into her breath and she crinkled her nose. The room smelt like a long-forgotten kitchen.

"So, why would someone clock you on the back of the head in the hotel car park and bring you to a kitchen, Del? They want you to cook them dinner?"

Stop it, Del. You need to take this seriously.

Delanie scowled at the dark thought. She was taking it seriously. Someone had abducted her. But whoever that someone was, they weren't that smart. For starters, they hadn't tied her up. Her wrists and ankles were still free, which meant she could kick the shit out of whoever came near her, or scratch their face off. Secondly, they hadn't taken her keys from the back pocket of her shorts, effectively leaving her with a weapon —of sorts. Clench her car keys between her fingers while making a fist and she had a pretty decent way of taking out someone's eye. Or puncturing their neck. Thirdly, they'd snatched her from the car park while she was with Jackie.

Del squinted into the darkness, picturing her best friend. That latter reason was probably the best argument for the low intelligence quota of her abductor. Who would abduct a girl whose best friend was not only a cop, a bloody good cop at that, but a friggen' were-Tasmanian tiger?

But now you're assuming the person responsible for this unexpected gloom and doom knows what Jackie is and who you are. What if it's a random snatch-and-grab? Just some nutter who saw you in the car park and thought, why not? She looks like an easy target.

Closing her eyes and clenching her fists, Delanie straight-ened to her feet. As scary as that scenario was, it was also unlikely. Not in Launceston, at least. The mainland, yes. Sydney or Adelaide, you betcha. But Tasmania? Nothing that random ever happened in Tasmania.

No, this was premeditated. Which, given the fact she was on her feet and had her keys already in hand, made the situa-tion not so much worrying, but puzzling.

"Whatever is going on, I'm not happy." Her grumble rever-berated around the room, bouncing back to her in soft echoes. Delanie raised her eyebrows. The room was bigger than she thought. "So where am I?"

"Far enough away from the hotel to make your friend shift."

The voice, low and deep and tainted with an accent Delanie could not place, sounded to her left and she turned. A shiver raced up her back and she clenched her fists tighter on her keys-slash-weapon. Someone stood in the darkness with her.

"I have left a trail, as such," the voice continued, disem-bodied by the deepening blackness of the room. Whatever was casting the red glow outside was going, leaving a cold lack of colour and light. "You may notice, when you stop thinking about tearing open my throat with those keys and how little light there is left in the room, that you no longer wear your watch, your necklace, your earrings or your bra."

Delanie jumped, her hands going to her wrist, throat and ears seconds before the unseen speaker listed the last item. She slapped her hands to her breasts. The feel of her nipples, pinched hard from the room's low temperature, rubbing against her palms through her shirt, brought a wave of hot anger to her face. The bastard had removed her bra?

"So, you are a pervert after all," she shot into the darkness.

A chuckle followed. "I did not look or touch, I assure you. I am not interested in you at all." There was a pause, and

Delanie got the feeling her newfound chum was moving. She couldn't hear a sound apart from her own rapid heartbeat, but something about the way the calmly spoken words rolled through the darkness made her think he, whoever he was, was moving to her left. Slowly.

"You are but a means to an end, Delanie McKenzie. Your bra was the only item of clothing I could deposit that would exude your scent and still leave you sufficiently attired."

Delanie narrowed her eyes, glaring into the black shadows. "A means to an end? My scent? What are you, a hunter?"

Another chuckle rolled toward her. "Exactly. I am a hunter."

"And I'm the bait?" Delanie crossed her arms, doing her best to keep her voice disdainful. A hunter. In Tassie. Right when Jackie arrived? Not good. "The only thing you'll catch with me as bait are debt collectors."

The chuckle came again. Closer. And definitely on her left. "I think we both know what I will catch with you as bait, Delanie McKenzie." Something touched her cheek and she flinched, disgusted shame flooded her face with heat.

A finger, Del. That's all. Just a finger. He's trying to freak you out.

"And what's that?" she snarled, fisting her keys. "Brad Pitt? Sorry. We broke up last week. I dumped him for Hugh Jackman."

"A shape-shifting thylacine," the voice answered, calm. "That's what I will catch. The only shape-shifting Tasmanian tiger to survive man's ignorance."

Delanie's chest grew tight. She stared into the darkness, trying like hell to see the man concealed there. "I'm not sure what medication you're on, mate, but I'd ask your doctor to cut the dose back a bit. A shape-shifting thylacine? As in a werewolf? A werethylacine? Seriously?" She laughed, a scoffing snort she hoped sounded believable. Jesus, how did he know what Jackie was? And why was he after her?

This is not good, Del. Not good at all.

"I applaud your loyalty, Delanie, but there is no need for artifice. The truth of Jacqueline Huddart's true species is something I have known for quite some time. At this point in time, I would say I know Ms Huddart's true nature better than you."

Delanie pulled a face, anger replacing her apprehension. "Is that so?" She glared into the deepening shadows. "Well, guess I don't have to warn you then what Jackie's going to do to you when she tracks you down. You know, the pain, the blood, the ripped open throat…that sort of thing."

The responding laugh sent a chill up Delanie's spine and the hairs at her nape stood on end. It was an empty laugh. An insane laugh.

A purposeful laugh.

There was a slight scraping noise, a shifting in the air beside her, and suddenly a man stepped out of the darkness. A tall man with skin like leather, hair blacker than pitch and eyes the colour of a cloudless sky. A tall man holding a wicked knife roughly the size and length of Delanie's forearm. "Ms Huddart is going to do exactly what I tell her to," the man said, tracing the tip of the knife's blade along Delanie's jawline.

Delanie's heart smashed into her throat, but she held her ground, staring hard into the man's cold blue eyes. "And what is that? What is the big, bad hunter going to make a tiny slip of a woman do?"

"Why, roll over and show me her belly, of course." White teeth flashed at her as he gave her a wide smile. "Right before I plunge my knife into her guts and mount her dead, stuffed carcass on my wall."

CHAPTER THREE

Marshall Rourke studied the woman glaring hard at him. She wanted to hurt him. She wanted to tear him a new one, and going by the absolute fury radiating from her in pungent waves—like the smoke from burning brimstone—she'd come damn near close to doing so if he gave her the opportunity.

Christ, he hadn't been prepared for this.

Didn't prepare for how hard your prick is while watching her either, did you?

No, he hadn't. From the first second he'd seen her in the airport, her petite frame almost swallowed by the crowd, the ancient potency of her *croi* making his blood sing and his beast stir, his body had been in a constant state of semi-arousal. That he'd reacted so quickly to the woman was a problem. That his inner beast enjoyed the entirely carnal reaction was even more of a problem. It was a complication he could ill afford.

When he should be thinking about the next stage of his plan, all he could do was think of the various ways he could press his body to hers.

The pit of his belly stirred and his balls grew heavy.

Damn it, Rourke. Get control of yourself.

He stood motionless, doing everything he could to project an air of calm confidence. It only took one look at Jackie—one long, lingering look—to know she'd attack if she sensed even the slightest hint of weakness in him. Whether as a cop or an animal, he couldn't tell.

Do you blame her, Rourke? Her best friend's been abducted. That wasn't part of your plan was it?

No, his plan had been to follow Jackie Huddart everywhere she went until Einar made his move. Then, after two freaking years of trying to catch the bastard, Marshall would finally take him out.

Instead, Einar had abducted an innocent human and Marshall's plan had gone to hell in a hand basket.

The same hot guilt that had flooded through Marshall the moment he'd realized what Einar had done surged through him again. Delanie McKenzie's abduction *wasn't* part of the plan. But his damn lust had let it happen, and he couldn't do anything about it now. Now, he had to rework the plan—the *original* plan, no matter how bitter and cutting the guilt flooding through him was.

Is that why you've made yourself known to Jackie? Instead of following her as she tracked Delanie's scent? That would have achieved your goal far more effectively. Follow her to Einar's obvious trap and catch the bastard as he tries to catch her.

Marshall stared at Jackie's face, unable to miss the fear and pain in her eyes despite the fury burning there.

That was why he'd approached her, why he'd thrown his well-organised plan to the wall. The agony and terror he'd seen in her eyes when she'd realized her friend had not just gone missing, but been abducted. Pain and fear *he'd* caused. *That* was why he stood before her now. The way his body stirred at the thought of comforting her, speaking to her, had nothing to do with it.

Yeah. Sure. Right. Jesus Christ, you're a piece of work, Rourke. You know that? A grade-A piece of—

The contemptuous thought didn't get the chance to finish. Before Marshall knew what was happening, Jackie attacked. So fast he didn't see her move.

One minute he was looking at her, the next, he was flat on his back, the heel of her shoe pressing into the base of his neck as she rammed her foot against his collarbone.

Holy smokes, how did she do that?

"I'm going to give you two options, Mr. Rourke." Her voice was even and smooth, like buttered whisky. She glared down the length of her petite body at him, eyes still unreadable, heel pressing harder to his throat. "You can tell me exactly where my friend is, or I can call the cops and have your Texan arse thrown into jail."

A cold ribbon of unease unfurled in Marshall's chest. It wouldn't do for the local authorities to be made aware of his presence in the country. He wasn't in Australia on official business. In fact, he wasn't on official business period. If his boss found out where he was, he'd face the dressing down of a lifetime, with a suspension and possible confinement period thrown in for good measure. The P.A.C. Unit Director had no tolerance for agents doing their own thing, no matter how right that thing was.

He shifted underneath Jackie's foot, the asphalt biting into his shoulder blades as he did so.

Jackie's heel shoved harder still to his neck, pressing on his windpipe and he stopped moving. "Time's running out, Mr. Rourke."

A low growl deep in his dual existence rumbled through his chest. He may be experiencing an increasing level of discomfort, but his beast, the ancient, primal creature that it was, seemed highly amused by his situation. And aroused.

Marshall stopped himself from rolling his eyes. Great. Just what he needed. A horny, laughing dire wolf tainting his judgment.

"Listen," he began, but her driving heel cut him short.

Christ, she was going to asphyxiate him with her goddamn size-six shoe.

Amber eyes regarded him. "Thirty seconds, Mr. Rourke."

"I know what you are."

Jackie's eyes widened—a fraction. "And what am I, Mr. Rourke?"

He looked up at her, her heel making it difficult to breathe, her sweet subtle scent making him want to drag in breath after breath after breath. "A were-thylacine."

Jackie Huddart didn't move. She became a statue, her stare fixed on him, her knuckles white. "A were-what?"

Despite the heel cutting off his air supply, Marshall grinned. She was good at hiding her surprise. With a face like hers—stunningly gorgeous and completely expressionless—she'd win a lot of poker matches. "A were-thylacine," he croaked, curling his fingers around her ankle in a tight grip. If he needed to he'd flip her off him. "A shape-shifting Tasmanian tiger."

Her poker-face didn't change. Neither did the position of her foot. "I think you've been watching too many movies, Mr. Rourke. This is Australia, not Transylvania."

He gave her another grin, the discomfort in his lungs beginning to turn into a painful burn. This was not how he'd seen this unfolding. "Transylvania is traditionally the home to vampires, Ms Huddart." He shifted slightly, the minute action earning him a sharp increase in pressure on his throat. "Australia however, is the home to many vampires and werewolves, Declan O'Connell being one of them." Her eyes widened again—the reaction to the Irish alpha wolf's name almost undetectable. She was good at hiding her emotions. Very good. But he was better at exposing them. He pressed his fingers harder to her ankle, the fine bones like hot steel under his grip. "Tasmania however," he continued, preparing his body, his beast, for whatever came next, "is the native habitat of the shape-shifting thylacine. To be precise, the last shape-shifting thylacine." He let her see his teeth in a grin he knew was borderline wolfish. "You."

Once again, her reaction surprised him. He expected to be attacked. Or for her to shift into her other form and then attack. What he didn't expect was for her to remove her foot from his neck and step back away from him.

He snapped to his feet, brushing down his backside, still half convinced she was going to throw herself at him with that same preternatural speed she had before.

Could be fun.

He looked at her, ignoring the suggestive comment, as enticing as it was. Having Jackie Huddart throw her tiny little body at him in the right circumstances was downright appealing.

"Tell me who has my friend."

Her voice was cold. Very calm, almost indifferent, but cold all the same. She stared at him, fists bunched, her small frame radiating an energy he understood all too well—pent-up fury and tenuous restraint. She was having difficulty controlling her inner beast. A state of being he existed in twenty-four seven.

Especially since Einar's "retirement".

The dark thought extinguished the rising heat in Marshall's body and he clenched his jaw. His ex-partner was never long from his mind. Nor were the man's actions since P.A.C. had "let" him go. Daeved Einar's activities were not only thoroughly documented by the Paranormal Anti-Crime Unit, they were classified security-level red.

That he'd contributed to Einar's freedom was an atrocity he could never forget.

"Who has my friend?"

Jackie Huddart's low growl snapped Marshall's mind from his ex-partner with a start, a part of him disturbingly pleased that she no longer assumed he was a part of Delanie's abduction.

But if she really knew…

He focused his gaze *and* his senses on the woman standing before him. The fingers of her right hand were wriggling. What did that mean?

You will have the time to figure that out. If she falls for this next bit.

"I can't tell you that, darlin'."

"You can tell me who took her, or I can arrest your arse and charge you with aiding and abetting an abduction." Her eyes flashed gold fire. "Or I can snap your neck and leave you here on the side of the road. In case you haven't noticed, we're not really in a busy part of town. It's after work hours on a Friday. No one will find your body for over forty-eight hours."

The pit of Marshall gut tightened. His inner beast growled. He studied her, weighing his options. He needed her. She, on the other hand, didn't need him at all. She'd find Delanie McKenzie without his aid, of that he had little doubt. But she wasn't expecting someone like Einar waiting for her when she found Delanie. She wasn't expecting to walk into a trap. A trap Marshall had a certain amount of responsibility for.

Ha, that's an understatement.

The idea of Jackie getting hurt had become inconceivable the moment her eyes connected with his. The moment she'd regarded him with steely, confronting strength when inside he knew she must be broken with worry and fear. He couldn't let her walk into Einar's trap unprepared. Besides which, he couldn't ignore the fact his best chance at catching Einar was still by Jackie's side. Staying near her and remaining undetected hadn't worked. All it had achieved was an ache in his groin that wouldn't quit and a guilt in his soul that wouldn't leave him. It was time to try something new.

Just pray to God you're not fucking it up even more, Rourke.

"I can't tell you who took her, detective," he said, emphasizing her rank. "But you need to believe me when I say the person who has taken Delanie will have her skinned and gutted before the cops can even think about putting out an APB." He paused. "Or before my body begins to rot, if that's the path you chose to follow."

The brutal description of her friend's possible fate drained the blood from Jackie's face. The first true reaction he'd elicited from her.

"I can help you, detective," he hurried, before her terror overrode what little control she still held. "I am here to help you. I know the MO of Delanie's abductor and I want to help you get her back."

Her jaw bunched and she stepped toward him, closing the small distance he'd left between them. He wished she hadn't. Her unique scent, unlike any he'd tasted before, filled his breath, and his balls, already heavy with a carnal interest, grew heavier. Oh, boy, he *hadn't* counted on this at all.

"Who are you, Mister Rourke?" Her heat folded around him, a thrumming contradiction to the icy rage in her eyes. "If I'm to trust my best friend's life to your oh-so-mysterious hands, at least tell me who you are."

He looked down into her face. A gentle wind blew at her hair, lifting the burnished chestnut curtain from her temples, and his chest squeezed. This close he could see the faint smattering of freckles across her nose. This close he could see the gold chips in her eyes. This close he could see the fine bone structure of her skull, the soft fullness of her lips.

This close his inner beast could feel the ancient *croi* of her inner animal.

Feel and crave.

Damn it, he needed to get himself under control. Now. "I'm no threat to you. That's all I can tell you." It was a lie—he was a threat. At least, what he was doing threatened her life, but he couldn't think about that now.

She studied him; face expressionless, eyes conflicted. She wanted to tell him to go to hell, but the fate of her friend held her tongue. The fingers of her right hand wriggled. "You have exactly thirty minutes to 'help me' find my friend. After that I will call the cops." She paused. "Or snap your neck."

Again, his inner dire wolf reacted to her—a deep, base reaction. It wanted her. It wanted to mate with her.

And so does your inner man, Rourke. Fess up.

A sudden lump filled his throat and he swallowed. He did. She was sexy. Sexy on every level. Dangerous sexy, feisty sexy, gorgeous sexy, petite sexy, determined sexy, animalistic sexy. He was attracted to her already. Wanted to taste her sweat, her sex, her cream. Wanted to feel her body move under his as his fingers entwined with hers. Wanted to look into her face while one orgasm after another claimed her. Wanted to ride each wave with her until they were both drained. Damn, as clichéd as it was, he'd never felt like this before.

Which made lying to her now all the more problematic.

"Thirty minutes," he said, holding his hand up as if taking the Pledge of Allegiance. "And it's Marshall."

Jackie didn't say a word. Just looked at him, poker face firmly in place. Yet her fingers were no longer wriggling. Which meant something, he just didn't know what. Yet.

He held out his arm, turning to his left as he gave her what he hoped was a reassuring, trust-me-I'm-the-good-guy smile. "My chariot's this way. It will get us to Delanie faster than your legs."

Still not a word in response. But she began to walk in the direction he indicated.

He grinned behind her back.

All right, P.A.C. Unit Special Agent Rourke. You've got her. She's with you. Now do what you came here for. Before she discovers just what that really is.

What are you doing? Are you insane?

The questions punched through Jackie's head—incredulous and accusatory. She suppressed the urge to fidget in her seat, staring fixedly at the road before her instead of looking at the man behind the Audi's leather-bound steering wheel.

Marshall Rourke directed the luxurious car through the quiet streets of the industrial area of St. Helens, the deepening dusk sky turning his face into a mask of shadows. He kept shooting her sideways glances, as if waiting for her to do or say something. He was on edge. She could detect it in the minute tension of his muscles. She did nothing to ease his current state. There was nothing about the situation she liked, no matter how quick and ardent her physical reaction to the man was. Finding Delanie was all that mattered. Besides, her sexual response to Rourke had little to do with the way he looked and everything to do with her stupid thylacine/human cycle. Of all the time to come on heat.

She curled her fingers into tight fists, driving her short, no-nonsense, cop fingernails into the centre of her palms. God, she wished she had her gun. That she was relying on a complete stranger to take her to her abducted friend made her antsy. Was she doing it because she was coming on heat?

She shot Rourke a quick look. No. Not because of her mutated human/thylacine cycle—although heaven help her if she got a whiff of the man's blood. As mysterious as he was, something about him made her feel, of all things, safe.

Which made no sense at all.

She pressed her nails harder to her palms. He knew what she was, he knew what Declan O'Connell was, he knew who Delanie was, he'd been following her since she landed in Launceston, and who knows for how much longer before that, and yet when her eyes made contact with his, she felt her animal relax. Even as a wicked sexual hunger made it stretch and preen and strain for release.

Jackie bit back a snort of disgust. This was why she'd stopped listening to the creature—raw instincts alone didn't make for a smooth existence. Just a confusing one.

She stared at the road illuminated by the fading sun and

streetlights only just flickering to life. The wind from the car's open windows whipped into the cabin, playing with her hair and filling every breath she took with Delanie's scent.

At least you know he's taking you to Del. He'd not lying about that. If he wasn't you'd have to incapacitate him.

Flicking Rourke another look, she suppressed a sharp sigh. Incapacitating him may not be as easy the second time round. She'd caught him unawares back on the roadside, but something about the straight set to his shoulders, the coiled strength in his biceps told her that was unlikely to happen again.

There you go, checking out his muscles again.

Jackie ground her teeth. Damn it, she *was* insane.

"Do you always growl under your breath when in a car, or is this just a one-time thing?"

Rourke's drawl made her start and she glared at him. Growling? Again? She was closer to losing control of her thylacine than she thought.

White teeth flashed in the muted glow from the Audi's dashboard. Grinning. He was grinning at her.

"I know you want to ask me a ton of questions," he went on, the grin on his lips echoed in the tone of his voice. "Hit me with one and I'll see if I can answer it."

Jackie narrowed her eyes. "Why are you so glib? Is it a defense mechanism?"

"I'm not glib. I'm sardonic."

"Ah, and that is so much better." Her fingers wriggled before she could stop them. "You want questions? Let's start with the obvious. Who are you? Who has Delanie? How do you know? And why do you want to help me?"

A low chuckle floated through the cabin. "That's alotta questions, darlin'. I guess I did ask you to hit me."

Jackie gave him a cool smile. "Trust me, if I hit you, you're not making lame jokes afterwards."

Rourke chuckled again. "And here I was trying to break the ice, and you're thinking about breaking my head."

As infuriated and worried as Jackie was, she couldn't stop her smile twitching into a reluctant grin. "Not your head," she said. "Your ambiguity."

"I'm sorry. If I could answer those questions I would. It would make you trusting me so much easier."

Jackie cocked an eyebrow. "Yes, I'm all for trust in this relationship. Oh, wait a minute, we don't have a relationship. We have a situation. You stalk me, my best friend goes missing, I kick your arse, you take me to her. That's our situation."

He hissed in a long breath. "Damn, darlin'. That's cold."

"No, that's the truth. Which is exactly not what I'm getting from you."

Silence followed her blunt statement, and the darkening shadows in the car's cabin hiding his expression.

She twisted in her seat, staring hard at him. "Who has taken Delanie?"

Another silence filled the Audi, before Rourke let out a sharp breath. "An enemy."

"Whose enemy? Mine?"

Rourke kept his stare on the road. "No. Yes." He made a face. "It's complicated, darlin'."

Jackie clenched her jaw. "Try me."

He didn't respond for a moment. Jackie studied his profile. High forehead, long, strong nose, blonde bristles not even coming close to taking the smooth perfection off his square jaw.

Perfection? Is that your damn thylacine libido talking or you?

"Someone wants something from you. Your friend unfortunately has been caught up in the trap."

His statement turned the twisting heat in the pit of her belly to a cold knot. "Someone? Who? And what?"

Rourke shook his head. "It's better I don't answer those."

"Better for who? You? Me? This mysterious someone?"

He shot her a quick look, the dashboard light catching in

his eyes for a split second, turning them to twin silver discs. "You."

The tone of his voice—flat, serious—made Jackie's stomach clench. She swallowed, not liking the sensation at all. "Okay," she said, staring at the side of his face. She wished he'd look at her. She wanted see his eyes again. She wanted to gage his reaction to what she was about to say. "Seeing as you're reluctant to share information, let me tell you what I know about you already."

His eyebrows dipped into a brief frown and his jaw bunched. "Okay, darlin'." He inclined his head a fraction in a shallow nod. "Give it your best shot."

"You're not a cop, but you've had training of some sort, possibly military, most likely government funded. You move like you are constantly prepared to attack or be attacked. You didn't like being bested back in the street, but there was a part of you that was impressed. Secrets are second nature to you. You try to pretend you're laughing at what's going on around you, but you are really observing every little detail. You catalogue everything you see for future use, either as a weapon or as a weakness. Your right arm moves slightly farther from your body than your left, meaning you are used to a holster being under your right armpit. This makes you left-handed, another trait you try hard to conceal by doing most things with your right—removing your sunglasses, scratching your nose, adjusting your shirt. But when you do something with your left hand the action is more fluid, less contemplated. You have a callous on your left thumb pad from years of cocking the safety on a gun. The indent on the inside of your middle left finger indicates your new weapon—most likely a Glock—is heavier than your old one. You've spent many hours at a firing range, and you tend to squint slightly with your left eye when you take aim." She cocked her head to the side. "You should do something about those wrinkles before you lose your Texan good looks."

She paused, noting with a perverse sense of satisfaction the white tightness of his knuckles on the wheel and the balled muscles in his jaw.

"You're older than you look, but not by much—maybe mid-thirties. You give off no scent whatsoever, which I have to admit, both irks and intrigues me, and you know what I am, which leads me to consider you yourself are not strictly human." She paused again, her throat tight at the fact.

If he was not human, what was he? Shifter? Demon? Or something else?

Rourke didn't say a word. Silence stretched between them as the Audi ate up the road.

Jackie cocked her eyebrow again. "How did I do?"

"You did very well."

She smiled at the begrudging compliment.

"Except I'm in my late thirties, thirty eight to be exact." He gave her a crocked grin. "In human years, that is."

Jackie's chest grew heavy. "What are you?"

He shook his head. "That's irrelevant to our situation."

She narrowed her eyes. "Our situation still is in a state of ambiguity."

He chuckled. "No, our situation is just as you stated. I stalked you, your best friend went missing, you kicked my butt and I'm helping you save her." He gave her another grin, this one not so lop-sided and way more mischievous. "Oh, wait, there's a new element. You think I'm good looking."

Jackie stared at him. After all that, the one thing he latched onto was a throwaway line about his looks?

A throwaway line completely unnecessary to proving your point.

She bit back a muttered curse. This was getting her nowhere. Except closer to a headache she didn't need and a state of interest she didn't want. She had to focus on Delanie. "I've had enough of the word games, Rourke," she snapped.

"Who the hell are you, who the hell has Delanie and what do they want from me?"

His grin disappeared and he turned his attention back to the road. "I'm the man here with you now, not the man holding your friend. Remember that."

Jackie shook her head. "What the bloody hell does that mean?"

"It means," he answered, directing the car into an abrupt right turn, "things are about to get nasty."

The Audi jolted to a sudden halt, the tires biting into what sounded like gravel seconds before Rourke released his seatbelt, flung open his door and leapt from the car.

Jackie blinked, snatching her stare from the man's empty seat. She looked out the window, the abrupt change in their "situation" making her chest tight and her pulse rapid.

What were they doing at the abandoned St. Helen's greyhound-racing track?

Is this where Delanie was?

The realization she was still sitting in Rourke's rental while the Texan stood looking at her from the Audi's grill smacked into her like an open palm. With a low snarl, she yanked her seatbelt off and shoved open her door, cheeks filling with disgusted shame.

She moved on silent feet to stand beside the man professing to be Delanie's only hope, wishing she had her gun more than ever. Her gun would not only help with whatever waited for them inside the racing grounds, but its solid steel weight and texture would keep her animal in check.

She didn't want to transform. Whatever went down behind the high, corrugated fence surrounding the track and derelict buildings, she didn't want to transform. Not unless Delanie's life depended on it. No matter what her animal and her body were trying to tell her about the mysterious Marshall Rourke, she didn't trust him. Not enough to let him see her shift.

Rourke leant at his hip to bring his lips even with her temple. "This is it, Detective Huddart."

She studied the dilapidated fence before her, the dying sunlight turning the rusted metal a dark old-blood black. Somewhere on the other side was Delanie. Lifting her chin a little, she drew in a deep breath.

The acrid stench of ancient dog piss, beer, excrement and rabbit threaded into her lungs, drowning out Del's scent. She curled her lip. The St. Helens' dog track had closed down years ago, but the remains of its purpose lingered in the soil—death and sweat and drinking. Dog's trained to run faster than any other, petrified rabbits used to frenzy them before a race, owners and gamblers alike drinking excessive amounts of alcohol as the greyhounds ran themselves almost to death chasing a lump of metal doused in rabbit urine. Mankind at its finest. It was the perfect place to hide from someone capable of tracking by scent.

Which made Jackie even more suspicious. Whoever took her best friend knew she would follow the trail here.

She took another breath, searching...seeking... "Damn it." She couldn't detect Del's scent at all in the putrid odors hanging heavy on the night air. It was all just muddied smells now.

She gave Rourke a level stare. "Are you sure?"

Sharp ice-blue eyes stared back at her, their intensity almost hidden in the growing darkness. "Yes."

The word sent a shiver down Jackie's spine. "How do you know?"

"I'll explain later, I promise."

Biting back a muttered curse, she turned back to the track, taking another breath. If she could just get a lock on Delanie's location herself she could knock Rourke out and deal with the situation without being distracted.

Distracted? Don't you mean turned on?

"Can you detect her?"

Rourke's voice seemed strained. She looked at him, noting the tightness around his eyes, the flaring of his nostrils. Her stomach knotted. Something didn't feel right. "No."

He turned his attention back to the track. "Building at three o'clock. Two different scents—one male, one female. Both very weak." He licked his lips, as if tasting the air. "He's tried to conceal their location. I smell fresh blood—rodent."

Jackie frowned, staring first at Rourke and then at the dark shape rising above the fence to her right. It looked like the old bar and cafeteria. Her stomach twisted again. How could Rourke detect Delanie's scent when she couldn't?

What was he to have such a highly developed sense of smell?

And why did she feel so aroused by the fact?

Her animal stirred, sending her pulse into an erratic tattoo. Her nipples pinched into hard peaks and her sex grew heavy. Her teeth pointed. Her flesh began to itch. Ripple.

Jackie drove her nails into her palms. *Damn it. Not now. Not now.*

"Let's go."

Rourke's growled command jerked her body back under control. He moved, long, lean frame somehow folding into the deepening night, crossing the graveled clearing in front of the track's gaping entryway on silent feet. Every step he took made the pit of Jackie's belly twist. The way he moved was almost familiar. It was like watching a foreign film without the subtitles. The story ensnared her but she couldn't fully comprehend it.

It pissed her off.

Casting the surrounding darkness one last look, she followed the Texan across the clearing, making no sound at all. Her palm itched for her gun. Her muscles itched to transform. Her animal growled for release. She fixed her eyes on the black shape looming up behind the fence, drawing an image of Delanie into her mind.

Her friend. Rescuing Del was all that mattered now. After Del was safe, then she would turn her attention to Marshall Rourke. Pin him down and extract his secrets.

Until then, he was just someone in her peripheral vision.

Stepping past the broken gate into the racing track's grounds, Rourke but a few steps in front, Jackie pulled another breath. Every scent she detected was old. Faded. She dropped into a crouch, touched her fingertips to the cracked concrete beneath her feet and then raised them to her nose.

Canine. Blood. Urine. Saliva.

Human. Urine. Sweat.

Bird. Shit.

She bit back a curse. No hint anyone had been here recently, let alone Delanie.

Straightening to her feet, she continued toward the building Rourke insisted her friend was in.

So why can't I smell her?

A soft scrape sounded to her left, shattering the silence.

Heartbeat tripling, she stared into the darkness, her animal vision seeing everything.

Which was nothing.

No indication anything had been—

A powerful stench hit her. Wild. Angry.

She gasped, the distinct scent of an alpha canine flooding her senses. Spinning about, she looked for Rourke.

Gone.

She was alone.

Sucking in another breath, she searched for the animal. The ghost of its scent tainted the sweet night air, ribbons of refuse and excrement twisting around the odor. Jackie frowned, her throat squeezing. Was it an animal? Maybe she was mistaken? Too much filth coated the scent to be certain. Made it difficult to taste.

She clenched her fists, her gut churning, her skin tingling.

Run, chase, track, hunt, kill.

Her thylacine surged upward, growling for release. She sank her nails into her palms, forcing control through her body. Just.

Something moved behind her.

She spun about, ready to—*transform*—attack.

A massive black blur darted behind a small brick building —a toilet block by its foul odor.

Jackie's pulse pounded in her ears.

She took a step forward, tasting the air again.

And smelt Delanie.

"Detective?"

The deep murmur at her ear made her jump. She struck out, her elbow connecting with something hard and hot.

"Oof."

Fists ready to strike, she snapped around, her stare locking on Rourke's face but an inch from hers.

"Damn, you're fast." The muttered exclamation slipped past his lips as he rubbed his hand over his abdomen.

Jackie ignored him. "I've found—"

"Delanie," he finished. Sharp blue eyes flashed silver in the moonlight. "Let's go."

He turned and loped away, heading for the derelict bar and cafeteria, fluid and graceful and fast. She followed, zeroing her senses on the almost nonexistent trace of her best friend.

Track, hunt.

The square building sat silent, its rust-blemished roof reflecting the waxing moon's glow, its serving windows covered with weather-bleached boards. A door at the back of the structure hung on a single hinge, the entry a light-devouring rectangle that seemed to mock Jackie. *She's in here. Are you brave enough to come in too?*

Jackie curled her lip. *Don't be bloody ridiculous, Huddart.*

Rourke veered left, his stride slowing somewhat. He shot her a quick look over his shoulder, indicating she should go right. Jackie frowned, a ripple flowing over her flesh. Her animal didn't like it. She didn't like it. Was it a perimeter search? Taking their foe by surprise? Or a tactic to divide and conquer?

Keeping her senses locked on Delanie's weak scent, she approached the cafeteria. The smell of burnt sausages, stale beer and vomit assaulted her, tried to overpower her friend's trace. She wouldn't let it. Pressing her back to the cool brick wall, she steadied her heart. This close to the open door, Delanie's scent was stronger, but not by much.

Jackie's heart smashed against her breastbone. Her hair stood on end and she wriggled her fingers.

Hunt, track, hunt, hunt, hunt.

She shut out the alluring, feverish want and inched closer to the black entryway.

A noise, like velvet rubbing against stone, whispered behind her, but she didn't look. There was no new scent, just the ghosts of dogs and humans long gone. Nothing to draw her attention from the inside of the cafeteria. Delanie. She needed to keep her focus on Delanie.

She drew closer to the door, the sour stench of human vomit and rotting meat slipping into her breath. All old. All tired.

Hunt, hunt, hunt, hunt, hunt, hunt.

Her pulse tripled.

The bricks rasped against her palms as she moved along the wall, tearing minute wounds into the pads of her fingers.

The noise came again. Closer.

She froze beside the doorway, ears straining.

Silence. Not even the sound of scurrying cockroaches.

She drew another breath—pinpointing Delanie's scent. Four metres inside the building, to the left. Her chest tightened. This close, it should be stronger. This close, she should be able to hear her friend breathing. This close, she should know Delanie was there.

But she didn't.

Trap, trap, run, hunt, kill, kill.

She closed her eyes for a split second, wriggled her fingers and stepped into the blackness.

Moonlight streamed into the building, pouring through a section of roof where the ironing sheeting no longer existed, illuminating the gutted kitchen and vandalized benches. Rubbish was strewn everywhere. Decayed rat carcasses littered the floor, discarded food wrappings and empty beer bottles blanketing them in refuse.

Jackie stood motionless, her blood roaring in her ears. Not a sign of Delanie. Not even a clearing of rubbish where she may have once been.

She scanned the filth. Nothing indicated someone had been here recently, let alone two someones. One of whom, Jackie was certain, would have been putting up a damn good struggle.

That's assuming Del's conscious.

Jackie snarled at the dark notion. She took a step deeper into the cafeteria, pulling in a long, deep breath. *Something* with Delanie's scent was here. The floral note of happy cheekiness Jackie had known most of her life whispered on the air, teasing her. Taunting in its fragile existence.

Closing her eyes, she shut everything in the derelict room out but the allusive hint of her best friend.

So faint. So faint.

She let her animal surge closer to release, closer to control. It was dangerous, but she didn't care. She needed to find her friend. Her body tingled. Her heart hammered. She felt a million pinpricks of icy fire raze her flesh. She felt every hair follicle thrum with ancient magick.

Hunt, track, run, kill, mate.

Her sex grew heavy, her breath short. She wriggled her fingers, controlling her Tasmanian tiger as it came closer to freedom, its heightened senses tasting the cool night air, feeling the vibrations of the earth, the shifting of the planet. Hearing the frantic heartbeats of petrified mice hiding in the refuse. She opened her eyes, scanning the moonlit debris under the far window, near the cafeteria's old freezer room. Delanie's scent tickling, mocking, teasing…

Track, run, kill, mate.

Mate, mate, fuck.

A glint of something gold caught her eye. Something tiny like an earring. Cast aside in the rubbish and filth. An earring just like the pair Jackie had given Del for her eighteenth birthday.

An earring on which Delanie's scent lingered, like beads of mist on a spider's web.

Delanie's scent and someone else's. Someone ancient and powerful and—

"Fuck."

Rourke's muttered curse smashed into Jackie's ears. She jumped, spinning around to stare at the man standing directly behind her, her pulse pounding, her thylacine growling.

Face etched in a frown, Rourke ignored her, raising his hand up to his face, fingers spread to study something on his palm.

Jackie's thylacine tasted the blood on the air before she saw it. A crimson trickle of pure male life force seeping over Marshall's wrist bone and down his arm from a wound she couldn't see somewhere on his hand. A trickle of blood ripe with potent pheromones and virulent power.

Her animal tasted the man's blood on the air. Tasted it and detected something different about it. Something ancient. Animalistic.

Fire erupted in Jackie's core. An ice-storm of primeval power followed. Her thylacine howled. *Shift, shift, mate, mate, fuck, fuck, fuck.*

Her body trembled. She staggered back one step, her stare snapping from Rourke's hand to his face.

Transform, shift, mate, fuck, fuck, fuck.

Rourke's frown deepened, his eyes unreadable silver discs in the room's cool light as he moved his gaze to her. "What's wrong?"

His voice—low and gravelly and far too sexy—stabbed into her core, a wicked blade of carnal stimulus. Her Tasmanian tiger clamored for release, its base instincts surging for control. Forcing the shift. Forcing the transformation from human to thylacine. From woman to bitch. A bitch in heat and wanting to mate.

Icy fire consumed her. Flooded her sex—*mate, mate, fuck, mate, fuck, fuck*—and she did the only thing she could to stop the shift claiming her.

She threw herself at Marshall Rourke, her hands fisting in his hair, her mouth crushing his, her tongue invading his mouth before the savage transformation could begin.

CHAPTER FOUR

Marshall's body exploded. The second Jackie's tongue plunged into his mouth, her sweet taste filling his breath, his being, the small gash in his palm from the building's broken window, were forgotten.

From the moment he'd opened the email with Detective Huddart's file, he'd become hooked. From the very first instant he'd smelt her soft, delicate scent, he'd become addicted. She was an enigma. Unique. And now here she was. Here they were. Bodies mashed together, hearts hammering in unison. Christ in a handcart, he was in trouble.

A whimper sounded in Jackie's throat, soft and animalistic and she pushed her hips harder to his, all but shattering his tenuous hold on his desire.

His cock flooded with hot lust, painful in its straining hunger. A burning vice squeezed his chest, stole his capacity for rational thought. There was a desperation in her actions he couldn't miss. He felt it in the heat of her body. A burning wildness that unnerved him. What she was doing now wasn't contemplated or restrained. But holy fucking Christ, did it make his blood hot. Did it make his beast stir.

He raked his hands up her back and buried them in her

hair, snaring the coppery-chestnut strands in fists so tight he felt his knuckles pop.

Jesus, she tasted good.

So fucking good.

A low gnarr rumbled in his chest and his blood thickened. Fuck. This was not the plan, not the course of action he'd set out to follow, but he couldn't stop. Not when she tasted so good.

Then fuck her. Mount her. Claim her. And then get on with the job.

The callous thought shot through his head, icy cold and vicious. He stiffened. God, what was he doing? He couldn't—

Jackie's hands tightened in his hair. She shoved her hips forward, grinding the soft hood of her sex against his dick, and scalding lust surged through Marshall. Destroying him. He plundered her willing mouth, his tongue mating with hers in frenzied desperation. Already it wasn't enough. He wanted more. His wolf wanted more. Dragging his hands from her hair, he grabbed her arse, squeezing each firm, toned cheek with brutal force as he yanked her harder to his hips.

She whimpered again, her teeth nipping at his bottom lip.

Sweet pain licked through him and he growled. Or was it his beast. He didn't know. Didn't care. He drove her backward, ramming her shoulders against the wall even as he shoved her legs apart with his knees and ground his erection to her soft heat.

Jackie tore her mouth from his, throwing back her head to offer him her throat. "Fuck, yes."

Her raw cry stabbed into Marshall's chest. Flooded his balls with molten need. He closed his lips around her neck. Bit into her flesh. She cried out again, arching her body into his, tugging on his hair as she did so. The heat of her sex scalded his straining cock, even through the material of their clothes.

He shoved his hips upward, dry-fucking her, his hands on her arse, his mouth on her neck, her jaw. He flicked his tongue into her ear and bit the soft, fleshy pad of her lobe. She groaned, one leg hooking around his calf, squeezing him closer to the junction of her thighs. "Yes." The word burst from her lips in a hoarse shout, bounced off the graffitied walls and came back to him tenfold.

His wolf snarled and a ripple of hot ice shot up his spine. It was ready to mate. It was ready to come.

Marshall jerked his mouth from her neck, staring into her face. Her eyes burned with primal lust. He sucked in a sharp breath and the musk of her pleasure coated his tongue. Fresh blood flooded his cock. Christ, he was too close. His beast was too close. If he didn't stop now, he didn't know who would penetrate her. Man or wolf.

Does it matter?

As if sensing his hesitation and wanting none of it, Jackie yanked her hands from his hair, snared the collar of her prim black shirt and tore it apart. "Suck," she ordered. "Now."

The pale moonlight painted the smooth flesh of her breasts in a silvery glow, the black lace of her bra a stark contrast to the creamy colour of her skin. Marshall's mouth filled with saliva. His cock jerked, his balls lifted. Jesus, she was beautiful.

He lifted his stare to her face, his blood roaring in his ears. "I won't be able to stop."

She stared back at him, the wild hunger in her eyes incinerating any other emotion there. "I don't care."

Each word rang with desperate need. Each syllable with raw want. It was too much. He couldn't fight any more. Why had he to begin with?

He shoved her legs farther apart with his knees, grinding harder to her pussy as he let go of her arse and cupped her breasts in his hands. Immediately, Jackie's nipples pinched into hard points. He dragged the pad of his thumbs over each tip, his beast growling at the keening noise the contact elicited from her throat. Her eyelids fluttered closed and she arched her back, rolling her damp sex harder to his dick. Her hands raked up his arms, her fingers tangling in his hair. She held him tight, her breath coming from her in ragged, shallow pants. Beads of perspiration glistened on her forehead, her chest. A tiny trickle of sweat ran down between her breasts. The sound of its path over her skin—mist on velvet—sent a scalding wave of liquid electricity through Marshall's body. Into his groin.

He dropped his head, catching the trickle with its tongue. Salty sweetness exploded in his mouth. Her taste. Her sweat. His cock pulsed and he growled again. She was as delicious and unique as he suspected. And as addictive. He wanted more.

Without preamble, he hooked his fingers under the lacy edges of her bra and pulled them aside.

Her nipples popped free and he captured one with his mouth, closing his lips over the distended nub. Jackie gasped, the sound turning into a moan as he suckled hard, his fingers twisting and pinching her other nipple in perfect sync with his mouth.

"Oh, God, that feels so good."

Her moan flayed what little control he held. He sank his teeth into her nipple, thrusting his cock upward in savage punches. The barrier of their clothes infuriated him. His dick felt like a solid shaft of pleasure. He dragged his hand from her breast, down her ribcage to the waistline of her trousers. He wanted to feel her wetness. No. He needed to feel her wetness. Like he needed to draw breath. Fighting with the buttons of her fly, he shoved his hand between their bodies.

The soft down of Jackie's pubic hair tickled his fingertips and he pulled a harsh breath in through his nose. Christ, even that intimacy drove him wild.

Jackie shifted in his hold, her hands gripping his shoulders as she levered her body slightly away from his. Granting him greater access to the heat between her legs.

He plunged his fingers down. Past the button of her clit. Along the wet lips of her pussy.

His cock jerked, his pulse tripled. He lifted his head from

her breast and stared down into her face, wanting to see her eyes.

They glowed. Amber fire. Primal desire.

Yes.

He shoved his fingers into her sex. Hard. Deep.

She threw back her head, her cry more like a howl. The beat of her heart vibrated through her body, down into her sex. She bucked into his hand, riding his fingers, her cunt gripping and squeezing.

He wriggled his fingers deeper, slipping in a third as he did so. She was so tight. So wet and so tight. He stared into her face, watching her pleasure dance across her features. She tried to hide it. He could see it in the measured pace of each breath she pulled. But it was there all the same. Pleasure he created. Pleasure he unleashed. He pulled his own steadying breath, taking the scent of her rapture into his being. His cock throbbed, its swollen length trapped by his jeans and Jackie's heat. With every thrust he made into her sex with his fingers, the back of his hand nudged his cockhead. It was agony and bliss at once. He wanted to throw her to the ground, rip their clothes from their bodies and bury his dick into her sex. He wanted to pin her to the wall with his hand and bring her to a screaming climax with his fingers. He wanted to drop to his knees and plunge his tongue into her folds. He wanted to mount her from behind. He wanted to rut. He wanted to fuck. He wanted—

To shift.

Molten ice shot up his spine. His muscles burned. His flesh tingled. His bones stretched.

He threw back his head, letting out a scream so loud plaster and dust showered down on them from the gaping roof.

He was going to shift. He was going to transform. And there was nothing he could do to stop it. Nothing.

"Fuck!" he roared, yanking his fingers free of Jackie's pussy.

He staggered backward, his stare locked on Jackie's face, his muscles distorting.

He drove his nails into his palms, sucking in lungful after lungful of night air. Focusing his senses on the filth and shit at his feet. Blocking out the potent sweetness of Jackie's desire.

He had to control himself. He had to stop the shift. If he didn't, he would claim Jackie here and now, mark her as his own, and his plan would be doomed to fail. How could he use her if she was his mate? How could he catch Einar if the one thing Einar hunted was the only thing Marshall could no longer use as bait?

Catching his ex-partner was the plan. Not claiming a mate. Jackie Huddart was a means to an end. He had to remember that.

He couldn't mate with her. Dire wolves mated for life and Jackie Huddart's life was all he had to catch a killer.

Bait.

That was what she was. That's all she could be.

Bait.

"Your friend's not here," he ground out, stepping farther away from Jackie. His beast howled, furious. His body screamed in denied agony. Halting the shift so close to commencement was like plunging naked into a frozen lake. Halting his desire was like stepping into a burning house. He turned his head, unable to look into her face. Unable to stand the wretched confusion and disgust he saw in her eyes. "We should go."

Silence stretched between them. Thick. Suffocating. He stared at the far wall, at the revelation some wannabe graffiti artists had spray-painted over its peeling plaster, *Don't worry. It's only kinky the first time.*

He wanted to look at her. To see what she was doing. Instead, he crossed the room, moving into the black shadows until he couldn't feel the heat of her body caressing his.

The faintest of sounds played in the silence behind him.

Jackie was moving. He clenched his fists, seeing her in his mind. Graceful and purposeful at once. Beautiful and menacing.

The sound stopped and Marshal held his breath. Waiting.

For what? For her attack?

He ground his jaw. If she did, he would have no choice. He'd subdue her and bind her. As woman or thylacine. He couldn't let her get away from him.

For all the wrong reasons.

Silence pressed upon him and, unable to resist any longer, he turned. He needed to know what she was doing. He needed to see her.

She stood in the far corner, beside the open doorway leading into what looked and smelt like an old freezer, her stare locked on something on the ground. Something Marshall couldn't see.

He frowned. What was she looking at?

In a fluid move, she dropped into a crouch, picked up the "something" from the floor and straightened to her feet once more.

Marshall's skin prickled. He drew in a quick breath, trying to detect what she held in her hand. Flowers. A hint of flowers and—

"Delanie," Jackie said from the other side of the room. She lifted her stare from her closed fist and gave Marshall a flat look. "She's been here."

Face expressionless, she opened her hand, showing him what she held.

Pale moonlight glinted off the small golden circle, catching the tiny diamonds embedded in the yellow band, turning them to pinpricks of white light. An earring. Just one. Looking abandoned and wrong on Jackie's palm.

Marshall's gut tightened. *Damn it, Rourke. Does Einar know your plan? Why would he have left something like this behind unless he was taunting you?*

"I gave her these as a gift ten years ago." Jackie's calm voice jerked his stare to her face. Her expression was detached. Somehow empty. Broken. "She had them in her ears today."

The statement fell in the taut silence between them, but before Marshall could respond, before he could destroy the space between them and take her in his arms, she crossed the room and walked through the doorway. Out into the cool night. Her shoulders square, her eyes unreadable.

Her scent lingering in the air. Tormenting him.

Haunting him.

He bit back a low growl and followed her from the cafeteria.

He hated himself. Jesus Christ, how he hated himself.

Delanie paced the small shack the hunter had deposited her in after removing her from the greyhound track's cafeteria, rubbing at her arms with her hands. She was cold. The linen trousers she'd worn to Richard Smith's funeral kept her legs protected from the dropping night temperature, but her light-weight cotton shirt did little to keep her warm. She was cold, hungry and frightened.

Not for herself. For Jackie.

Stopping at the shack's only door, she uncrossed her arms, curled her fingers around the rusted knob and gave it a sharp tug. Just as it had the ten previous times, the door refused to budge. Delanie bit back a curse. The place may look like a dump, but the door—the only way out—must have come from Fort bloody Knox.

"Damn it."

Her mutter echoed around the confined space and Delanie winced. Even to her own ears, she sounded petrified.

No, Del. Not petrified. You can't be petrified. Petrified isn't going to get you out of this situation. Petrified is going to get Jackie killed. Suck it up, woman, and get out of here.

Delanie rolled her eyes. God, she was an annoying pain in the arse. How did Jackie ever put up with her?

Fixing her stare on the door—a tricky task given the irritating lack of light in the room—she walked backward, her heels stumbling over the odd empty can and bottle until her backside bumped the wall behind her. Whoever Jackie's hunter was, he had a thing for derelict buildings. First the abandoned cafeteria at the dog track, and now this, whatever this once had been.

The inconsiderate bastard. If you're going to abduct someone and keep them prisoner, at least do it somewhere nice. And warm. Preferably with a television and, oh, I don't know, a direct phone line to the cops!

A mirthless snort sounded in the back of Delanie's nose. Yeah, sure. That's what the psycho was going to do. Take her somewhere public. She'd never been hunting before. Shit, she'd never been fishing before, but she'd watched enough animal documentaries to know the hunter always had the same approach. Separate their target from the safety of numbers, get them away from protection and attack.

Wherever she currently was, she would bet her freebie Prada stilettos it was nowhere near people.

From what she could gather, the hunter was leading Jackie away from the populace. Taking her from one place to another in an attempt to draw her from the safety of civilization.

And Jackie would follow. Delanie had no doubt. Her best friend would get Del's scent in her nose and track her right to this very spot, and when she did, the insane bastard would plunge that evil, massive knife in Jackie's belly and kill her.

You have to stop that from happening, Del. You have to get out of here. Now.

Delanie stared at the closed door on the other side of the shack, focusing her entire energy on the large black rectangle. She bent her knees slightly, springing up onto the balls of her feet. Readying.

Balling her fists, she bunched her shoulders, dragging in five long breaths. *This is gonna hurt, Del.*

Too bad.

She burst forward, sprinting full force at the door, right shoulder lowered. Clenching her jaw and squeezing her eyes shut, she collided with the solid panel of wood. And bounced backward.

Splintering pain exploded in her shoulder. Up her neck. She staggered away from the door, shoulder a world of pain, her head a whole universe. Her heel snagged on something hiding in the filth on the floor, and before she could regain her balance, she fell, landing on her arse with a teeth-clicking snap.

"*Fuck!*"

Her furious scream shattered the silence of the room, breaking into a choking sob at the very end. She dropped her head into her hands, hot tears stinging her eyes. Oh, God. What was she going to do?

"Have you hurt yourself?"

The hunter's calm voice snapped Delanie's head up. He stood in the open doorway looking at her, his expression concerned, pale moonlight outlining him in a silvery white glow.

She leapt forward, shutting out the pain in her body and the fear in her gut. Running for the open door. For the night beyond. She had to get away. Away. She had to warn—

The hunter smashed his fist into her chest.

Agony exploded through Delanie. Hot and total. She stumbled back a step and collapsed, red shards of pain stabbing into her lungs. Black stars burst before her eyes and she pressed her hand to her left breast, gasping for breath.

Crossing the shack's threshold, the hunter swung the door behind him, giving her a worried frown. "Now, that was a silly thing to do, wasn't it?"

Delanie glared up at him. "Go fuck yourself," she rasped, pain ripping her chest with each word.

"While I appreciate the need for masturbation, sexual release is not my priority at this moment."

Hate surged through Delanie's veins. "That's right. Your priority is butchering an innocent woman, isn't it?"

The man's frown furrowed deeper, and he shook his head. "Butcher is such an ugly word. A negative word. What I do is…" he lifted his gaze to the right, as if contemplating, "…eradicate."

Delanie shot up her eyebrows, cold fingers of horror threading through the burning pain in her chest. "Eradicate?"

"Besides," the hunter continued, returning his sharp blue stare back to her. "Jacqueline Huddart isn't a woman, is she? She is a shape-shifter. A paranormal creature."

Removing her hand from the burning ball of pain in her chest, Delanie shook her head. "She's a woman," she snarled, pushing herself to her feet. Fresh black stars blossomed behind her eyes, and for a sickening second the shack seemed to tilt and sway around her. "She was a girl," she continued, planting her feet more firmly on the floor. Anger rolled through her. Tight anger. "And a teenager. At eight she fell from the top of my bunk bed and broke her wrist. At twelve she stacked my pushbike and cut her knee so badly she needed six stitches. At sixteen she had her heart broken by Travis bloody Callister and cried for a week." She fixed the hunter with a hot stare. "What kind of paranormal creature does that?"

Emotionless blue eyes regarded her. "A clever one."

"And that's it? That's your reason for wanting to kill her? She's clever?"

The hunter shook his head, his lips curling into a smile that screamed you poor dumb child. "No, Delanie. I want to kill her to see her die."

Delanie widened her eyes. Hot disgust churned in her gut. "To see her die?"

A smile curled the corners of the man's mouth, a wistful look falling over his scarred face. "I killed a manticore in Brazil in 1875. Its last act was to defecate. I killed a keron-kenken in Russia in 1915. The last seconds of its life were spent sobbing and squealing for mercy. I am quite fascinated with the reaction to death. Every paranormal creature's life perverts the natural order of the world, you see. They draw the essence of the world into their existence. They feed on it. It nourishes them. Strengthens them. Gives them their power." He turned his gaze on Delanie, his smile friendly and relaxed. "They are parasites. As with all parasites, the very last moments of their existence, the very last second before they expire, their *croi* magnifies. Their fight to survive intensifies their life essence, and the moment their existence is terminated, that essence is released."

"And you are there to what? Absorb that power?" Delanie curled her lip, letting him see her contempt. "You're going to kill my best friend, the last of her kind, just to suck up her power?" She shook her head. "Doesn't that make you a parasite too?"

The hunter laughed, a soft, carefree sound that sent an icy spear straight into her chest. "No, no, no, Delanie." He crouched down, bringing his gaze level with hers. Delanie flinched, scurrying backward, not wanting to be close to him, but he didn't seem to notice. Or care. "I do not absorb their power. I do not wish it, nor need it. I am very old. I have my own power, one much more in tune with the earth and her magick. I have hunted and killed creatures that do just that however. Creatures who kill for no other reason than to absorb the *croi* of their prey." His friendly smile stretched wider, his blue eyes dancing with excitement. "It is better for the world they no longer exist."

"But Jackie is not like that." Delanie's heart thumped, a wild beat that made her chest ache. "She's just..." She faulted. What was Jackie, exactly? A human? An animal? Or a...

Monster?

The hunter raised his eyebrows. "Just?"

"She's my friend," she finished on a whisper, her throat tight, her mouth dry. Oh, God, Jack. What do I do? How do I convince him? "My best friend."

With a shake of his head, the hunter leant forward a little, his stare locked on her face. "Your friend is unique, Delanie. Her magick is unique, and as such I long to kill her to see what she does when she dies. And to look into her eyes when I plunge my knife into her belly and have her see me. Have her see the man who tracked her down, hunted her, caught her. That is why I am going to kill Jacqueline Huddart."

Cold fury incinerated Delanie. She screamed, throwing herself at the man, fingers hooked, aiming for his impersonal, insane eyes.

Hands moving so quickly she didn't see them, the hunter snatched her wrists, yanking her arms wide apart. He smiled, a small furrow dipping between his eyebrows. "Now, now, Delanie McKenzie. This is unbecoming." His fingers drilled into the soft underside of her wrists and his smile vanished. "And pointless."

He threw her across the shack, slamming her into the far wall. Before she could fall to the floor, before her body could register the pain tearing through her, he leapt on her. Sinking his fingers into her neck, he jerked her upright. "Hush now, Delanie," he murmured, eyes wide, smile once again stretching his lips. "Or I will rip your throat open and paint the very wall behind you with your blood."

CHAPTER FIVE

"I think we need to—"

"No," Jackie cut Rourke's obvious statement short, refusing to turn her stare from the Audi's passenger window and the dark bush blurring past them. "We don't."

Her animal growled, a low rumble in the pit of its existence. That the damn thing was still horny, still wanting to break free and mate with the Texan irritated the hell out of Jackie. That she agreed with the sentiment pissed her off even more.

Her skin prickled and she knew Rourke was looking at her. Which annoyed her further still.

She heard him stir behind the wheel, and the car picked up speed, taking them away from St. Helens and deeper into the bush surrounding the sleeping coastal town. "You don't know what I'm going to say."

Jackie pulled in a long, steadying breath, the subtle leather of the luxury car doing nothing to lessen the potency of Rourke's scent.

"'I think we need to talk about what happened back there in the cafeteria,'" she said, finishing what he'd begun. She gave

Rourke a quick look over her shoulder before returning her stare to the night-covered countryside outside the car. "To which the answer is, no. We don't."

"I don't make it a habit of making love to someone I've only just met, Detective Huddart."

A hot, wet spear stabbed into Jackie's core at Rourke's statement. She ground her teeth, wishing the traitorous response would go to hell. "We didn't make love." She turned from the window and gave him a flat stare. "We didn't even fuck. You were fully dressed and my feet never left the ground."

The corner of Rourke's mouth twitched. "And that's your benchmark for sex? Your feet off the ground? I'll remember that for next time, darlin'."

Jackie's sex constricted. Next time? *Oh, God, yes, next time.* "There's not going to be a next time," she snarled, both to the infuriating man behind the wheel and herself. Mainly herself. "This time only happened because…"

She stopped, the pulse in her neck leaping away.

Rourke cocked an eyebrow. "Because?"

She didn't answer. She couldn't. The rest was too shameful to finish.

Rourke studied her, his eyes glowing silver in the cabin's shadows. "Because your inner animal was on the verge of taking over, of emerging, and the only way you could prevent that happening was to release the tension another way."

Jackie's heart stopped. She stared at the Texan, her lips tingling, her blood roaring in her ears. "How did you…" Her mouth felt dry. Drier than the Simpson Desert. "How did you know?"

Silver eyes held her stare. Rourke's expression was collected. Controlled. "Because it's the very reason why I stopped." He turned back to the dark road ahead, the car's powerful headlights piercing the night's blackness. "If I'd kept going back there in the cafeteria—and trust me, I really wanted to keep going—*my* inner animal would have taken over. My inner animal would have emerged and it wouldn't have been a man mating with you. It would have been a wolf."

Wolf.

The word made her breath catch in her throat. Wolf? He was a shifter. Just like her. A bloody werewolf from America. No wonder he moved so quickly, could detect Delanie's scent when she couldn't. No wonder the animal inside her—

And then the rest of his statement penetrated the stunned realization roaring in her head and she gasped.

Mating with you.

The statement sent a tight shard into Jackie's core and her sex constricted, still wanting release. Her clit throbbed, her nipples ached.

Mating with you.

Her thylacine rumbled with need, lurking too close to the surface for Jackie's peace of mind, hungering not only release, but Rourke. A primitive, carnal hunger that made her pulse pound and her head spin.

She needed to mate. She needed to release the tension. She couldn't focus on finding Delanie until she did. Christ, she could barely concentrate on anything but Rourke's heat, the taste of his lips, his saliva. The earthy musk of his scent.

Jackie froze, her breath catching in her throat. His scent. She could smell him now.

And you have since you first kissed him. That's why your animal is straining for release—Rourke's scent is in every breath you pull, in every molecule of air you draw into your lungs. He's there. He's in you already.

And you want him to be, don't you?

Her blood roaring in her ears, Jackie closed her eyes. God, yes. She did. More than anything. Chemistry? Primitive animal lust? Physical need? She didn't know the reason why, she just did. She wanted Marshall Rourke. Completely.

Opening her eyes, she turned her stare from the black landscape outside the Audi to give the Texan a steady look. "I want—"

"I can't."

The interruption came from his lips in a flat growl. He stared back at her, silver eyes reflecting the glow from the dashboard, expression unreadable, jaw square.

Icy rejection curled around Jackie's heart. She clamped her hands into fists, driving her nails into her palms. "How do you know what I'm going to say?"

"Because I can smell your heat."

His answer stabbed into her. The ancient animal prowling in her being snarled, anger and hunger making it agitated. Edgy. Suppressing a snarl of her own, she ignored the pain slicing into her chest. It was good he'd refuted her. She needed to get her act together. Rourke's rejection was just the slap in the face she needed. She was a cop, for Pete's sake. She needed to behave like one. Her friend's life was at risk. That was all that mattered.

Straightening her shoulders, she gave him a hard glare. "Who has Del?"

Rourke didn't answer.

Jackie grit her teeth harder. "I've had enough of the games. Who has my friend?"

Rourke's knuckles whitened on the steering wheel. He studied the road, every muscle in his body growing tense. Jackie could taste the irritated energy rolling from him in tangible waves.

"Either tell me, let me out now or face the consequences."

"What consequences?"

"Tasmanian tigers were known for their powerful jaws, Rourke. Do you really want to know what it's like to feel your throat ripped open?"

He didn't say a word—for a short, tense second.

"Who. Has. My. Best. Friend?"

He let out a sharp breath that sounded more like a snarl. "A man called Daeved Einar. He is an ex-P.A.C. agent."

"Pac? What the hell's that?"

Rourke's jaw bunched and his hands gripped the steering wheel harder. "Paranormal Anti-Crime Unit. A top-secret US federal government division that polices the actions of non-human beings."

A sharp and wholly surprised laugh burst from Jackie. She raised her eyebrows, her stomach twisting even as she shook her head. "Paranormal Anti-Crime? Top secret? US government? Fair dinkum, I think you've been watching too many movies."

Rourke flicked her a dark look. "You live in this world, detective. You know what's in it, what other creatures share this planet. Who do you think protects the humans from their natural predators? The cops? The *human* cops?"

"PAC-Men?" Jackie laughed again, the sound scornful and disbelieving. "You're telling me the human race is protected from the evils of paranormal nasties by an agency named after a nineteen-eighty's arcade game?"

A low growl rumbled up Rourke's chest and his nostrils flared. "In 1995, P.A.C. prevented the mass slaughter of over five hundred humans when a higher order gargoyle lost a bet to a djinn. In 1969, P.A.C. ended the bloody reign of a wendigo who had been feasting on young humans in Northern California. In 2004, P.A.C. shut down a human child-trafficking organisation run by a master vampire in Germany. One hundred and eighty children from powerful political families across the world were lost before we killed the blood-sucking bastard. Stolen from their parents and drained of their blood so undead creatures with too much money could get their rocks off on the innocent blood of supposedly untouchable children." He gave her another quick look, this one dark.

Tormented. "P.A.C. exists because it needs to. I only wish it didn't."

Jackie studied him, a lump growing thick in her throat. "*We* killed the blood-sucking bastard? You're an agent."

Another brief, tense silence followed. "Yes."

A cold numbness settled in Jackie's stomach. She licked her lips, her tongue dry. "And this Daeved Einar is your ex-partner."

Rourke's head snapped around, his shimmering stare locked on her face. "How do you know that?"

Jackie gave him a level look. "Your pulse rate went up when you said Einar's name, almost doubled when you called him an ex-P.A.C. agent. It doesn't take a cop to draw the connection. You're emotionally invested in this hunt. Maybe as much as I am."

Rourke shook his head, an expression of awed unease flitting across his face. "Damn, you're good."

Something like triumph sheared into Jackie's cold agitation. She narrowed her eyes, keeping her fingers balled into tight fists. "You told me before Del was being used as bait. What does Einar want with me? As far as paranormal creatures go, I'm pretty sedate."

Rourke twisted his hands on the steering wheel, turning his attention back to the road. "I don't want to tell you that."

"I don't want to break your nose with my fist, but I will if you don't answer me."

The Texan bit back a low mutter, shaking his head. "Okay, darlin'. Daeved Einar was P.A.C.'s poster boy for many, many years. An agent of the highest rank, with more accolades and commendations than could be pinned to his chest. When he was assigned a job, it was done. Quickly. The trouble with P.A.C. agents, we tend to be a little emotionally unstable. Imagine a homicide detective's mind after years of hunting killers. Sick killers. Now, imagine that mind when the killers really are monsters. Imagine decades, and in Einar's case, almost four of 'em hunting said monsters, getting in their head and existing there. Imagine what that does to a psyche."

Jackie suppressed a shiver. She knew all too well the mind of creatures not of the human world. She was one. When she was lost to her thylacine existence, she existed purely on instinct. Hunt. Feed. Mate. Kill. She had little doubt the instinct of a creature born in hell—or whatever place the real monsters of the world came from—would make her dark place seem like a kid's playground. But that still didn't answer her question. Why was Einar after her?

"Two years ago, Einar was retired from the P.A.C.," Rourke went on, as if he sensed Jackie was going to ask the question he'd been skirting from the very moment he'd popped up in her life. "Since that retirement, he's taken up a new hobby." Silver-glowing eyes turned to her for a split second before Rourke returned his stare to the night outside the car. "I need to stop him."

The numb tension in Jackie's stomach intensified. She didn't like the way Rourke said the word hobby. Even less than she liked the way he said retired. "Why was he retired? What kind of hobby?"

Again, Rourke held his answer for a long moment. Again, he bit back a low mutter that sounded a lot like "fuck". He lifted one hand from the steering wheel and dragged it through his hair, turning it into a choppy mess. "He was retired due to excessive force on the job. He tortured an innocent succubus to death. It wasn't the first time he'd done such a thing."

"And his hobby?" Jackie prompted, her gut churning. She didn't like where this was going, but she couldn't stop it now. She wouldn't stop it. The bastard had her best friend. "What does Einar like to do with all his new free time?"

A ragged sigh tore from Rourke, and he shook his head. "Jesus, darlin', you have no idea how much I don't want to tell you this."

Jackie swallowed, anger turning the lump in her throat into a hot ball. "Too bad."

Knuckles bleaching whiter still, Rourke stared fixedly at the road. "His new hobby is hunting paranormal creatures. Hunting them and killing them. For the challenge. For the sport."

Jackie lifted one eyebrow. "Don't you need a license for that?"

Her flippant comment made Rourke frown. "Do you understand what I'm saying? You're his next target. He's hunting you."

Jackie turned to her window, watching the blur of gum trees go by. "I'm a shape-shifting Tasmanian tiger, Pacman. I've been hunted my entire life. My kind have been hunted into extinction. One lone hunter with a screw loose isn't going to send me screaming into the hills."

"It should," Rourke shot back, his broad Texan accent thick with what Jackie could only assume was anger. "You don't know what Einar is capable of."

"Abducting an innocent woman is the first thing that comes to mind," she said, giving Rourke a level look. "Skinning her and gutting her the second."

"You remember what I said?"

"I don't forget anything, Pacman. Comes with the thylacine genes."

He shifted in his seat, an uncomfortable grimace pulling at his lips. "I may have exaggerated a little when I said that."

A cold itch began in Jackie's stomach. She twisted about until she faced Rourke completely, fixing him with an unwavering, unblinking stare. "Why?"

"Because I needed—"

He stopped, his lips turning white as he compressed them into a tight line, his gaze locked firmly on the road. Jackie balled her fists before her fingers could wiggle. For some reason, he'd come close to letting something slip.

Something he didn't want her to know. But what? And why?

Because he can smell your heat?

Shutting down the insidiously enticing thought, she narrowed her eyes, studying Rourke's brooding profile. "Why are you helping me get Delanie back instead of tracking down your ex-partner? Why are you here with me?"

He ignored her, tilting his head to the left a little, his eyes narrowing. "I can't detect Delanie's scent anymore."

Rourke's abrupt, disconnected announcement made Jackie blink. "Excuse me?"

Without a word, the Texan yanked the steering wheel to the left and slammed his foot on the brake. The Audi screeched to the side of the road, stones and dirt and gravel peppering its underbody like bullets. He released his seatbelt and threw open his door, climbing from the cabin to stand beside the car in the space of a heartbeat.

"What the bloody hell are you doing?" Jackie flung open her own door and shot to her feet, glaring at him over the Audi's low roof.

He lifted his head, silent, his hand raised in a *shhh* gesture.

A low growl echoed through Jackie's head and she drove her nails into her palms. Irritation shot through her, a living spark of energy so close to the surface she could almost taste the ozone on her tongue. Damn the man. She was getting sick of this. It had to stop.

"I no longer have Delanie's scent." Rourke swung his head toward her, silvery-tinted eyes reflecting the thin moon. "Can you smell it?"

His statement sent a cold shard into Jackie's chest. She lifted her head, putting her nose into the slight breeze and pulling in a long breath.

Wild, native jasmine rushed over her olfactory nerve, threaded through with melaleuca, acacia and eucalypt oil. Rich, night-dampened soil and wallaby dung followed, an animalistic undertone that went straight to Jackie's thylacine. The creature surged through her, the sweet taste of Tasmania, the birthplace of its magick, giving it strength. Making her skin prickle and her muscles burn.

With a low groan, Jackie shoved the transformation down. Not yet. Not unless she really needed to.

For fuck's sake! And when's that? When Del's dead? Wouldn't that be a touch too late?

"Can you detect her?" Rourke's voice danced around the edges of her awareness, worry and impatience cutting the words. She tuned him to a lesser frequency, narrowing her senses on the taste and sounds of the night.

The road they traveled, the road Rourke had taken them on, lead away from St. Helens, following the Bay of Fires southeast toward the coastline. A briny hint of sea spray flittered over the earthy bushland scents, salty in Jackie's nose. It tickled a memory, like a lone strand of hair brushing against the back of her bare arm. She frowned, ignoring it. It wasn't important.

"Jackie?"

She closed her eyes, loosened her hold on her animal. She needed the heightened senses of the ancient creature. She needed its primordial force entwined with the land around her. Parting her lips, she pulled another breath into her body—past tongue and olfactory bulb at the same time. An oily taste smeared the surface of the sweet air. Petrol. Rubber. A car had driven the same road she and Rourke now stood beside. Three hours ago? Maybe less.

She lifted her head, relaxing her hold on the thylacine within further still.

A ghost teased her. Fragile flowers brushed with terror. A minute particle of aroma almost lost in the loud cacophony of odors and tastes. Teasing her. Taunting her. Just beyond detection.

Beyond detection of your human senses, don't you mean?

Jackie opened her eyes, a cold finger of dread drawing hideous patterns in her belly. She couldn't change. Not with Rourke so close. Not with the heat in her blood and sex and core. She didn't want to be lost to her animal again. She wanted to be her. Detective Jackie Huddart—human, not an animal more connected to the land than possible.

And every second you hesitate is a second Del is still in danger.

She fixed her gaze on the dark road stretching before her, her heart thumping so hard she could barely form rational thought. A car had driven along the road's bitumen length but three hours ago. An old car, its engine highly tuned but with a failing catalytic converter. A car with its windows down? Letting the wind suck into its cabin? Whipping through the long, red head of one of its passengers? A car that may have carried her best friend in its belly?

"Detective Huddart?"

The deep male voice singed Jackie's nerves—a distant heat she had to deny. She needed to find Delanie. She needed to— *shift, shift, hunt, hunt, track, mate*—transform.

Scalding fire poured through her body, turned her blood to mercury and her muscles to liquid. A million pinpricks of heat rained over her flesh. She threw back her head, mouth wide, letting the power of the ancient land stream past her lips, over her tongue and teeth, into her body. Letting it fill her, incinerate her from within, release her even as she released her control over the animal she was and surrendered to its existence.

A soft tearing sound, delicate fabric rent asunder, whispered to Jackie as her clothes were destroyed, but she barely noticed. Didn't care. Clothes? Why would she need clothes?

Affinity flooded through her. Timeless connection to the timeless land around her. She threw back her head and howled, the last of the transformation taking her—bones tearing apart and reknitting, muscles reforming, skin stretching, agony beyond comprehension.

And then the cool gravel pressed against the pads of her paws, the night wind rippled through her fur and Tasmania flooded into her being. Her homeland. Her territory. She lifted her muzzle, tasting the air and the floral/fear texture of Delanie McKenzie's scent flooded into her being.

As did the virile scent of a male wolf.

The craving, urgent heat in the pit of her belly erupted into demanding want. She swung her head, her ears catching every little sound, the vibrations of the earth running up her legs, along her spine, down her tail. A wolf stood behind her, his true form hidden by the awkwardness of human form. She bared her teeth, letting him see her tongue before turning back to the road.

She had to do something. Something her human deemed important. Something the creature within her desperately longed for. She had to...*find Delanie.*

Track.

The night flowed over her as she ran, caressing her coat with cool fingers. It felt wonderful. Intoxicating. Thylacines were not by nature fast runners, but then she was not a typical thylacine. As a Tasmanian tiger, she ran to hunt. As a human, she ran for fitness. When she did, she ran fast. Very fast. The fluid strength of her muscles powered her forward with unerring agility and she brought that human characteristic to her animal form. And it felt good.

The heat in her core grew thicker. She drew the sweet air into her body, its taste like ambrosia in her nose. Colours and sounds thrummed about her. Earth, soil, animals, birds, trees, moss, stones, insects—the scents of them all flooded through her. Fed her. Nourished her.

Lifting her muzzle, she drank in the scents, hunting for one. Human. Female. Flowers and fear.

An image of a tall human female flittered through her head, her hair long and red like the dying sun.

Yes. That's her. Find her.

She burst forward, tail wagging, the frisky fire burning in her sex telling her to play, to return to the wolf behind her and mate even as her human told her to track.

Find her. Please, stay focused. Find Delanie.

Another image of the human female flashed through Jackie's head, the woman's distinct scent singeing over her nerves. Her human's fear was growing. She was scared. Very scared.

And very angry.

The emotion tasted hot in Jackie's nose and a growl rumbled in her chest. She increased her speed, Delanie's scent consuming her. Her paws pounded the road, the hard surface biting into her pads. It had been too long since she'd run this way. Too long since she'd been released to do so. When she found the female, she would run some more. Run and play with the wolf. Bite his ear, his tail, his neck. Roll with him. Lick his balls. Let him mount her and—

Focus!

Jackie flicked her ear at her human's roar. She surged forward, fear/flowers in her nose. The wind blew into her face, tickled her whiskers, sang ancient songs of ancient beings. The spirits of the land whispered timeless words of the dreaming. The magick of the country called her. Welcomed her home. Beautiful, compelling songs in perfect harmony with the wolf now running behind her, free of his human form. His strong heartbeat reached her ears, echoing hers, his pounding lope kissing the ground, sending messages of his strength, his power through the earth, up into her body through her legs. He was behind her, but she could still taste his musk, his hunger and the wanting fire in her belly—

Focus!

Fear laced the silent command. Her human was worried.

Jackie's tongue lolled from her mouth, over her fangs, and she swished her tail. Her human had nothing to fear. Tracking the female—

Delanie

—was fun. Easy. Her scent grew stronger with every tree passed. Soon she would find the female human—

Delanie, damn you! Delanie.

—and then she would run and play and—

No. I will not be lost again.

Cold rage flooded Jackie's veins. An image of two women filled her mind—one tall, one short. Both laughing.

The human memory scraped at Jackie's psyche. She snarled, her human's unease twisting into her natural impulses.

Human. She was human too. She had human friends, human connections. She had human dreams, human desires. Human fears.

Delanie. Delanie was in trouble. She needed to find her. Save her.

The blackness around her became a blur. She moved through the night. Rourke followed her, a massive dark wolf of immeasurable power and age whose heat called to hers, but she remained focused only on one thing. Tracking Delanie's scent. Finding her. Finding her friend.

The bush on either side of the road grew dense. Old trees and vegetation threaded with new trees and scrub, melaleuca strangled by roaming lantana vines. Salt and seaweed tainted the wind. The soft sound of lapping waves skipped over the gentle rustle of leaves and grass. They were drawing closer to the Bay of Fires' waterline, following the deserted road as it wove around the inland body of water. Jackie lengthened her gait, Delanie's scent becoming thin in the briny air. Faster. She needed to be faster.

A sudden gust of wind lashed at her side, ruffling her short coat, pouring over her tongue. She skidded to a halt, lifting her head and pointing her muzzle into its strength.

There. On her left. In amongst the scrub and ancient eucalypts.

Another gust of wind raced through the trees and with it came the stench again—metallic and cloying and fresh.

Human blood.

Delanie's blood.

Cold dread slammed into Jackie's chest. She streaked forward, leaping over vegetation and bush, weaving through the tangled mess of growth lining the road. Behind her, she heard the wolf do the same, his paws barely making a sound as he followed her into the scrub.

She ran, Delanie's scent coating her nostrils, streaming over her olfactory nerve. Close. She was close.

Moonlight flickered above her, its pale light lost in the canopy above, but Jackie didn't notice. Delanie's scent directed her, led her through the bush, farther away from the road, the waterline until, in a clearing almost devoured by creeping vines, she came upon a wooden structure.

Del!

The human within her strained for release, fear and hope turning her natural thylacine wariness into charged urgency. She stood still, studying the shack. It stood silent. Dark. Revealing nothing.

Without a sound, she slunk closer to the structure, stare locked on its sole door, nose skimming the ground. A myriad of odors filtered into her breath: plant and animal alike. Tasmania. Wild Tasmania.

Jackie's heart thumped and she lifted her head, her tail switching. Inside. She needed to go inside. Inside away from the intoxicating, delicious smells threading into her body.

Lowering her muzzle to the ground, she tasted the scents again. Tasmanian devil, echidna, snake, bandicoot. Saliva filled her mouth, dripped from her teeth. She ran her tongue over her muzzle, her whiskers. The scents called her. She pressed her nose harder to the soil, scuffing its sandy grains. New smells. New tastes. Wallaby. Plovers. Skinks.

Her tail wagged.

Deep in her existence, a sound roared. A sound she should know. A voice? What is a voice?

She lifted her head, looking at the shack. She was meant to do something. She was meant to go inside.

She cocked her head to the side, tail flicking side-to-side in a low, agitated arc. Why would she go inside? Inside the thing made by those on two legs? Those that hunted her and killed her family? Those that kept her caged for so many, many moons she almost ceased to be? Why would she go inside? She didn't want to go inside. She wanted to run. She wanted to play. To feed. Wallaby had been on this very spot, only a moment ago. Young. Weak. Abandoned by its mother. The scent tickled her and she ran her tongue over her whiskers again. She wanted to feed.

A soft noise behind her flicked at her ears, and a new scent trickled into her breath. A male scent. She turned her head, the insistent heat in her core becoming an inferno of hungry need as an animal stepped out of the bush. Silver eyes burned at her in the darkness and she lifted her tail. She wanted this one. She remembered his smell.

The roar sheared through her again, louder. She bared her teeth, swinging her head back to the shack. Why was she standing there? Why wasn't she—

Inside. Inside. Go inside now!

The command screamed in her head. She flinched, shame and guilt slicing into her. She was there for Delanie. Her friend. No matter what form she was in, Delanie was her friend. She needed to find her now. Before the hunter hurt her. Or worse.

She leapt forward, forcing the insistent need in her belly down. The night-damp grass and soil matted her fur, chilled the pads of her paws, and she focused her attention on those sensations, not the carnal call of her heat. The shack smelt wrong, but she needed to go inside. Pressing the tip of her muzzle to the edge of the shack's door, the old wood like iron on her nose, she nudged it open.

The still air hung heavy with human—delicate floral scents

cut through with acrid terror. Jackie stood in the doorway, scanning the shack's sparse interior, her ears low, her bristle raised.

Nothing. Delanie's scent—thick in the confined space, sour in its fear and bitter in its anger—the only remains of its recent occupation.

Wherever her friend was, it wasn't here.

Stepping into the shack, she put her nose to the ground, seeking answers. The human female's sweat tainted the dusty floor, but not her blood.

Jackie lifted her head, studying the small dark area. Nothing left by those that walked on two legs to tell her anything. Just the smell of human rage and fear. She swished her tail. Nothing here. Nothing—from the far wall, like a potent imprint of life, wafted the coppery ting of human blood.

Head lowered, ears flattened, she crossed the small space, her nose locked on the scent.

Hunt, hunt, track, track.

Something cold and metal lay amongst the dust and dead insect bodies. Something small, circular.

Watch.

The word floated through her head and she flicked her tail, her heartbeat quickening. The watch belonged to the one with the long red hair who was always kind to her, always in her heart.

Delanie.

She nudged the cold metal thing with her nose, the rich coppery taste of blood trickling into her breath. Faint, yet there. She touched her tongue to the smooth surface.

Delanie's blood—a tiny drop—slicked her taste buds and her heart beat harder. Faster.

A soft sound cracked the silence behind her and she snapped her head in its direction, her stare falling on the wolf.

He stopped at the door, filling its width with his massive frame, his silver eyes watching her, his tail still.

Jackie's muscles thrummed, a base urge she could not understand claiming her. She held the wolf's pinning gaze. Didn't look away. His musky scent flowed into her breath, a scent of dominance and power and stretching time. Made her want to drop to her belly and submit to his force, even as it stirred a defiance deep within her existence as incomprehensible as the need in her belly. She let out a low growl.

An invitation.

A warning.

The wolf's ears twitched. Silver eyes dilated, changed colour. Silver to ancient ice-blue. His inescapable stare held her imprisoned. A violent shudder wracked through his form, vibrating through the very earth into Jackie's body. His thick black fur shimmered with unseen light, his blue eyes sparked with white fire and then he stood before her on two legs. Furless, tailless. A wolf in a man's body.

A naked man's body. Panting, sweating, his muscles coiled, his desire long and thick and hard jutting up from between his corded thighs.

"Jackie."

Rourke's raw whisper scaled Jackie's senses.

Explosive want detonated in her centre. She leapt at him and transformed mid-flight.

Her palms slammed into Rourke's bare chest, driving him backward under her force. He tumbled, his hands knotting in her hair, his mouth claiming hers, crushing it, his tongue delving between her lips before his back could even make contact with the floor.

She slid down his body, straddling him, gripping his hips with her inner thighs, his sweat-slicked flesh hot against hers. Her sex, sodden with desire and want, pushed at his cock, the rigid organ parting her folds with ease.

God, she'd never been so wet.

Fisting her hands in his hair, ignoring the cruel knowledge what she was doing was insane, was dangerous beyond all measure. Her tongue mated with his, her heart hammering so hard she could barely draw breath. She rolled her hips slightly away, up the flatness of his abdomen before, with a low growl in her chest and mind, she shoved backward. Impaling herself on his cock.

CHAPTER SIX

Fuck, he'd never felt someone so tight. So fucking tight. Marshall thrust into Jackie's sex, his mind gibbering in ecstatic disbelief, his body incinerating from within. He moved inside her, pumping into her gripping heat, filling her with every inch he had.

She whimpered, the sound like aural ambrosia to his desire. Holy Hell, he wanted her. Wanted this. So much so he couldn't stop. He didn't care it fucked up his plans. He didn't care it created a weakness he may never recover from. He wanted to fuck Jackie, mate with her, claim her, unlike any female—animal or human—he'd had before.

Plunging his tongue deeper into her willing mouth, he drove his heels into the ground, planting his weight more firmly on the floor so as to gain greater force in his thrusts. She whimpered again, a guttural noise that sent shards of wet electricity to his balls.

He tore his hands from her hair, raked them down her back and cupped her arse, squeezing each cheek with brutal impatience. He wanted to touch all of her. At once and immediately. He wanted to mark every delicious part of her body as his own. Fuck if he would ever let anyone else have her. She was his. *His.*

The thought raised a growl in his chest—whether his or his beast's, he didn't know or care—and he dragged his hands back up to her hair, tangling his fingers in its silken strands. He nipped at her bottom lip, drew it into his mouth. Sucked on its fullness before, desperate to taste her further, her sweat, her cream, he tore his mouth from hers and slid his lips down her throat.

She rolled her head back, bowing her neck, her sex constricting on his cock as she rode his penetrations in harmony with his mouth's exploration. He traveled the firm column of her throat, up to her jaw, her ear. Capturing her earlobe between his teeth, he nipped its softness, suckled it gently. Her flesh tasted sweet on his tongue and he moaned, sliding his mouth from her ear down to her jaw, her chin. "Christ," he murmured against her flesh, tightening his fists in her hair to roll her head to the side, exposing the other side of her neck to his mouth. "You taste good. Delicate and subtle, like the air in the Rio Grande after rain." He slanted his lips across hers again, dipped into her mouth with his tongue, traced her teeth. "It's addictive. Powerful. I can't get enough of you."

Jackie's groan vibrated down her throat, into her chest and she arched on top of him, rolling her hips to take him deeper still. "Please," she gasped, her nails sinking into his shoulders.

Squirming tension twisted in Marshall's groin. "Please what, detective?"

She didn't answer. Just shook her head and rode him harder, her thighs gripping his sides, her nails scoring his flesh.

Staring at her face, its pleasure-enrapt beauty mesmerizing, he smoothed one hand from her hair and stroked his fingers down the line of her spine. A shiver rippled through her body, pinching her already hard nipples into puckered tips. He smiled and tasted her collarbone with a string of lingering kisses. "Tell me."

She shook her head again, licking her lips as she closed her eyes.

A little pulse beat wildly below her ear and he pressed his lips to it, breathing in her scent through his nose as he smoothed his hand from her back to her ribcage. "Tell me," he ordered against her neck, punctuating each word with a tiny bite. "Tell me what you want me to do to you."

Jackie's breath quickened. Grew shallow. Ragged. "I want..." A hitching moan fell from her as he moved his hand between their bodies and captured her nipple between his knuckles. She arched her back, grinding her sex harder to his cock. "Oh..."

Marshall squeezed her nipple again, freeing his other hand from her hair and placing it on her shoulder. He pushed— gently but with undeniable command—creating space between them enough to cup her other breast and palm its swollen weight. "You want me to suck your nipples?"

The question was a statement. Before Jackie could respond, he grabbed her arse with both hands and moved into a sitting position, the sudden action stabbing his cock against the inner wall of her pussy.

She cried out, the sound raw and loud, her back arching, her sex taking him deeper still.

He grabbed each breast as the cry burst past her lips, scooped them together and rolled his thumb pad over each pinched nipple. "Shall I take these into my mouth, detective?" He looked up into her face, the heat in her eyes sending new blood to his cock. Without waiting for her to respond, he lowered his head and closed his lips over one nipple, drawing it into his mouth with gentle suction, flicking his tongue over its tip in soft stabs before moving to the other.

"Jesus!" Jackie groaned, pushing her hips forward, her

hands raking his back, scoring lines of exquisite pain across his flesh with her nails.

Marshall's cock grew thicker, harder in her pussy and he dragged his mouth from her breasts, moving it to her neck. She whimpered, letting her head fall to the side as he explored her jawline, the shallow dip below her ear. He pressed his tongue to the rapid beat dancing there, pinching her nipples as he did so, enjoying the raw moan slipping past her lips. He created that sound in her. He created the pleasure it signified.

The knowledge filled him with power, and he growled, sliding his arms around her waist and up to her shoulders. He curled his hands into her hair, holding her locked to him, his balls swelling with heat so tight and heavy he felt sure he would lose his mind. He was close to coming. Very close, and he so much wanted to do more to the woman impaled on his shaft.

Mark her. Claim her.

Gazing into her shining amber eyes, he pulled in a ragged breath. "I can't control the wolf in me for much longer, Jackie."

His statement made Jackie's eyelids flutter closed for a second before she shifted on his lap, taking him deeper, deeper still into her sex. "Then don't."

A growl rumbled in his chest, his wolf's growl. He thrust into her, stabbing her core with driving need, each stroke growing faster, faster. She rode him completely, her stare locked on his face, her lips parted, her breath rapid. Her sex squeezed his cock in a series of pulses, each one increasing in strength until she threw back her head and let out a long raw sound. The howl of an animal in rapture.

It was too much. Marshall's tenuous hold on his control incinerated. His wolf howled, racing for release, turning his already burning muscles to liquid fire. Wanting to mount her, claim her, mark her, mate, fuck...

He had to stop it, he had to—

Mark her as your own.

He let out a roar, his orgasm consuming him, flooding her

sex with his seed as he fisted her hair, yanked her head to the side and sank his teeth into her neck.

The cool night air bit into Daeved Einar's flesh, turned his breath to mist as it passed his lips. He stood motionless beneath a tall tree, its dense foliage concealing his whereabouts, hiding him amongst a curtain of slender light-grey leaves and long bottle-brush-type flowers, their cloying fragrance over-powering any scent he may excrete while watching those in the shack.

He curled his hands into two tight fists, cold rage and disgust unfurling in his stomach. How considerate of them to leave the door open.

Stare locked on the two "humans" within the structure's walls, he studied their actions, noting the smooth, feminine muscles of the female and the coiled, ropey muscles of the male.

The male.

Rourke.

A soft crack shattered the heavy silence in his head and Einar bit back a curse, the dull ache in his jaw telling him he'd ground his jaw so tight one of his molars had fractured.

He pressed his fingers to the side of his face, not daring to rub in case the two in the shack heard the scraping sound of flesh-on-flesh. He ran his stare over the naked form of his ex-partner, mindless to the erotic display. The rage and disgust in his gut twisted into a knot. Marshall Rourke was a dire werewolf.

Disgust turned to contempt and he narrowed his eyes. Icy pain sliced into his head but he ignored it. It was irrelevant, inconsequential. Compared to the revelation he'd just discovered, a broken tooth was nothing. Marshall I'm-Too-Fucking-Righteous Rourke was a dire wolf. How did he not know that? How had the cocky Texan kept that little fact a secret? They'd been partners for years. Years fighting the "good fight", working so closely together in the hunt and extermination of dangerous paranormal creatures they'd shared the same fucking toothbrush, and he was only discovering now the man was a fucking *dire* werewolf? A creature as extinct as the thylacine Einar now hunted?

And yet, it explained so much. His phenomenal sense of smell, his preternatural strength and speed, his failure to age in the entire duration they were partners.

His pathetic empathy for paranormals below his own standing.

No wonder he'd never shifted into his wolf form in all the years they were partners. He'd been keeping a big, fat secret.

Einar sank his nails into the centre of his palms. Rourke had fooled him. Fooled the P.A.C. suits as well. All P.A.C. agents were creatures of paranormal origin—they had to be—but only those approved by the Executive Director. A dire wolf, an animal classified extinct for over ten thousand years with little available data known on its behaviour and psyche, was not on that list. Einar himself had needed to jump through more hoops than he'd found comfortable when joining P.A.C. So many hoops *his* true origin had come close to being discovered.

If the suits had known the Texan was a *dire* werewolf, not just the common Northern Hemisphere werewolf he purported to be, lying for years about his true species, they would have been less inclined to believe Rourke when he'd stood against Einar during his "trial".

A silent snort of contempt sounded at the back of Einar's throat at the word. Trial. Witch-hunt was more appropriate. What P.A.C. failed to understand was he kept them all safe. His "savage, unnecessary brutality" kept everyone safe. The second they'd forced his retirement—thanks to Rourke's bleeding heart testimony—the suits had handed mankind to the barbaric beings that perverted the world on a silver fucking platter.

Kill them both. Right now.

The enticing thought slashed through his head and he stiffened. It would be easy. Very easy. His eyes narrowed and he studied them in the moon's pale glow. They had no idea what was going on. Too busy with the depraved sins of the flesh, too busy fucking each other's brains out. He could slip into the shack unnoticed and slice Rourke's throat open before the dire wolf's sickening howls of pleasure died away. He could plunge his blade into the thylacine's chest, right between the breasts Rourke now mauled, and pierce her heart.

Then do it.

He lifted his right foot, his pulse quickening, his hand stealing to his knife.

And stopped.

No. He didn't want to rush Huddart's kill. He'd spent too many months hunting her to not enjoy her final moment, and if Rourke was here, there was a distinct possibility other P.A.C. agents were as well. He couldn't risk their interference. When he killed Jacqueline Huddart, he wanted to relish every slow moment. He wanted to drink in the terror shining in her eyes. He wanted to bathe in the fear leeching from her pores. There was no quick kill for the thylacine. The last of her kind deserved a long, considered death, nothing as crude as a single, fatal penetration. Besides, now he knew what Rourke was, well, his ex-partner deserved the same treatment. There was no way he was going to miss the chance for payback.

Letting his gaze run over the naked forms of his prey, he considered his next move. He had to separate them. Somehow, he had to get them alone.

He thought of the human female trussed to a tree deeper in the bush. He'd moved Delanie Mackenzie to watch Huddart track her scent, curious if the thylacine would transform to do so. How did he use this to solve his Marshall Rourke problem?

Rourke could never resist a damsel in distress.

A slow smile pulled at Einar's lips and, without a sound, he stepped backward, away from the shack and the copulating perversions within.

He knew what to do. And all he needed was a little bit of the human's blood soaked into her brassiere.

Items very easy to arrange.

Jackie cried out. Marshall's teeth sank into her flesh and exquisite pain exploded through her body. She came, again and again, each climax like a detonation of charged heat in her core. Each one driving her higher and higher to the next.

Oh, God, how could this be happening?

The animal inside her howled, consumed by the primitive pleasure of Marshall's bite. Base rapture flooded through her and she arched her back, the dominating force of his teeth on her neck making her cry out again.

Marking her. He was marking her. As his territory. As his mate. He was marking her and she should be stopping him. Tasmanian tigers mated for life. Once the male marked the female with his bite, once his saliva mixed with her blood they were bound together forever. She should be stopping Marshall, but she couldn't.

Since the very second she'd seen him across the crowded airport, her very existence hungered for him. Had recognized him. Her body had known this moment would come long before her stupid, backward human brain could comprehend what was going on. Two alphas finding each other. Two equals in every aspect. Two animals, two humans, one undeniable connection.

She should be stopping him—she wasn't ready to be mated, to be marked—but she couldn't. She didn't want to. Her thylacine didn't want to.

"Oh, Christalmighty, Jackie," Marshall groaned into her

neck, his hands falling from her hair. He grabbed her arse and yanked her harder to his hips, sinking his cock deeper into her sex even as the wild shudders of his orgasm began to subside. "Jackie, Jackie."

He moaned her name, the sound raw and utterly exposed. His hands slid from her backside and he curled his arms around her waist, holding her close to him. Closer and with more reverence than anyone had held her before, his head buried into her neck, his breath hot and rapid on her flesh.

Jackie stayed motionless in his embrace, her hands still fists in his hair. Her sex throbbed, a fading beat still potent enough to make her whimper. God, what had they done?

What were they going to do now?

Fuck, fuck, mate, mate.

She slammed a mental door on her thylacine's rapturous suggestion, her throat tight. What had just happened was insane. She was kidding herself otherwise if she thought differently. Two animals, two humans? What the fuck was she on about? She was an Australian cop hunting the lunatic who'd abducted her best friend and Marshall was a wolf unlike any she'd ever seen... Hell, unlike any she knew even existed. Mated or not, there was no way in hell she could succumb to the call of her needs again.

Heat.

The single word slipped through her mind and Jackie froze, her eyes widening. She sucked in a sharp breath. She was in the peak of her cycle, and they hadn't used any protection.

Oh, God. What was she thinking?

You weren't. It was all instinct. Animal instincts. This is what happens when you forget what you are, Jackie, and let your thylacine rule your actions. This is what you get for releasing it. This is what you get for—

"Jesus Christ, Jackie, I'm sorry."

Marshall's low growl against the curve of her shoulder jerked Jackie from the grim thought. He moved against her, lifting his head from her neck to drag his hands through his hair. He didn't look at her. Not at first at least, and when he did Jackie's chest squeezed tight at the tormented contempt in his eyes.

"Christ, I've fucked this up." He shook his head, scraping his hand down his face before dropping his forehead to her shoulder. "Shit. Shit. Shit."

Jackie blinked, her gut churning. This wasn't quite what she'd expected. "Hey." She nudged him with her shoulder, running her hands down his back. His skin was smooth and warm, the muscles underneath long and sinewy. Her thylacine stirred in appreciation and the heat between her thighs grew damp. "Hey," she said again, shutting out the realization he was still buried deeply in her sex.

Marshall didn't move and a wholly disquieting sense of unease began to gnaw at Jackie. What was going on? Just what in the bloody hell was going on? "Marshall?"

He didn't respond.

"Marshall?"

For a split second, she felt the Texan's arms hold her tighter, and then he pulled away from her. Slightly. He looked at her with an unwavering gaze, his eyes reflecting the weak moonlight, his jaw clenched. "I bit you."

Jackie returned his steady look, her heart hammering. "Yeah, I kinda figured that out."

His Adam's apple jerked up and down his throat as he swallowed. "I should apologise."

Jackie narrowed her eyes. "Should?"

He didn't say anything for a long moment and then, with a muttered growl, he shook his head. "I should, but I can't." He slid his hands up her back, a slow caress that sent sensual shivers all the way to her core. "I've fucked everything up, Detective Jackie Huddart. Nothing has gone the way it was meant to, the way I planned, but I can't apologise for biting you. For marking you as mine." He shook his head again, his stare growing intense. "I want you, Jackie. I don't know what it is about you, but I want you. The very idea of not being able to touch you, smell you any time I want makes me crazy. The thought of someone else touching you, anyone else touching you, pushes me beyond crazy to a dangerous place." He stopped, swallowed, closed his eyes and turned his head away. "Fuck, the thought of Einar getting his hands on you pushes me beyond even that place." He let out a sharp sigh and returned his stare to her face. "I am an animal at soul, Jackie. A savage animal with a savage history. I am over two hundred years old, have killed more monsters than I care to count and have no discernable future that I can see beyond killing more."

Jackie's chest grew tight. So tight she could barely draw breath. She opened her mouth, knowing she should say something, but honestly clueless to what that something should be. What did she say?

Marshall shook his head, his eyes haunted. "I have little to offer anyone, Jackie, including myself let alone a life mate and I swear to God and all things holy, I did not set out to mark you as mine."

"But you did."

Jackie frowned at her own words. They weren't accusatory or angry, and given the situation, either was appropriate. No, they were...what? Confused?

Hopeful?

Oh, you truly are *insane, Huddart.*

Marshall let out another sharp sigh and she felt his body tense.

"I did."

She studied him, waiting for him to say more. When he didn't, when he just held her close, his heart thumping so hard she could feel it in her core, his gaze holding hers, unreadable and inescapable, she let out her own sigh. "So, what do we do now?"

He slid his hands up her back and gave her a wry, lop-sided grin. "We save your best friend and I deal with my ex-partner."

Jackie raised her eyebrows.

And before she could say that illusive bloody "something" she knew still waited to be said, Marshall leant forward and kissed her.

CHAPTER SEVEN

Delanie tugged at the length of rope tying her to the old gum tree. The steely fibre cut into her wrists, a slicing burn that made her eyes water and her temper boil. Damn it, how the hell was she to wear her watch now?

What watch? The psycho nut-bag took your watch, remember? Along with the earrings Jackie gave you and your bra.

She tugged again on her bindings, earning nothing from her efforts but more pain and frustration. Damn it, when she got out of here she was going to…

Slumping awkwardly against the tree, the short length of rope pressing against her chest, Delanie bit back a sob. A dull weight fell to the pit of her stomach. Get out of here? Who was she kidding? She wasn't getting out of anywhere. The hunter was a certifiable lunatic, and if Hollywood had taught her anything, certifiable lunatics who carried big knives were not likely to leave witnesses to their lunacy alive.

Another sob worked its way up her throat, thick and choking, and she closed her eyes. She couldn't see anything anyway, so what was the point? The bush around her was darker than pitch, the moon too thin and new to cast any light, the stars too far away to do anything but taunt her.

"Oh, God, Delanie, now you're just being melodramatic."

Opening her eyes, she squinted into the darkness, trying like hell to make out her surroundings. She wasn't giving up. Not after all the shit the hunter had put her through already. So what if she was tied up out in the middle of the bush? Big deal. She'd survived the Boxing Day sales in Sydney. Five hundred pushing, inconsiderate shoppers all fighting for the best bargain made this look like a picnic. A much, much darker picnic, albeit, minus the food and friends and folding chairs, but a picnic all the same. It even had the annoying bugs buzzing at her face.

Delanie huffed at the unseen insect dive-bombing her ear, wishing she could swipe at it with her hand. She didn't want to be here. She wanted to be in her motel room with Jackie, sharing a bottle of white wine and doing her best to convince her best friend not to go back to the mainland.

The dull weight sitting heavy in her gut rolled and she chewed on her bottom lip. She had to get out of this. She had to warn Jackie what the psycho nut-bag was planning to do.

Pushing herself from the tree trunk, she returned her attention to the rope knotted around her wrists. She would get out of this, damn it. Hollywood could go stick their gory, blood-soaked clichés in their ear. The heroine's best friend didn't always die. Sometimes she came back for the sequel.

Delanie glared at her wrists. "And I plan on being in the sequel." She bent over, raising her wrists to her mouth. She'd get out of this bloody insane situation even if she had to gnaw her way out. She'd paid a fortune for her caps. It was about time they earned their keep.

"I assure you, Ms McKenzie," a friendly voice uttered behind her, making Delanie's blood ran cold. "You will not be able to chew through that rope."

She snapped upright, the sight of the hunter stepping toward her through the darkness slamming her throat shut. "Let me go, you sick fuck."

The second she snarled the words she wanted to take them back. Her skin broke out in a clammy sweat and she tensed, waiting for the sick bastard to strike her.

He didn't. Instead, he laughed, the relaxed sound making her stomach roll some more. "Tsk tsk, Ms Mckenzie. Surely by now you know I'm not going to let you go." He moved closer, the waning moonlight catching in his eyes for a second and Delanie shrank back, ramming herself against the tree.

God, he looked like a walking corpse. An insane walking corpse.

Oh, Lord, help me.

The man's smile stretched wider. He lifted his right hand to her face and Delanie bit back a cry, flinching as he lightly patted her left cheek. "Now I have two traps to set, you are more important than ever." He chuckled. "In fact, I would not be able to do this without you, Delanie."

A sob burst up her throat and she shook her head, unable to stop the tears stinging her eyes. God, she was pathetic. "Please," she croaked. "Just let me go. Please. I won't tell anyone. I promise. Just let me go and leave Jackie alone and I won't tell anyone."

Pathetic, Delanie. Pathetic.

The hunter's face creased into a worried frown and he lowered his hand from her cheek. "I'm worried about you, Delanie. This is not at all becoming."

"Fuck becoming!" she screamed, throwing herself at him.

Hot agony detonated in her shoulders as the rope snapped tight, jerking her backward. She cried out, yanking at her bindings, blinded by her tears.

He chuckled again. "That's better. I like this Delanie McKenzie more."

Delanie thrashed against the rope, each wild tug cutting her wrists deeper. She felt her blood seeping from the ragged wounds and didn't care. She couldn't do this anymore. She'd had enough, damn it. Enough.

The hunter didn't move. "Keep it up, Ms McKenzie. The more you fight now, the less I will have to make you bleed."

His words punched into her like a fist. Her knees collapsed and she slumped as far as the rope would let her, half-dangling, half-standing, her face wet with tears and sweat and snot. "Jackie is going to kill you," she mumbled, staring through the tangled mess of her hair at the ground near her feet. "And when she does I'm going to watch and laugh my arse off."

The air shifted beside her as the man stepped closer and placed his hands to her wrists, his fingers working the knot there. "It is an interesting notion, Ms McKenzie. But a foolish one."

The second the rope released its tension from her wrists, Delanie moved. She slammed her knee upward, smashing the hunter's balls into his groin. He screeched, buckling over, his hands flying to his crotch as he did so.

Delanie slapped her palms to his head, smacking his ears with two fierce whacks. "How's that for foolish, fucker," she spat, shoving him backward and sprinting like hell.

The trees reached out for her, snatching at her as she ran through the black bush. Her wrists throbbed and her lungs burned, but she didn't care. She'd had enough, damn it. Enough.

Stumbling over the uneven terrain, she fought to stay on her feet. She couldn't fall now. She ran harder, sucking in breath after breath, the cool night air singeing her windpipe, cutting like razor blades. And still she ran, not even slowing as her right ankle rolled beneath her. She'd had enough, damn it. She wasn't stopping. Waving her arms wildly to regain balance, she ran. Over rocks and fallen trunks, branches lashing at her face, her legs and arms, gouging at her flesh, tearing at her hair.

She ran, forcing her legs to keep pumping. She couldn't see for shit, but she ran. Somewhere nearby was a road. The hunter had driven into the bush on a gravel road. When she found that road, she'd find even ground. When she found even ground, she could run faster. When she ran faster, she'd find help. Help. Help for her. Help for Jackie.

She'd had enough. Enough.

A branch hooked her ankle, the right one, and blinding pain ripped up her leg. She stumbled, a cry tearing from her throat. *No.* She hit the ground, unseen rocks and sticks gouging into her palms and knees.

Get up, you pathetic idiot!

She scrambled to her feet. Pushed herself forward. Running. Again.

Birds squawked and screeched, furious to be disturbed from their slumber. Surprised animals scurried out of her way. She balled her fists, running harder.

Enough, damn it. She'd had en—

"Where are you going, Delanie?"

The hunter appeared before her. Just like that. As if some curtain had been jerked upward, revealing the nasty fucker standing directly in her path, a curious smile on his face.

Delanie screamed, throwing herself backward, even as her feet continued to propel her forward. Gravity betrayed her. She fell, her feet going out from beneath her, her arse hitting the ground.

"That looked unpleasant," he commented, head cocked to the side.

Delanie flung herself onto her hands and knees. Scrambled for traction. She lunged away from him, bursting into a limping sprint, her heart slamming against her breastbone. No. No, oh God, no. No.

The hunter appeared before her again. Just like that, there. "This is becoming tedious, Ms McKenzie."

"No!" she screamed, staggering backward. She caught herself before she hit the ground, stumbling over her own feet, dead wood, jagged rocks. Turning, she ran away. Straight into Einar's chest.

"And now," he snarled, "it's becoming boring."

Icy pain lashed her arms and, with a horrified gasp, Delanie watched a thick length of rope—the very rope stained by her very blood—snake around her wrists in blurring speed and smash them together. Rope untouched or guided by any hand.

Her breath punched from her lungs and she collapsed to the ground, gaping at her bound wrists.

"I really wish you hadn't done that, Delanie," the hunter chided and she jerked her stare up to his face.

"What are you?"

He gave her a wide smile, his right hand slowly withdrawing from behind his back, the long blade he held glinting in the new moon's weak light. "I've already told you that, Ms McKenzie." He cast the knife a casual look before returning his gaze to her face. "Remember? I have my own power, one much more in-tune with the earth and her magick. Were you not paying attention?"

"What the fuck does that mean?" She glared up at him. She twisted her wrists but they didn't budge. The rope wrapped around them only pulled tighter.

The man chuckled. With blurring speed, he hooked his left hand between her bound wrists and jerked her to her feet. "It means you can't ever outrun me." He lowered his face to hers, his eyes catching the thin moon's glow. "And neither can Jacqueline Huddart."

And with one quick stroke, he plunged his blade into her side.

Jackie's heart smashed against her breastbone. She kissed Marshall back, the velvet heat of his lips on hers making her head spin. Of their own accord, her arms slid up around his shoulders, and she tangled her hands in his hair, holding his head as she rolled her hips forward.

His shaft was still buried in her sex and she felt it spasm, grow thick and long. It was a connection she could no more deny than ignore, but it was not the connection making her blood tingle in her veins. Making her pulse slam in her throat.

Not the connection making her surrender to the wild heat igniting in her core again.

Mated.

Marshall's existence called to hers. She could not think of it any other way. Every molecule in her body felt him on every level imaginable. And then some.

Felt him and hungered for him.

She growled, rolling her hips forward again, taking his stiffening cock deeper into her centre as she plunged her tongue into his mouth. God, she wanted all of him. Lunacy. The whole thing was lunacy, and she wouldn't have it any other way.

Mated.

The very notion made her already spinning head light. She tore her mouth from Marshall's, desperate for air. He moaned in protest, scoring a hot path along her jaw, down her throat to her shoulder, his fingers curling over her butt, squeezing each cheek with fierce pressure.

Oh, God, Jackie. Stop. You don't have time…time… Delanie…you should be finding… Oh, God, that feels so…yes…

Her thylacine muted the disconnected thought with a low gnarr, consumed with pleasure and elemental need.

Mate, fuck, mate.

"Damn it, Jackie," Marshall groaned against her collarbone. "I know I should stop…" He nipped at her neck, raking his hands up her back as he thrust harder into her pussy. "I should stop…"

She closed her eyes, rolling her head to the side to grant his mouth greater access to her throat.

Fuck, mate, fuck.

A noise slipped past her lips. A whimper? A protest? An agreement? She didn't know. Didn't care.

She rolled her hips. Took him deeper. Her flesh on fire, her blood roaring in her ears.

"Christ, you feel so right." Marshall's lips tasted her shoulder, her jaw. His heels rammed into her arse cheeks as he pumped into her, filling her completely. "So fucking right I can hardly think."

"Then don't." Jackie panted, her pulse a sledgehammer beneath her ear. "Just make me yours."

The gasped command seemed to ignite a fire in Marshall's desire. His lust for her became wild. With a growl deeper and more menacing than any she'd heard, he pushed her onto her back. Grabbing at the undersides of her knees, he yanked them up beside his hips, slamming his cock into her sex with fierce force. The dirt and grit on the deserted shack's floor pressed into Jackie's flesh, but it didn't matter. This was how animals claimed each other. Raw and savage and feral. This was how an alpha male took his mate—aggressive dominance and base need. He pumped into her, harder, harder, each stroke marking her more and more his. She scratched at his back, tore at his shoulders with her blunt nails, thrusting into each penetration.

"Look at me, Jackie." Marshall's thunderous whisper snapped her stare to his face, and her pussy constricted at the fierce intensity in his eyes. His need to possess her, own her, burned in their piercing blue depths, so blazing it stole her breath.

A whimper vibrated up her throat, the sound caught by Marshall's mouth as he crushed her lips with his. He assaulted her mouth. No, he fucked her mouth with his, his tongue claiming her just as surely as his cock claimed her sex. She met his ferocity and returned it, sinking her nails into the back of his neck as she bit his bottom lip, sucked it, tasted it.

There was nothing gentle about the way they took each other. Nothing tender or sweet.

"Fuck!" Jackie arched her back, slamming her heels to the floor, her arms spread wide. She bucked her hips forward, ramming her sodden, throbbing sex to his groin. He slammed into her. Again and again. Liquid electricity shot through her and she cried out, bucking once more. Christ, he wasn't just mating with her, he was taking full and utter possession.

Her thylacine howled, reveling in the unadulterated pleasure flooding through her. Surrendering to the animalistic nature of their copulation. Jackie cried out again, on the very brink of orgasm, her flesh tingling, her breath shallow. One more thrust and she would explode.

He drove his cock deeper into her. Hard.

"Yes!" The brutal penetration detonated Jackie's climax. She came, hard, fast. Shudders wracked her body. She clung on to Marshall, the constricting pulses pushing her beyond even the instinctual primitiveness of her animal. Turning her into a creature of pure pleasure. Jackie McKenzie no longer existed. The cop, the human, the Tasmanian tiger, the shape-shifting thylacine, all incinerated by the pleasure consuming her. "Yes!"

Marshall thrust into her still, his hands pinning hers to the ground. He loomed over her, staring into her face with iridescent silver eyes, his nostrils flaring, his skin slicked with sweat. "Mine," he growled. "Say it. Mine."

"Yours," Jackie cried, voice hoarse and choked. "Oh, fuck, yours now and forever."

His growl became a roar and he sank his teeth into her neck again, biting her with such force pain ripped through her shoulder. She snatched at his hair, fisted her hands in its length.

Mine, mine.

She heard the words in her head. Felt them in her soul.

Mine.

Marshall thrust into her, and just as she felt her own animal surge for release, just as she felt her climax reach its mounting peak, he threw back his head and howled, his rhythm lost to his rapture as he pumped her full of his seed.

Mine.

Marked.

Mated.

He collapsed, pressing her to the floor, his body wracked by fading shudders, his flesh slicked with sweat, his breath ragged, his muscles lax.

Jackie skimmed her fingertips up and down his back, forcing her breath to steady, willing her heart to slow down. She closed her eyes, all too aware how much she loved the feel of the Texan pressed against her, how quickly she'd become addicted to it.

Think, woman. Think. You've just mated for life with a complete stranger. He knows your most intimate of secrets and you still only know what he's told you. Which is sweet bugger-all.

A cold pressure wrapped around her chest and she opened her eyes, staring at the shack's corrugated iron roof and the black sky visible through the gaping cracks and holes. Not only mated, but marked. There was no other way to describe their second savage copulating. It wasn't love making. It was rutting.

Swallowing a thick lump in her throat, she lifted one hand to her neck. Her fingers brushed over wet flesh, tiny slivers of pain radiating through her from the light contact. Marshall's bite had not just emotionally marked her; it had physically marked her as well—punctured her skin and drawn blood. She could feel the moisture on her fingertips, could smell her blood and his saliva on the still night air.

Deep within, her thylacine stirred from sated bliss and Jackie bit back a moan, realization dawning on her. She could smell Marshall's saliva. She could smell his sweat. She could smell his very pheromones.

Her sex contracted with eager need at the thought, and she squeezed her eyes shut. There was no going back now. She could smell and taste him on the very air. She could feel his breath disturbing the very fabric of existence. She could hear his heart beat and his blood flow through his veins.

Mated.

She gnawed on her bottom lip, staring at the rusty, rotten roof.

"Your fingers are wriggling."

Marshall's low murmur made Jackie start and, cheeks heating, she snapped the hand on his back into a fist. Damn it. That he said something meant he'd noticed it before. *Bloody hell, Jackie. Aren't you meant to be an expert at hiding your emotions?*

He lifted his head, studying her with unreadable eyes. "Why do you do that?"

She clenched her jaw and looked away. "I don't know what you're talking about."

"Hmm." The ambiguous sound vibrated through his chest a split second before he rose to his feet and moved away from her. "We have to go."

She looked at him, doing everything in her power to keep her stare from caressing the lean perfection of his naked body. A heavy pulse thumped in her neck. His back and butt was the stuff of female fantasies—fantasies she'd never harbored until he'd thrust himself into her life. A life of which he was now so inextricably a part. So why was she feeling so...edgy?

"I have spare clothes in the car." He threw her a quick look over his shoulder, but even in the shack's almost non-existent light she could see his gaze did not fall on her. Her pulse quickened and her stomach knotted.

She straightened from the floor, brushing the grit and dirt from her arse as she glared at the back of his head. "You do this often? Destroy your clothes while out and about?"

"Not for over six decades."

His voice was flat. She frowned, the knot in her stomach growing tighter.

"I have a set for you too."

Jackie's eyebrows shot up. "You expected me to transform while dressed?"

"Yes."

A hot worm of anger wriggled into Jackie's tight stomach. She frowned, glaring at Marshall's back. "So glad one of us knows everything about the other."

He tensed, and for a moment she thought he was going to turn and look at her. Her heart quickened and she bit back a groan. God, she wanted him to look at her. She wanted to see his face, to know what he was thinking. To see how he was feeling. She wanted him to see her—standing before him, naked, exposed.

Fair dinkum, Jackie, you need to get a grip. For Del's sake if not your own.

He didn't turn, however. His muscles coiled, as if responding to some stimuli she could not see or feel. He crossed to the shack's only doorway, the pale moonlight painting his bare skin in a faint silver wash. "I will see you at the car."

Before she could respond—*in what way, Huddart?*—he shifted into his wolf form, a wolf larger and more thickly muscled than any she'd seen, and loped off into the blackness of the night.

Jackie stood still, glaring at the spot in the doorway the wolf—Marshall—had just vacated. Her inner animal howled and growled for release, scraping at the tenuous threads of her control. Hungering for freedom.

Hungering for Marshall.

She curled her hands into fists, driving her nails into her palms as she squeezed her eyes tight. She couldn't shift. If she did, she was lost.

She opened her eyes and stared at the empty doorway again. "God, I wish I had my gun."

Her mutter shattered the silence of the shack, like the first rumble of thunder from a distant storm and she let out a sharp breath. "Fuck it."

She crossed the shack, snatching up Delanie's watch as she

did so, the coppery scent of her best friend's blood chilling the squirming ardor in the centre of her being.

"Fuck it," she muttered again, gripping the delicate piece of jewelry hard. She stood on the shack's threshold, studying the night before her, tasting the massive wolf that was Marshall on the air, and then began to run.

Naked.

Human.

Confused and pissed-off.

Wishing she had her gun.

Rocks and stones and dead twigs jabbed into his paws as he ran. The cool night air rippled through his fur, a seductive caress that normally would have made his tongue loll out with joy. The sweet potent scents of small animals scurrying away from him, leaching fear and shock, some emptying their bladders as they did so, would normally make him yip with happiness.

Instead, Marshall ran through the Tasmanian bush with his teeth bared and his muzzle creased.

What had he done?

He pushed himself harder, ignoring the evocative call of his beast. It had taken him many, many decades to be able to keep his dire wolf's id in check when transformed. The primitive wolf was powerful in every way, and more than once Marshall had lost time to the animal. Lost time and control. There was nothing comforting about waking up naked and covered in blood, with only flashes of incomprehensible memories to fill in the missing hours. The last time Marshall let his wolf's id control him, he went on a killing spree. True, those torn to shreds had deserved to be—a nest of vampires who'd prayed solely on children—but the loss of control still haunted him to this day.

His inner beast needed to be kept firmly in check at all times, most especially when he ran in wolf form.

He'd never, never needed to keep it in check during sex.

And then along came Detective Jackie Huddart.

A harsh growl rumbled up his chest and he pushed himself faster. If he didn't, he'd turn, run back to the shack and take her again.

As wolf or man?

The thought unnerved him. Over two hundred years of being in control of every molecule in his duel existence and he couldn't answer that one question.

He increased his gait, welcoming the discomfort in his paws and muscles. If he focused on the pain, Jackie's presence behind him faded.

Yeah, sure.

His ears pricked and he growled again. He could hear her running behind him. On two legs.

An image of Jackie running naked and human filled his head—her long limbs hard with smooth muscles, her skin pale and almost luminescent in the darkness, her breasts free and—

His paws stumbled and he scrambled for balance.

Focus.

The dark command cracked through his mind like a shot and he flattened his ears to his head. He shut her out of his senses, concentrating on the earth under his paws instead, the repetitive thump of his heart.

Stop thinking about her. Focus on Einar. Remember why you're here.

Cold disgust twisted into his chest. He was here to catch a cold-blooded killer, not mate with the woman he was using as bait.

Again his paws stumbled beneath him. Fuck. He'd mated with her. What had he been thinking?

No thinking involved, Rourke. You wanted her. You took her.

He curled his muzzle and growled again, the sound vibrating in his chest less animal, more monster.

He could still taste her blood and sweat in his mouth. It fueled a heat simmering in his loins he knew would never be extinguished. Once dire wolves mated, the bonds connecting the two together could never be severed. No matter the distance.

His ancestors—long long extinct—had not been subtle when it came to mating. The males took who they wanted, when they wanted them. No discussion, no arguments. The word rape did not exist when his kind first transformed, but it existed now. He may be the last dire wolf shifter alive, but that didn't excuse what he'd done to Jackie. She may have been a willing sexual partner, she *was* a willing sexual partner—of that he had no doubts—but to mark her as his. To mate with her…

And what of her thylacine mating rituals? There was scant intel on the Tasmanian tiger as an animal, let alone as a shape-shifter. Before he'd left the US he'd learnt all he could about her kind—tenacious predators, the top of the food chain in Australia until man's arrival on the continent, ferocious defenders of their young, solitary. Nothing in his intel told him if thylacines mated for life. He'd marked Jackie as his own, tied his body and spirit to her, but what did that mean to Jackie?

What did she think of him now?

Christ, you're fucked up, Rourke.

He was. His thoughts smashed through his head like the debris from an explosion. Pummeling him, tormenting him. How was he to use Jackie now that she was irrevocably a part of him? He couldn't use her as bait anymore. He couldn't, even if he wanted to, which he didn't. So how did he find Einar now? How did he lure his ex-partner out of hiding without the very prize the bastard hunted? What was his purpose if not to stop the very monster he'd set free on the world?

How did he tell Jackie he couldn't live without her?

Fuck.

The acrid smell of tar and gravel seeped into his breath and he ran harder, shoving the tumultuous confusion away. Weaving through the thinning trees, he leapt out of the bush, his paws thumping onto gravel-laced bitumen. The road.

Tail flicking, he sprinted up the empty stretch, stare locked on the distant shadow of his hired car. He'd change into his spare clothes, holster his gun and when Jackie arrived he'd explain everything.

Everything.

He had no idea what to do next, but he knew he didn't want her not in his life. He'd figure all the shit that came with his existence out after he told her that. After he told her dire wolves mated for life and his life was now hers. After he—

A slick scent of flowers and sweat slipped into his nostrils and he skidded to a halt. His heart smashed against his breastbone and his hackles rose.

Delanie McKenzie.

Deep within his subconscious, his beast growled. It surged for control, blood-lust and fury fueling its fight.

Marshall pushed his muzzle toward the silent shape of the Audi, tasting a ghost of the human female's perspiration on the air. Einar had brought her here—or something belonging to her.

He stood motionless, straining to detect any sound around him.

The night was silent. He'd left Jackie way behind, her distant human footfalls so faint he could barely feel them through the earth. Even the nocturnal critters inhabiting the area seemed to have vanished. Escaping the monster moving about their territory.

Which monster, Rourke? You, or Daeved Einar?

Stare fixed on the car, head low, nerves strung tight, he moved forward.

Four steps from the Audi, another scent licked at Marshall's senses and his heart beat harder.

Delanie's blood.

In a blur of painful distortion, he transformed, destroying the short distance between him and the car on human legs. He snatched his Glock from where he'd stashed it under the back driver's-side wheel arch before chasing after Jackie. Flicking off the safety, he held it low in both hands, studying the immediate area around the car. Einar had wounded Jackie's best friend. The scent of her blood was faint, almost undetectable, but there all the same.

Marshall peered into the blackness, narrowing his focus down onto that faint scent.

The woman was scared. Her fear laced the coppery ting of her blood, singeing his nostrils. Despite how weak the scent was, he could still smell her fear. It squeezed his tight throat. In his gut, he hadn't believed Einar would harm the human, but it looked like his gut was wrong. His partner was a callous being capable of untold atrocities—and many Marshall could tell of —against paranormal creatures, but he'd never deliberately hurt a human before until now.

To do so meant Einar wanted Jackie Huddart badly. Delanie was his trap.

Marshall's throat squeezed tighter still. He wasn't going to let Einar get her.

Shooting his dark surroundings a quick look, he hurried to the Audi's trunk and popped it open. He didn't have much time. Jackie would arrive soon and he had little doubt she would not detect her friend's scent. If he didn't go and retrieve Delanie quickly, Jackie would. Or she'd go after Einar herself if she discovered he was there waiting for her. Marshall couldn't have that. He couldn't put Jackie in that kind of danger. He had to move quickly.

Studying the direction Jackie would emerge from, he shoved his legs into the spare pair of jeans he'd packed earlier. Ignoring the shirt and shoes, he tucked his Glock into the back of his waistband. He didn't need a shirt and he would run faster and more quietly in bare feet.

With another look at the dark terrain, he took off, following Einar's and Delanie's scent. Tracking them off the road and into the scrubland. Trailing their path over the vegetation. Heading north. Closer to the ocean's edge. Farther away from the road and any signs of civilization.

Marshall's lips curled in a cold grin. Einar thought he was laying a trap for the Australian cop?

Einar was wrong.

Dead wrong.

Jackie stopped running.

She stood motionless, nose lifted to the air, her heart beating so loud she could hear nothing but its rapid thump.

She narrowed her eyes, pulling in a deep breath. "Oh, my God."

Hot, prickling anger flooded through her and before she could choke it back, a raw sob burst from her lips.

Del. She could smell Del's blood. Strong. Powerful. The scent of her best friend's blood filled her nose, slipped down her throat.

Closing her eyes against the distracting night, she drew another breath, deeper this time.

Fear and sweat threaded through the scent and Jackie's heart rate doubled. He'd hurt her. The bastard had hurt her.

Her thylacine stirred, furious.

Forcing both herself and the creature within her to be calm, she pulled another breath, seeking the source direction of the scent of Del's blood.

South.

Wherever Marshall's ex-partner was now, Delanie was south and that's all that mattered.

What if she's not? What if it's just her blood?

Shutting out the chilling though, Jackie opened her eyes and, without hesitation, transformed into her Tasmanian tiger form, bursting into a dead sprint. Moving through the bushland on all fours, faster than she could ever run in human form. South.

Delanie was south and close.

Very close.

So close Jackie could almost taste her on the soft breeze.

She had to be.

I'm coming, Del. I'm coming.

She ran south. Heading for her best friend.

CHAPTER EIGHT

The scrubland turned to sparse vegetation. Squat, spreading plants covered in prickly leaves and spiky flowers crunched under Marshall's feet, cutting into his soles. Low, spindly bushes snared at the legs of his jeans, tugging at his gait.

He gripped his Glock tighter, lengthening his stride. Delanie's scent was growing stronger. Much stronger. The closer he drew to the beach, the more potent the female's scent became. It filled his every breath now, not just a tickling tease in his nose.

Scanning the darkness before him, he searched for any visual sign of her. With her scent as strong as it was, he should be able to see something.

Nothing. Yet.

The scratchy growth beneath his feet turned to gritty sand, and the constant sound of waves breaking made him frown. Where was she? On the beach? What kind of trap could Einar set on the beach?

He narrowed his eyes, a sense of unease began to itch in his gut. This felt wrong. He slowed his sprint, straining to hear anything that would tell him where Delanie and Einar were.

A faint beat thumped through the air, so soft he almost missed it under the sound of the crashing waves to his right.

He cocked his head, listening.

A heartbeat.

But whose?

He continued forward, moving in a half-crouch over the sandy dirt, Glock ready. The thin moon cast the stretch of beach in pale light, turning the white sand to a silver swathe, illuminating nothing but the obvious. There was no one there.

But you can smell her. She has to be here. Her scent is—

A black shape lurched in the shallow waves, rolling backward and forward in the water's pull.

Marshall froze.

He fixed his stare on the rocking form. Narrowed his senses onto its waning heat.

His mouth went dry and his pulse smashed into rapid life.

Shit. It's—

"Delanie."

He lifted his head, turning his nose into the wind, trying to pull some hint of his ex-partner from the gentle off-shore wind playing over him.

Nothing. Except the stink of fish, seaweed, brine and Delanie.

Marshall returned his stare to the lolling form in the surf. There was no sign of Einar. Not on the wind, the sand, the surrounding scrub. He knew his ex-partner. He knew him well. Very well. There may not be a sign of him, but he was here. Somewhere. This was a trap. A trap for Jackie.

Then he won't be expecting you, will he?

He burst into a dead sprint, propelling himself across the sand, letting his dire wolf flow through his muscles even as he held tight control over his human form.

The cool water splashed over his feet and ankles, soaked the hem of his jeans as he ran through the waves. He dropped into a crouch beside the motionless female and grabbed at her shoulder, rolling her onto her back and pulling her face from the water.

"Delanie?" He whispered her name, scanning the scrub line for signs of Einar.

She didn't respond, and he dared to tear his stare from the black surroundings to shoot her a quick look.

Wet red hair strangled her face in tangled strands, covering her eyes and nostrils, clinging to her cheeks and lips. The waning moon turned her flesh a ghastly white, and if it weren't for the weak thump of her heartbeat vibrating through her body, he would have thought her dead.

Another shallow wave rolled up the shore, lapping into Marshall with gentle force. Delanie lurched to the side, limp and boneless, the wave lifting her from the sand and carrying her forward until she bumped into his legs.

Shit. Whatever Einar had done to her, she was out cold.

With a harried glance at the blackness skirting the beach, he shoved his gun into his jean's waistline at the small of his back and snared Delanie's right wrist.

Worry gnawed at his control. If his ex-partner was planning on snapping the trap, now would be the time to do it, when Marshall had both hands full.

Hauling Delanie out of the water, he threw her over his shoulder and straightened to his feet. Every muscle in his body tensed, expecting the bullet or cross-bow bolt or knife.

None came.

The uneasy itch in Marshall's gut grew stronger. What was Einar playing at?

Stop fucking worrying about it and get the woman to safety.

Left arm hooked around Delanie's leg, right hand anchoring her to his shoulder by her wrist, Marshall spun toward the scrubland and ran.

The sand stuck to his wet skin, clung to his damp jeans, turning the material to course sandpaper that rubbed at his calves and ankles. He ignored it, running up the beach, Delanie's weight pushing into his shoulder.

Something hot and damp seeped into his skin and he pulled in a quick breath.

His beast growled, already too close to the surface. Blood. Fresh blood.

He ran faster, the feel of Delanie's blood trickling down his arm and back pushing him harder still. The longer he had her slung over his shoulder, the longer the wound in her stomach would weep. He had to get her dry and warm.

Hard, compressed sand gave way to soft and loose the farther he ran away from the water. The tiny grains moved under his pounding feet like liquid, throwing his balance continually into turmoil. He gripped the unconscious woman harder, his stare fixed on the bush just beyond the pearly strip of beach. He'd expected his ex-partner's attack by now. Einar would have taken full advantage of his vulnerable situation, but there was neither sign nor scent of him.

The itch in his gut grew wild. Shit. This all felt wrong.

This wasn't the trap, Rourke. You know that, don't you. At least, not the trap for Jackie.

Cold dread flooded through him, turning the itch into a maelstrom of fury. Shit, his ex-partner knew he was here. And had played him.

And there's nothing you can do. You can't leave Delanie. She's bleeding, she's unconscious and she's likely got half the Pacific Ocean in her lungs.

He bit back a guttural curse. *Shit. Shit, shit.*

The low scrub tore at his wet jeans as he ran into the bush. Something sharp sliced into the sole of his right foot. He grunted, stumbling a little before righting himself and increasing his pace. Hot disgust fought with the cold dread eating into his control. How could he have been so goddamn stupid?

If Einar wasn't here watching Delanie, then that put him somewhere else. Somewhere…

An icy fist squeezed Marshall's heart and he sucked in another deep, sharp breath. Hoping, praying.

There wasn't a hint of Jackie's scent on the air. Which meant she wasn't following him.

And she would be following you, Rourke. If she detected even a whiff of her best friend's scent back at the car, she would be following you. If she's not, it's because she can't.

"Fuck!"

The word sounded more like a snarl.

"Divide and conquer, Rourke. Divide and conquer." Daeved Einar had lived by the adage, repeating it often to Marshall when they'd first been assigned as partners. Einar used the principle well. In fact, he was a master at it. More than one alcove of demons had been decimated thanks to his ability to separate the strong from the protective number of the weak. Marshall himself had been impressed with the technique—until he'd started to witness what Einar did to the strong once vulnerable.

"Fuck."

He turned his run into a sprint, Delanie's boneless weight pressing heavier on him with each step. Sweat beaded on his forehead, trickling into his eyes in stinging rivulets, but it was the woman's blood slicking his shoulder and arm that worried him. It painted his flesh with its sticky heat, flowing with alarming speed from the unseen wound in her belly.

If he didn't get her off his shoulder soon, she'd likely bleed to death.

Shoving the grim thought from his mind, as well as the unnerving fact she hadn't made a sound or even twitched since he'd found her, he raced through the night. At this point in time his best option was getting her back to the Audi and—

And what? Call an ambulance? Leaving her to possibly die while you go looking for Jackie? While you hunt Einar?

Marshall's dire wolf growled deep in his soul. The latter option appealed to it. Greatly.

A burning prickle up his spine and in the base of his skull made him grind his teeth and he forced the beast back down, restraining it—barely. He couldn't shift now. He had an injured woman to look after and if there was anything he'd learnt about Jackie Huddart in the last twenty-four hours it was this —if he abandoned Delanie McKenzie to come after her, if he left Delanie unattended, bleeding and unconscious, Jackie would rip his throat out herself.

The last thing he wanted was his life mate pissed at him.

Life mate.

The word flicked through his head and he stumbled. His life mate. The woman he was bonded to forever—both physically and spiritually. Unplanned, unexpected but so goddamn right he couldn't think about her without his core existence growing warm. His life mate separated from him by the one man who would take great pleasure in bringing her more pain than imaginable. The one man hell bent on killing her. Butchering her for his own demented, unhinged enjoyment. And Marshall had led that one man to her as surely as if he'd wrapped her in a bow and handed her over. The simple bait-and-terminate operation was now a nightmare beyond any he could have foreseen.

Shit, could this mission have gone any more off the rails?

Before he could consider an answer, the sticks and rocks beneath his feet gave way to rough gravel, followed instantly by crumbling bitumen. Marshall swung his stare from left to right, a shallow punch of relief sinking into him. He was back on the road.

He dragged in a long breath, his chest tight.

Let there be a hint of Jackie. Please, God and all things holy, let there be a hint of Jackie.

The silent prayer was bitter and unanswered—Marshall and all things holy had long since parted company. The air hung heavy with eucalyptus oil and other plant life his Texas senses were not familiar with, its cool dampness undercut with the faint tinge of the distant ocean, but there was no hint of the Sydney detective. In either human or Tasmanian-tiger form.

If she had been following him, if she had detected her friend's scent, she hadn't made it this far before—

He cut the thought dead.

He needed to keep his head clear, and thoughts of Jackie in Einar's deranged hands did not make for a rational mind.

Shifting Delanie slightly on his shoulder, he headed for the Audi. First things first. Make sure the woman wasn't going to die. After that…

Do what has to be done, Rourke. Disconnect your heart and do what has to be done. Until Einar is neutralized your heart is just an organ required to keep you alive. That's it.

He clenched his jaw and ran for his car, his disconnected heart aching for the woman he would never be disconnected from.

In the distance, the Audi still stood silently on the side of the narrow road, Jackie nowhere to be seen. He curled his lip in a snarl of contempt. He'd been fooled by his ex-partner. Einar had always considered him a victim of what Einar called a knight-in-denim-thinking-with-his-dick complex. His partner had ridiculed him often about Marshall's propensity to rescue damsels in need of a good slap. Tonight, Einar had used that against him. He'd dangled Delanie's scent under his nose and separated him from Jackie.

"Christ, you're an idiot, Rourke."

A low moan at his chest made him start. He tensed, twisting his body to look at Delanie's face.

Her eyes were still closed, her skin still shockingly white.

"Delanie?"

She didn't make another sound, and Marshall suppressed a low growl. Even unconscious, it seemed the woman agreed with him.

Straightening, he hurried along the road, searching the night air for any signs of Jackie. That he couldn't detect any made the itch in his gut flare again. If she hadn't made it to the car, where was she? What scent was she following?

If any?

The answer to that question made his blood cold.

He reached the Audi, gut a churning mess, throat tight. His shoulder screamed at him, his leg muscles burned. Popping the trunk, he snatched out his shirt and jacket, throwing them on the stretch of gravel between the car and the scrub. He lowered Delanie onto them, the cloying stench of blood attacking his sinuses the second her belly left his shoulder.

Ah, shit.

Crouching down beside her motionless form, he parted the blood-soaked edges of her shirt, careful not to touch the seeping wound beneath.

He hissed in a quick breath. An oozing hole punctured her side, its edges raw. Marshall clenched his jaw, hot fury boiling in his veins. He recognized his ex-partner's handiwork all too easily. Einar loved the sensation of his knife sinking through living flesh, and it seemed he'd lost his distaste for harming humans.

A thick lump formed in Marshall's throat and he swallowed it. He could only imagine Delanie's screams as Einar did this to her. Einar would not have stabbed her while she was unconscious. He would have wanted to hear the result of his pleasure.

"If for no other reason, this is why I am going to make you suffer, you bastard."

His course whisper sounded like a roar in the silent night and he scrunched up his face, forcing composed calm to flow through him. He needed to keep his focus on the woman before him, not on what he was going to do to his ex-partner.

Opening his eyes, he returned his attention to the wound. Fresh blood, almost black in the faint monochromatic light, oozed from its hideous hole. He skimmed his fingertips along the flesh directly above it, drawing in a quick breath as he did so.

The metallic tang of blood filled his nose. Only the metallic tang.

Marshall let out a ragged sigh of relief. Einar's blade had not punctured or sliced Delanie's intestines.

So, the wound wasn't to maim or kill, but just to make her bleed? Why? He was your partner long enough to know you could track anything, whether they were bleeding or not, so why make her bleed? In fact, it wasn't her blood you tracked. The ocean washed away any scent of her blood, so why make her—

Cold realization rolled through him and he bit back a curse. He didn't need Delanie's blood scent to track her, a dire wolf's sense of smell was phenomenal. Once he had a scent, he could track it no matter how old or weak. All he needed to track Delanie was the faintest hint of her body odor—a few molecules on the air or ground and he would find her. Jackie however, wasn't a dire wolf and what limited intel he had on the thylacine told him a Tasmanian tiger's sense of smell wasn't their strongest. *He* didn't need Delanie's blood to find her, but did Jackie? If he didn't know the answer to that question, what were the odds neither did Einar? Which meant his ex-partner would go to extreme lengths to make sure Jackie followed the scent trail Einar wanted her to.

Marshall scraped his hand down his face. Damn it, how long had Einar been following him and Jackie? What had he seen?

He knows. He knows what you are. And now he knows he will use that to his advantage. Like trapping you with your own fucking abilities.

Marshall clenched his fists. "Damn it!"

He skimmed his fingertips over the wound in Delanie's side again, his skin prickling with rage, disgust and dismay. Einar had cut the human to lure Jackie away. He'd used her best friend to isolate her from that which would keep her safe. A protective, angry dire wolf.

"Jesus, Jackie," he muttered, staring at Delanie's wound. "I'm sorry."

Throat thick, he snapped to his feet. He had to get Delanie medical care. He couldn't hunt Einar until his life mate's best friend was safe. Yanking open the passenger door, he pulled out the small first-aid kit he always carried with him from the glove compartment. There was not much to it—disinfectant wipes, sterile gauze bandages, a tube of Neosporin, a roll of sticking plaster and needle and thread—but hopefully it would be enough to stop the bleeding.

Returning his attention to Delanie, he studied her in the dim yellow light cast by the Audi's cabin light and hissed in another breath. The extra light highlighted the dark blood pooling beneath her, seeping into the soft suede of his jacket. Fuck, he had to move quickly.

He tore open one roll of disinfectant wipes with his teeth and gingerly wiped at the cut. Even through the cotton, Delanie's skin was cold to the touch, and he had to stop himself shaking his head.

Keep it cool, Rourke. Keep it composed. You can't rush this, no matter how much you want to.

When he'd cleaned away as much blood as he could without pulling the cut open, he ran a quick inspection over the wound. There was no muscle or ligament damage, which was a good thing. Maybe it wasn't as bad as—

Shit.

New blood began to seep from the ragged hole. Bright red and glistening in the waxing moonlight.

Shit.

He tore open another roll of wipes and sopped up the blood, making sure to clean away any traces of salt and sand he missed the first time. His field dressing techniques were a little rusty—there wasn't that big a call for medical help from the paranormal nasties he collared, and neither he nor Einar ever sustained enough damage to their person to require it.

He chuckled a mirthless snort as he disinfected Delanie's wound again. Who would have thought he'd regret not being injured in the line of duty?

Grabbing at the roll of gauze, he snagged its end with his teeth and unraveled it a little. Just enough to press against the flat plane of her belly beside Einar's stab wound. If he wrapped it firmly enough around her waist, he should be able to stop the—

Shit!

Fresh blood seeped from the hole. Fuck. What the fuck did he do?

Frustrated worry gnawed at his control. He didn't want to tell Jackie he'd let her best friend bleed to death.

He shot the sterilized needle and tiny spool of surgical thread a quick look. He wasn't a surgeon. Jesus, he'd never stitched on a button, let alone a human.

Fuck. Fuck, fuck, fuck.

Blood continued to ooze from Delanie's side. Shit, did he stitch it? He didn't know. *Shit.*

"Fuck it," Marshall snarled under his breath. He snatched the needle from the first-aid kit, sliding it from its sterile casing.

The silver-metal alloy burned like ice against his fingertips, and he ground his molars together, desperately trying to drag up any memory he had of his field-dressing training.

"Wound must be clean and free of debris. Skin must be dry."

He stared at the needle, his pulse pounding in his throat. Damn it, how the fuck could he concentrate with that thumping through his head?

"You're not planning…to use that on me…are you?"

The barely audible rasp shattered the silence and Marshall started. He snapped his stare to Delanie's face, a whoosh of air bursting from him when he found her looking up at him.

He gave her a lop-sided grin, knowing it probably looked wan and relieved at once. "I was thinkin' about it."

She shifted slightly on her back, wincing as she twisted her body enough to look at the bleeding hole in her side. "I'm not…a fan of needles."

Marshall let out a sharp chuckle. "Me either."

Her gaze returned to his face, and he suppressed a worried frown. She may be talking, but she was still in pain. A lot of pain. It clouded her green eyes like fog.

"I'll make you a deal," she went on, her voice croaky. "You put that away and…wrap me up in bandages…" She coughed, and winced again. "And I promise…not to bleed to death."

"Deal."

He ripped open the last packet of gauze in his kit and pressed it lightly to her wound, lifting her hand with his right and placing it on top of the material. "Hold this here," he ordered, keeping the words calm as he grabbed the largest roll of bandage he had. Now that stitching into her flesh was no longer an option, he felt better. More composed. "This is going to hurt."

"Not as much as it did happening."

Delanie's wry response made him chuckle. He unfurled the bandage around her waist, stretching it gently with each pass over the stab wound.

She flinched each time, but didn't make a sound. Not until he'd finished, at least. "Okay, tall, blonde and handsome, you've saved me," she said, studying him with narrow eyes, and Marshall had to smile at the strength returning to her voice. And the suspicious glint in her eyes.

"Now, who the hell are you?"

Jackie sped through the bush, Delanie's smell thick in her nose. Low tree branches and scrub tore at her sides and muzzle, snagged in her fur, but still she ran.

The deeper into the bush she went, the stronger Del's scent grew. More potent.

Human blood cut her friend's distinct odor, its coppery overtones sour with fear. Jackie let her tongue loll from her mouth, taking the scent into her body. The blood was arterial —rich with life and oxygen. Jackie could taste its vitality even through the choking stench of fear coating it.

She ran faster, for the first time in her strange life willingly letting her animal control her. That her thylacine could sort out Delanie as fiercely as her human soul spoke volumes. More than words ever could. When she found Delanie, her human friend was just going to have to accept the fact there would be lots of face licking taking place. Jackie doubted she'd have any luck at all reigning in her thylacine's relief and joy.

But first you have to find her.

She snarled at the thought, its menace making her hackles rise. She would find her. That's what she did. She hunted, she tracked, she…*mated.*

A growl slipped up her throat, a blurring memory of the other animal, the massive wolf who'd marked her as his, filling her head.

After she found the human female—*Del, damn you*—she would return to the wolf and show him what it meant to be mated to a thylacine. He was in for a surprise. Her kind had never been known for their passive nature.

A hot flutter rippled through the pit of her belly. The human she was found the notion of wild mating with the man who was sometimes a wolf more appealing than she wanted to let on. It was only in the honest state of her thylacine form, a state with little understanding of the concepts of deceit and subterfuge, that she acknowledged the true depths of her attraction to the male. Yes, when she found the lost human female, she would return to the male and—

The faint sound of a twig breaking under slow pressure brought her to a skidding halt. She stood motionless, gazing into the scrub around her. She detected the rapid heartbeat of two startled echidnas to her left, a bush rat and a multitude of skinks, but nothing large enough to break wood.

Her bristles rose, the blood-tainted scent of Delanie feeding her agitation.

Above her, almost silent, an owl swooped through the coolly humid air. The bush rat let out a terrorized squeak and scurried away. For a dizzying second she wanted to leap on it. Chase it down. Tear its soft belly open and warm her throat with its innards.

And then another twig snapped—louder. A bigger twig— behind her. She spun around, ears flat, teeth bared, and broke into a sprint again. The sound came from the source of Del's scent.

Branches snatched at her but she pushed through their insistent fingers. She was close.

Close.

The scrub grew sparse, patchy, and she leapt over one particularly stunted bush, ears flat to her head. A small clearing opened up before her, coarse yellow grass crunching against her paws. She took one step and froze.

The scent of Delaine's blood saturated the air.

Del.

She flicked her stare around the clearing, her muzzle wrinkling at the dark shadowy shape lying amongst the grass to her left. In two silent steps she was on it, her hackles rising as she pushed her nose to it.

Material. Wire. Sweat. Skin. Blood.

A shudder rippled through Jackie, and with a million rips of fire tearing at her existence, she transformed back into her human form.

She crouched down, her knees popping, the short grass scratching at her bare butt as she reached for the blood-soaked bra lying by her feet. Her fingertips brushed the sodden satin and her throat slammed shut. "Oh, fuck, Del."

"I am not sure which form I find more appealing."

Jackie was on her feet, staring into the dark bushland beside her before the smooth male voice finished forming the words. "What the fuck have you done with my friend?" she snarled, searching the blackness for any sign of the speaker. "Where is she?"

"Human scientists believe the modern thylacine to be over four million years old," the man she assumed was Marshall's ex-partner spoke again, this time to her right. She jerked around, finding nothing but the empty bush and dark night. "The pure thylacine closely resembles the wolf, dog *and* cat, but is not of the same genus of any of them. It is the largest carnivorous marsupial to ever evolve." A low chuckle rolled toward her, the sound bending until it came from behind her. "And like all marsupials, has a pouch in which young are born and protected."

She spun about, every hair on her body prickling. Why couldn't she detect Einar? How could the bastard move without her seeing him? Hearing him?

"I must admit, on learning of your existence, I found myself wondering how you carry young in your human form but I see you do not have a pouch."

The droll statement snapped Jackie's attention to the fact she was without clothes, and she dropped into a crouch again, the idea of Einar seeing her naked making her sick.

"Oh, please." His laugh floated at her from the front and, in a sudden shimmer of silver light, he stood before her, tall, lean and holding a long, hooked knife in his right hand. His iridescent blue stare fixed on her face. "Do not be modest on my account."

He swung his arm toward her, the knife turning to a blur as incandescent as his eyes.

Jackie threw herself backward, striking out with her left leg as she did so. The ball of her foot smashed into his wrist and a jarring shudder shot down her leg, spearing into the base of her spine. She heard a grunted *oof*, the sound both surprised and angry, before—heart thumping into her throat—she leapt to her feet and burst into a dead sprint.

She was unarmed and naked. She wasn't ready for this fight.

Einar appeared before her. That same shimmering light slid away from him like liquid mercury, and he grinned down at her, blocking her path. She stumbled to a halt, her heels scraping at the ground, her stare locked on his cold, calm eyes. "You cannot out run me, Jacqueline Huddart." He moved, a frightening fast blur of form and colour that crashed against Jackie with crushing force.

She fell, her own feet tripping her, and before she could do anything but gasp, Einar straddled her chest, his knees pinning her elbows to the ground, his arse squashing her breasts. He shook his head, lips twisted into a down-turned pout, his stare drilling into hers. "I'm disappointed. This was easier than expected." He touched the tip of his knife into the dip at the base of Jackie's neck and she bit back a sharp hiss of pain. "Still, the thylacine was not known for its fighting prowess."

Jackie fixed him with a flat glare. "True, but you're not sitting on a thylacine at the moment, are you?"

She whiplashed her legs upward, wrapped her calves around Einar's neck, locked her ankles together and slammed her legs back down to the ground.

Taking Einar with them.

His head hit the dirt, followed by his legs and chest as he crumpled over himself, a grunt vibrating through his body. Jackie didn't take the time to appreciate his discomfort. She smashed her heel into his jaw, driving his head backward.

"Didn't expect that, did you." Grit and stones and grass bit into her bare hip and butt. Her sweat stung her eyes. She didn't care. The bastard at her feet had hurt Del. He was going to—

Silver light tore at the darkness, and suddenly she was alone on the ground.

She leapt to her feet, lips bared in a silent snarl, her thylacine surging for release.

Hunt, track, kill.

"You are correct, Jacqueline." Einar's voice wafted on the air like diffused fog. "I was not expecting that."

Jackie narrowed her eyes, searching the bush around her for Rourke's ex-partner. The small gash at the base of her throat stung, as if boiling acid seeped into the wound. She clenched her fists, shutting out the pain. "Where is my friend? What have you done to her?"

"Delanie McKenzie is alive," Einar responded from wherever he stood hidden in the darkness. She couldn't pinpoint his location. His voice came at her with no discernible point of origin. "Possibly. It depends on how quickly your lover gets to her, I have to say."

His off-handed comment churned Jackie's stomach and her throat squeezed tight. Possibly? Her lover? A ragged breath slipped past her lips and she bit back a disgusted groan. Oh, God, not only had the man hurt her best friend, he'd seen her and Rourke together in the shed. He'd watched them copulating like...like...

Animals.

She shut the thought out of her head, focusing instead on the unseen Einar. Why couldn't she see him? She opened her mind to her thylacine's spirit, letting the creature's ancient magick flow through her. All around her, the land, the trees, the earth whispered, disturbed by a force she still could not detect. Daeved Einar. Her flesh crawled with the sensation of his gaze roaming over her naked body, but she stood motionless, determined not to show him any weakness. Be damned if she'd cower because of him. "This was a trap."

"And you both took the bait." A low chuckle followed his smug answer and the wound in her neck seemed to throb with molten heat at the sound. "As I knew you would."

She turned her head slightly to the left. Her ears heard

nothing to tell her Einar was there, but the connection her thylacine shared with the ancient land on which she stood, a connection sometimes whispered about in reverence by the country's original people, told her reality was blemished there. As if something not belonging to this world, this place, defiled it. She narrowed her eyes again. "What are you? Because I know you're not human?"

Silence answered her and Jackie suppressed the urge to smile. Her proclamation startled him.

"Very astute, detective." The smug arrogance in his voice was gone, replaced by a cutting irritation, his unusual accent thicker with each word. "How can you tell?"

Jackie bared her teeth in a cold grin. "Haven't I already illustrated you don't know everything about Tasmanian tigers?"

A hissed breath cut the night and icy air struck her from behind, like a wall of angry winter. With preternatural speed, she dropped into a crouch and spun around, striking out as Einar materialized before her. She smashed her right fist into his knee, her left fist into his groin. He let out a wail and staggered backward, his gaping mouth revealing pointed teeth glistening with saliva, the hideous hooked blade slipping from his fingers.

Without hesitation, she lunged for it.

The second her palm slapped the smooth hilt, the tiny puncture wound in her neck erupted in blistering agony and she screamed, collapsing to her knees.

Einar leapt at her, a blur of enraged disbelief. "No!"

She lashed out, swinging her arm up in a tight arc, the pain in her neck choking her.

The blade sank into Einar's right thigh with a wet thud, just below his crotch. He squealed, the cry loud and ear-piercing. Silver light poured from the entry wound and, eyes wild, face contorted, he wrapped his fingers around the hilt and disappeared.

Leaving Jackie on all fours, the black night pressing down on her like a shroud, her heart slamming with painful force.

She didn't wait to see if he returned.

She ran. Heading north. Back to Marshall.

Transforming into her thylacine form mid-stride.

CHAPTER NINE

Delanie studied the man crouching over her. He'd said a total of ten words to her since she'd demanded he tell her who he was. "Marshall Rourke. I'm a friend of Jackie's," he'd said. And then, when she'd asked where Jackie was all he'd said was, "I don't know."

After those ten words, he'd not uttered a sound. First, he'd checked the freshly bandaged knife wound in her side so generously given to her by the psycho hunter. Then he'd called someone on a cell phone he'd pulled from under the driver's seat of the black Audi she was lying beside, muttering something she couldn't hear. *Then* he'd paced backward and forward beside said Audi, staring into the bush to the south like he was trying to rip it out with his mind.

She'd watched him the whole time, her side throbbing like a son of a bitch, the wound feeling like it was on fire. Hot fingers of pain kneaded their way into her belly, down her legs, up her spine. It was only the curious actions of her saviour that kept her from crying. Or demanding he tell her what the hell was going on.

Worry ate at his expression. Which wasn't at all comforting.

After ten minutes of watching Tall, Dark and Pacing, she'd had enough. Struggling up onto her elbows, she fixed the back of his head with a level look. "I don't mean to sound ungrateful," she said from the ground, flinching a little when her saviour swung a very intense stare her way. "But if you don't tell me what's going on, I'm going to force myself to my feet and bleed all over your—"

A cry of pain choked her flippant declaration before she could finish it. She collapsed back to the gravel, the knife wound erupting in an agony so total for a split second she wished she was dead.

Rourke was by her side in half a second, the worry on his face tenfold. "You need to stay still," he said, and even in Delanie's state she couldn't miss the growl in his words. "Unless you want me to stitch you up."

He brushed his fingers against her side directly above the knife's entry point, and Delanie bit back another highly undignified cry. "Fuck!" she ground out instead, trying to move away from his hand.

"Fuck," he echoed on a mutter, his American accent broad. He lifted his gaze to her face, sharp blue eyes unreadable.

Uh-oh. Not a good sign, Del.

She swallowed, her mouth suddenly dry. She felt cold. No, she felt hot. God, she felt...weird.

"Can you describe the knife that cut you?"

She frowned at Rourke's question, trying to look at her side without moving. Was that fresh blood? Why were her lips numb? Christ, she was boiling. Where was—

"Delanie." Rourke's voice commanded her attention and she jerked her stare back to his face. Damn, he was good looking. Who was he? Why was he—

"Can you describe the knife used to cut you?"

She swallowed again, her throat coated with burning dust. "Big...kinda...kinda curved...pointed." She closed her eyes.

Her side didn't seem to exist anymore. In its place, an inferno blazed. "Silver...with some kinda...pattern..."

"Fuck," he muttered again.

She forced her eyes open, scraping her dry tongue over her lips. "Whas...the problem?"

He swiped at his mouth with the back of his hand. "I need you to stay still, Delanie. Do you understand? You need to stay still."

She nodded. At least, she thought she did. She wasn't really sure anymore. She felt...wrong. "Is Jackie okay?"

Her saviour let out a ragged breath. "Christ, I wish I knew."

The raw torment and pain in his voice made Delanie's throat squeeze. "Can't you go after...find her?"

Rourke scrunched up his face and dragged his fingers through his already disheveled hair. "If I leave you, she'll kill me."

Despite the pain engulfing her side, Delanie snorted. "Guess you really do...know Jackie."

Rourke snorted back and shook his head, exasperation fighting with worry on his face. "You could say—"

He shot to his feet before finishing, spinning one-eighty degrees into a semi-crouch, his left hand reaching for the gun tucked into his jeans at the small of his back.

Delanie tensed. And then hiccupped out a weak laugh of relief at the sight of an animal she knew very, very well bursting out of the bushes. "Jesus...Jack," she croaked, slumping back to the road as the Tasmanian tiger loped toward the Audi. "Make us worry...why doncha."

A cold, wet nose touched the side of her neck, soft whiskers tickled her jaw and then Jackie's fingers threaded through hers, her best friend holding her hand with such force Delanie almost asked her to let go. Almost.

She rolled her head and looked up at Jackie, giving her a

small smile. "Took your time, girlfriend. You been playing…fetch?"

Jackie pulled a face. "Found a couple of teenagers playing Frisbee. Couldn't resist." She smiled, the relaxed action crinkling the corners of her eyes.

If Delanie didn't know her friend as well as she did, she'd think the smile real. Jackie however, was as worried as Marshall Rourke.

"I see you've been up to your usual tricks," Jackie went on, sliding a quick sideways glance at Rourke where he stood silent at the Audi's tailgate watching them both. "Do anything to get the attention of a good-looking guy, won't you?"

Delanie chuckled—and then winced as a scalding dart of pain speared into her ribcage. "Don't think it's me…he's interested…in."

Jackie's eyes widened, and to Delanie's immense surprise and enjoyment, a pink blush tinged her cheeks. "Shush, you lunatic," she mumbled.

Delanie chuckled again, risking life and agonizing pain. She didn't care. Her friend was safe. Pain didn't stand a chance of ruining her mood.

As if to prove her completely wrong, another blistering dart sank into her side, this time shooting through her body like an electricity storm. She snapped into a rigid arch, hissing in a sharp breath.

"Del?" Jackie frowned, her grip on Delanie's fingers growing tighter. Before Delanie could tell her not to worry, Jackie snapped her head toward Rourke. "What happened to her?"

The American's expression turned dark. "Einar."

"Do you have your gun?"

He nodded once, eyes narrowing. "Why?"

Jackie turned back to Delanie. "We have to get her out of here."

Rourke took a step closer, his hands going to his hips, his

stare locked on the back of Jackie's head. "What happened, detective?" His voice sounded like a growl again. "Where have you been?"

Delanie gazed into her best friend's eyes. They were chips of amber ice—cold and hard and angry. "I met your ex-partner."

At Jackie's words, Marshall Rourke moved. Quicker than Delanie had seen anyone move before, including Jackie. He dropped into a crouch beside them both, studying Jackie's face with such intensity even Delanie wanted to squirm. "Are you okay?" His gaze slid to Jackie's neck and his nostrils flared. "That fucking bastard." He reached out with his right hand, placing his fingertips on a small, blood-crusted hole at the base of her throat.

Jackie swiped his hand away, and it suddenly dawned on Delanie her friend was naked and not remotely concerned about being in that state of undress in Marshall Rourke's presence.

"I'm fine."

Rourke shook his head. "And I'm a beagle."

Delanie blinked at the man's bizarre retort and then was hit by another wave of agony in her side. Another...another...

Oh, no.

The world swam, black fire spread through her, radiating from Einar's stab wound, and she cried out.

Oh. Oh...

"Del?" Jackie's voice—stretched with worry to a harsh gasp —came at Delanie from a distance, but the pain was too much. Too much. She writhed on the ground, eyes squeezed shut, trying to escape it. Trying to—

Someone scooped her up. Strong arms hauling her from the side of the road. Pinpricks of light stabbed at her closed eyes and she cried again, cowering from the assault. Her side erupted in new agony, tearing through her like a monster.

Oh, oh, oh, no. It hurts. It hurts, oh God, it hurts.

The world shifted and she heard a growl, the sound too animalistic to be real.

I'm delusional.

The thought floated through the black fire seconds before she felt something firm yet soft press against her back.

"I'll stay with her." Jackie's voice slipped over the pain, and for a brief moment Delanie wondered why her best friend was here in hell with her. She tried to open her eyes, tried to tell Jackie to run. "*Run. The hunter's after you. He'll find you even here.*" But the fire roared through her, a column of black agony filling her throat.

Cool fingers brushed her temple, scalding her flesh and she flinched, jerking away from their brutal touch.

"What's happening to her?" Jackie's voice scraped at her ears like steel wool and she whimpered.

No. No, no, no.

If an answer came, she didn't hear it. How could she over the inferno devouring her from within? Eating her alive.

"Del?"

The black fire roared through her. Consumed her.

"Damn it, Marshall, what's happening to her?"

No answer came. Nothing came. Except the agony of the burn, the blackness of the agony, and the image of a man with an evil knife and dead eyes.

And then they too were devoured by nothing, and Delanie felt herself turn to ash.

Einar screamed and slammed his fist against the wall. The plaster cracked and fell to the ground in a shower of white dust, turning the toes of his boots grey. The knife wound in his thigh detonated, ice and fire and black void and he let out another yell, punching the wall again.

She had stabbed him with his own blade.

The shape-shifting cunt had not only escaped him, she'd stabbed him with his own knife.

Dark poison throbbed through his veins, snaking out from the neat hole in his right quadriceps, turning his thigh to a blizzard of agony. His flesh had never been rent by his own steel before. He could feel the blade's poison turning his blood to death with every beat of his heart.

Fuck.

She'd escaped him. She'd stabbed him.

How the fuck had she beaten him?

He turned from the wall, ignoring the numb ice in his leg. There was more to her than he thought. More to the perversion behind her transformative magick. Something to do with this cursed country. A connection?

The black ice in his thigh grew colder, scalding his blood, blistering his flesh. He spat out a guttural curse, driving his nails into his palm. He would need to address the wound soon, before its poison reached his heart. If that happened…

He knew what the magick of his knife did to his kind and it made what it did to paranormal abominations pale to a paper cut.

None of that mattered at the moment, however.

He'd taken Jacqueline Huddart for granted and she'd escaped him. For the first time since leaving his realm to join P.A.C. over fifty years ago, he'd been bested by a paranormal abomination. Not to mention, fooled by a fucking wolf in man's clothing.

Einar snarled, an image of his ex-partner rising through the black pain fogging his brain. Marshall Rourke would suffer for this. Einar would pin out the stinking, flea-ridden werewolf and skin him alive, rending him of his human flesh and feeding it to him one bloody strip at a time.

The thought filled his groin with heat, but he didn't enjoy the sensation for long. Another surge of icy pain throbbed through his thigh and he collapsed, his leg crumpling beneath him.

"T'aht!"

The curse burst past his lips, the hitching breath of his native language sounding peculiar in the silent human house. He dragged himself across the carpeted floor to the closest piece of furniture—a wide bed with a sunken mattress and gaudy duvet—and climbed onto its edge, staring up at the ceiling. The house he had commandeered was far from the luxury he was used to in his own abode, but it was serviceable for his needs now. A ground base of operations while he hunted Jacqueline Huddart. The previous occupants currently resided in a state of comatose ignorance, unaware of their new guest, frozen in perpetual terror until he deemed them worthy of release or death.

Humans were such pathetic things. Easily entranced. Easily controlled. All it had taken was one word spoken from his lips in his true language and the family who lived in the house had meekly lain on the floor of the room where he'd first appeared, their minds his to do with as he wanted.

Pathetic. Why they deserved protecting from the horrors walking amongst them he never knew. If those very horrors didn't pervert the She-God's world so much, he'd gladly leave them to feast on the humans at will.

Scalding ice speared up his torso, growing close to his heart, and he choked back a gasping breath. If he didn't tend to the injury in his leg now, he would be dead by sunup.

Struggling upright, he touched his thigh with steady fingers. The flesh around the puncture seemed to boil even as he watched it, sloughing away from his muscle, staining his trousers with wet ichor, turning the course fabric black with blood. He drew in a slow breath, picturing the poison running through his veins. There was only one antidote to its fatal magick, and he doubted he would find a virgin fae in Tasmania. The cunts were hard enough to find in his realm, let alone in a backwater human piss-hole.

He traced the clean edges of the lesion with the tip of his right index finger, dipping it into the raw flesh with increasing pressure. Excruciating agony shot through his thigh and he hissed, pushing his finger deeper. Until he could return to his home, he needed to stem the poison's spread. Imprison it so it could not enter his heart.

He pushed his finger harder into the cut, turning it into a narrow hole, opening it wider and wider. Sweat beaded on his forehead. Black smudges danced in his vision.

He drew an image of Marshall Rourke to his mind, pulling strength from the thought of killing the werewolf. The pain subsided, the black smudges fogged to the edges of his sight and, bending slightly at the waist, he bowed his spine enough to align his mouth directly above the wound on his inner thigh.

He stared at its glistening black entry. Watched fresh blood, like liquid night, ooze from it.

Rolling his tongue against the back of his throat, he worked up a mouthful of saliva, leant closer to his leg and let it dribble from his lips.

Searing heat ripped through him. He wanted to arch his back, to throw back his head and scream. Instead, he stayed motionless, spitting more and more of his saliva into the hungry wound. His muscles convulsed, spasm after spasm torturing him, threatening to snap him from his position, but he fought it. The poison from his blade would only be stayed by complete saturation. He would need to drench the wound with his own saliva until his mouth was dry and incapable of producing more. Then and only then, could he move.

And when he did…

He focused on the image of Marshall Rourke in his mind.

Five years as partners. Five years pretending to be friends. Pretending to share the same goals, the same ethics. Until the

SAVAGE TRANSFORMATION | 151

night Rourke had reported him to the head of P.A.C. for excessive violence against an assigned suspect.

Einar closed his eyes, continuing to spit into his wound. P.A.C. had been the perfect existence for him. The hunt, the torture, the destruction of all those he deemed deserving of death. A perfect career for someone who loved the hunt as much as he did. He was not a violent man, no matter what the Im'oisian elders had declared. Their grounds for expelling him to the human world were ludicrous, but he'd found a second home, if you will, as a P.A.C. agent. He'd concealed his true form with a simple incantation, presenting himself as a simple mage of limited magical ability. No one had suspected what he was and all hailed his phenomenal skill at "bringing to heel" those he enjoyed killing the most. What dark elf wouldn't enjoy a life destroying creatures whose very existence was a front to the Word and the Law of the She-God?

And he had done it so well. For so long. Until Marshall Rourke.

Curling his lip, Einar spat harder at his leg. He wouldn't just skin Rourke when he found him. He'd slice his throat, hang him up by his ankles and let his duplicitous blood drain from his veins until he was almost dead. Then he'd skin him. Alive.

No wait. Change that. As the Texan's blood dripped from his body, Einar would gut the thylacine bitch in front of him and then skin him alive.

Wet heat flooded his groin at the thought and his mouth filled with fresh saliva. Perfect. Exactly what he needed.

The hunt called him. Even through the agony of his knife wound.

The Audi purred to a halt under the high street light, rumbling with restrained power before Rourke killed the engine. Jackie lifted her stare from Delanie's sweat-slicked face, worry eating at her. Her best friend had not regained consciousness the entire drive back to St. Helens—and with the G-forces pressing on Jackie's belly the duration of the trip, she suspected the drive went a lot quicker than it legally should have. Rourke had pushed the sports car to its limits, driving with silent determination and focus, and she hadn't cared. Not one little bit. Delanie's life seemed to be rapidly deteriorating and the sooner she was in the ER the better.

Jackie frowned out the back passenger window, studying the deserted car park around them. Where were they? She scanned the surroundings, looking for the St. Helens hospital, finding a dark, boarded-up shopping centre beyond the asphalt instead. Her stomach knotted. "What the hell are you doing, Rourke?" Brushing a damp strand of hair from Delanie's forehead, she shot Marshall a quick look. "Why have you stopped here?"

Instead of answering, he shoved open his door and leapt from the car, pulling something small from the back pocket of his jeans as he did so.

Jackie bit back a muttered curse. Damn him. What was going on?

She returned her gaze to Delanie's face, adjusting her position slightly so Delanie's head rested deeper in her lap. The blue denim of the jeans she'd hastily pulled on before climbing into the Audi looked black compared to her friend's ghastly white skin, and Delanie's purple eyelids and ashen lips made her already unsettled stomach churn. She let out a frustrated sound. She didn't want to move or leave Delanie alone. Since Marshall had laid Delanie out on the Audi's plush backseat, the white gauze bandage wrapped around her torso pink with blood, she had barely shown any signs of life. Jackie had kept her fingertips pressed to her pulse, the erratic beat disturbing her as much as it told her Delanie was alive. Her friend had made no whimpers, no moans or groans. Nothing. She'd just lain on the backseat, limp and motionless, sweat rolling from her, the heat radiating from her body so hot Jackie feared her insides must be boiling.

"I don't know what's going on, hon," she murmured on a whisper, tucking the damp strand behind Delanie's ear, "but we'll fix it. I'll fix it."

The promise squeezed Jackie's chest and she closed her eyes. Guilt gnawed at her. Her mouth filled with bile and a soft sob escaped her. She had done this. If she hadn't come home, back to Tasmania. If she hadn't let Delanie pick her up from the airport. If she hadn't been Delanie's friend to begin with.

She opened her eyes and looked down at the still woman, hot tears turning her vision to a blurred smudge of muted colours. "I'm sorry, Del. Oh, God, I'm so sorry."

Delanie didn't move.

Jackie lifted her gaze back to the window, swallowing the thick lump in her throat. What the hell was Rourke doing? Was he lost? Asking for direction? Didn't a car like this come with a GPS?

Anger rolled through her, competing with the guilt coiling in her soul like a pissed-off snake. She wriggled her fingers, sharp, jerky movements that brought no relief or calm to her state of mind. Bloody hell, this was ridiculous. She couldn't just sit here while her best friend died in her lap.

Loathed to move Delanie's head, she strained to see the Texan beyond the glass. Where was he? Why would he drive them to an empty car park? What was he thinking?

Her fingers wriggled again, and deep within her soul, her thylacine growled, eager to be away from this turmoil. To run. To hunt. To kill. She closed her eyes, snapping her fingers into a fist. God, she wished she had her gun.

And who would you shoot, Jackie?

The ominous thought stabbed into her like a shard of ice and she let out a choked sob. "Stop it." She could feel guilty and angry later. Now all that mattered was Delanie.

She stretched her neck to look out the window again,

ignoring the blistering pain that flared in the tiny wound at the base of her throat. She had to trust Marshall knew what he was doing. No. She did trust Marshall. As screwed up as it was, she trusted him with Delanie's life and she trusted him with her life —a state she'd never experienced before with anyone except the woman close to feverish death. Jackie had seen the worry in the Texan's eyes when he'd helped her lift Delanie into the Audi. She'd seen his concern etch deep lines into the sides of his mouth every time his gaze dropped to the stab wound in her neck. Whatever reason they were sitting in a shopping-centre car park, she had to believe the man she was now mated to for life knew what he was doing.

"Just wish he'd tell me," she muttered, blinking at the tears still threatening to overwhelm her. She looked back down at Delanie's deathly face. "Before I thump him one."

She didn't have time to snort at the hollow threat. A sudden roar shook the car, vibrating all the way through Jackie's body. She twisted on the seat, craning to look out the window. It sounded like a chopper. A bloody close chopper.

White light flooded the car park, illuminating everything with blinding force, and she tensed, her right hand automatically reaching for her absent gun, her left splaying over Delanie's chest. "What the hell?"

The door behind her opened and cool night air streamed against her back from outside. She jerked around, the sudden chill covering her arms in goose bumps, and gazed up at Marshall. "What—?"

"We need to get Delanie to specialist care ASAP," he shouted, his voice barely audible over the roar above the car. Wild downward wind whipped his hair around his head and Jackie leant sideways in the seat, peering out the open door at the sky above the car.

The black belly of a large helicopter hung high overhead, a massive spotlight bleaching the ground from the aircraft's snub nose. As she watched, it keeled slightly to the left and began a smooth horizontal descent, far enough away from the Audi to not be dangerous, close enough to tell her the pilot knew exactly what he was doing.

She twisted until she could look up at the Texan, her hand pressing flat to Delanie's chest. The rapid beat of her friend's heart filled her with dread. As did the baking heat emanating from Delanie's body. "P.A.C.?"

He nodded, his expression guarded. "Sorta."

The helicopter's downforce tore the ambiguous answer away. Jackie turned her stare on its black shape, a sense of something very like foreboding squeezing her chest tight as it came to a perfect landing in the empty car park ten metres away. She shook her head. She didn't like this.

A firm hand touched her shoulder and she started, jerking her glare back to Marshall. "I'm not leaving her."

He studied her with unreadable eyes. "The chopper can't take anyone else, Jackie."

Before she could tell him to find another chopper—or go to hell, she wasn't sure which—the other back door opened and a man built roughly the size of an office block leant into the car, black sunglasses hiding his eyes from view. "She doesn't have time for you to argue, Detective Huddart."

His voice rumbled around the car's interior like a thunderstorm, an accent Jackie couldn't identify rolling over each consonant.

Jackie glared at him. "I'm not leaving her."

Black lenses regarded her.

"Lift her out, Hillerman." Marshall's command punched over Jackie's shoulder. "She's running out of time."

The office block nodded once and, moving with fluid speed, slid his massive arms under the small of Delanie's back and lifted her from the seat. She bowed in his hold as if boneless, one arm slipping from her stomach to swing in a limp arc beneath her.

"No," Jackie cried out, scrambling forward.

"Detective," Marshall shouted, his fingers gripping her shoulder with increasing pressure, holding her back. "Jackie."

She spun around on the Audi's backseat and shoved her palms against his chest. "Let me go."

He didn't budge, his expression revealing nothing. "Jackie. This isn't going to save her."

"And you can?"

He didn't answer and she let out a sharp snarl. Pushing him aside, she leapt from the car, sprinting around its hood toward the chopper. She had to stay with Del. Keep her safe. Hold her hand until she opened her eyes and said something witty and sarcastic. She couldn't let them take Delanie away from her. She couldn't—

Her hair lashed at her eyes as the helicopter's whirring propellers thrust the air down to the ground with powerful force. She stumbled backward, the pit of her belly sinking as the black craft lifted from the asphalt and rose into the night sky.

Tears stabbed at her eyes and she let out a growl, the sound far less human than it should be.

Del...

"Time is against us, Jackie." Marshall's voice came from behind her. Close. "If Delanie doesn't receive treatment soon she will die."

Jackie spun around and smashed her fist against his nose. "You fucking bastard!"

He staggered backward, blood seeping from his right nostril, his stare never leaving her face. "Jackie, you need to trust me."

"Trust you? You didn't say a bloody word in the car! Why didn't you tell me what you were doing?"

He shook his head. "Because you would ask too many questions. Questions I can't give you the answers to."

Cold fury tore through Jackie and she growled again. The wound in her throat throbbed with stinging heat, fingers of fire sinking deep into her chest, but she didn't care. "I have had enough of this secretive bullshit, Rourke. You've just sent my best friend away in a helicopter with a stranger who sounds like he's from a bad James Bond movie to wherever the fuck knows where. I have no idea if I will ever see her again, if she will even be alive by sunup and you're talking about answers some US agency I've never heard of won't let you divulge?" She clenched her fists harder, every molecule in her body charged with rage. "Tell me where he's taking Delanie. Now."

Rourke's jaw bunched. "I can't do that, detective."

She narrowed her eyes. "Then I can't do this anymore."

She turned and looked up into the night sky, trying to locate the chopper. She'd get a fix on its direction and call up the Tasmanian State police commander. Fuck that, the Australian Federal Police commissioner. It wouldn't take long for the Feds to track it down.

The world around Jackie swam. Black smudges blossomed in front of her eyes and she blinked, her throat erupting in pain so hot it incinerated her breath before it slipped into her lungs.

She blinked again, black fire devoured her from the neck out and the world tilted on a sickening axis.

Arms that felt like corded steel slid around her back and knees, lifting her from her traitorous feet. "Gotcha," a deep male voice—Marshall's voice—murmured in her ear. He pulled her closer to his hard body, the warmth of his bare chest chilly against her fevered face.

"I feel...wrong..." The words fell from her lips in a slur. Her throat burned, her eyes throbbed.

"Shhh," Marshall whispered against the top of her head. "Save your voice for later."

The world span once more and she clung to his neck. "What...what..."

Marshall shushed her again. "How are you going to chew me out later if you don't save your energy?" He carried her back to the Audi, each step he took sending jolts of agony into her body.

"I haven't...finished...with..." A finger of intense pain speared into her chest and she bit back a whimper.

Marshall chuckled—the sound low and distant. "Yeah, I kinda figured that." Leaning into the car, his arms holding her tighter to his torso, he laid her gently on the backseat, brushing the hair from her eyes. "Now shut the hell up, will you."

She looked up at him through black burning fog, and even though her body felt like it was on the verge of spontaneously combusting, she couldn't miss the worry in his face.

"Just hold on for a little longer, darlin'." His Adam's apple jerked up and down his throat and he ran the pad of his thumb over her cheekbone in a touch so light she wondered if she'd really felt it at all. "I can fix this, but you've got to hold on for me."

Fingers of fire bored into her body. Squeezed her lungs. Sank into her head. She closed her eyes, the Audi's muted cabin light like knives piercing her eyeballs. "Don't...call me darlin'."

He chuckled again. From a long, long way away. From the other side of the world. "That's my girl."

She heard a solid thunk, the glaring light vanished and more fingers drilled into her skull.

God, don't let me die.

A deep gnarr scratched at the edges of her brain, as if another entity pawed for escape. An image of an animal flittered though her head, maybe a wolf, maybe a dog, black stripes marking its back and hindquarters and tail. It looked at her, golden amber eyes scared. Lost.

Beautiful. So beautiful. What are you?

The animal's ears flattened to its head and it lifted its muzzle, a soundless cry warbling in its throat. Its throat. Fire danced over its throat. Burning in a single flame at the base of its long neck, singeing the russet fur.

Jackie reached for the animal, the pain raping her body

nothing compared to the agony in her heart—the animal's heart.

Beautiful creature. I will help you. I will…

The animal's head swung back toward her and looked at her with human eyes. *Her* eyes. And then a man appeared, a man within a man, as if two beings inhabited the same space, one gaunt and tall and leathery with empty eyes and wiry strength, the other with pearlescent black skin and long silver-white hair and lean sculpted muscles. The man stepped up behind the animal, a dead smile stretching lips both sensual and thin. He raised his left arm high, a wicked silver knife reflecting blood-red light gripped in his fist and Jackie cried out—*no!*—seconds before he plunged the knife down into the beautiful animal's side. Into the creature's chest. Into its heart. Her heart. Jackie's heart.

She cried out. Liquid fire spewed from the wound. Enveloped her. Engulfed her. She writhed under the man's knife, the man no longer two men, now just one, his glossy black skin and shining white eyes glistening with the animal's blood, with her blood. She struggled against the knife, against Einar's blade. The animal, the thylacine, bucked and thrashed. The animal that was her. Her duel soul, her duel existence. Fire poured from the hole in her side, up her chest, into her muzzle and down her throat. Choking her, burning her from within. The last thing she heard was Einar's laugh and the faint distant sound of Marshall calling her name.

CHAPTER TEN

Jackie opened her eyes and squinted at the low yellow light pressing all around her. Where was she?

She rolled her head to the left, ribbons of warm pain threading through her chest as she peered at the wall opposite her. A framed print of a fishing boat hung at a crooked angle above a white Formica desk, a gold lamp straight from the sixties sitting atop the chipped surface.

She frowned and pulled a slow breath.

Musty air slipped through her nostrils, dry and stale, and her frown deepened. It smelt like a hotel room. Why was she in a hotel room? What hotel room? Where was she?

She let her gaze slide to the window, the pale glow behind the garish drawn curtains telling her it was close to dawn. God, how long had she been out?

The mattress shifted beneath her, dipping deeply to her right and she jerked her head around, staring up at Marshall, her stomach lurching as the world spun in sickening rolls.

"Hey, hey, hey." Marshall placed a hand on her shoulder, looking down at her with a dry grin. "Better you keep the movements slow and steady for a while, ok, darlin'?"

She lifted her hand to her face, rubbing at her eyes. They

stung, like she'd stood too close to a bonfire, staring at its raging flames for too long. "You've brought me to a hotel room, Pacman?" The base of her throat throbbed and she swallowed, the simple action more painful than she expected. "Does this mean we've moved on from derelict buildings and abandoned shacks?"

He chuckled, tracing a gentle line down her temple with the back of his knuckles. "Sorry it's not the Hilton."

A soft laugh bubbled up Jackie's throat and she cringed, the scratching pain hitching her breath. "I'll forgive you. Did the thought happen to cross your mind to put some clothes on me?"

Another laugh rumbled in his chest. "Well, it did, but…" He shrugged, a lopsided grin playing with the corner of his mouth.

Her belly flipped-flopped at the subtle meaning in that smile and she let out a soft chuckle of her own. "I take it I'm going to—"

Live.

The word no sooner formed in her mind when she remembered Delanie. She sat up, every muscle and sinew in her body protesting the abrupt move. Waves of dark fogginess rolled over her, the base of her throat throbbing harder, but she tuned it all out and focused her stare on Marshall's face. "Is Del okay?"

He didn't answer. Not straight away, at least. "They are working on it."

Jackie narrowed her eyes. "They?"

His expression remained neutral.

She ground her teeth, guilt and anger slinking into her chest. "Why am I here in a hotel room, sitting up with nothing more than a killer sore throat while Delanie is with the oh-so-secretive 'them'?"

Marshall's jaw bunched at her sarcasm. "Einar's knife penetrated Delanie McKenzie's body completely." His tone was brusque. Clipped. "Your wound was only a shallow nick."

Jackie cocked an eyebrow at him. "I'm not stupid, Rourke. You should know that by now. What aren't you telling me?"

He sat silent, his gaze locked on her face for a moment before he raked his hands through his hair and stood up. "We suspect the weapon Einar used to stab you both was elvish."

"Elvish? As in pointy ears, mystical realms and J.R.R. Tolkien?"

He rolled his eyes, frustration pinching his eyebrows together. "You know, darlin', for a shape-shifter, you know next to nothing about the paranormal world."

Jackie gave him a flat glare. "You know, mate, for a wolf, you know next to nothing about pissing off an angry, wounded bitch."

He studied her, and for a split second Jackie wondered what definition he'd given to the word "mate".

What definition did you give it?

She stopped her fingers before they could wriggle. "So, your ex-partner is an elf?"

Marshall shook his head, his attention flicking to her hand before returning to her face. "No. Fae, even light fae, are not employed by P.A.C. Einar must have procured the weapon from an illegal trader."

Jackie's head swam with sudden prickling heat and an image flashed at her through the pain. An echo of a memory she could barely recall. A tall man with glossy black skin, silver white hair and cruel, sensual lips, a long, wicked blade marked with intricate glyphs gripped in his long fingers. She frowned, slumping a little on the mattress, and pressed her palm heels to her eyebrows. A dull ache filled her head. Her throat hurt.

Why was she picturing such a man? Who was he?

The image flashed through her head again, this time over-laid by another. She sat straight, fixing Marshall with a steady stare. "Daeved Einar is an elf. A dark elf."

Marshall shook his head again. "No. That's impossible. Dark elves are forbidden to walk the human world. They have black skin and—"

"White hair and eyes that seem to glow silver hate," Jackie cut him off.

He blinked, a sharp breath escaping him in a stunned grunt. "I would not have said it quiet so poetically, but yes." He dragged his hand down his face, his gaze flicking around the room. "Jesus, how could Einar traverse to our world? Disguise himself? How did he fool P.A.C.?" He looked back at Jackie. "Dark elves exist in a subterranean realm separate to the human world. The laws of their She-God forbid they move beyond that realm. Like humans, there are many different races, all however, are dangerous. What makes you think Einar is one of them? How do you know?"

"I saw him." She frowned again. "I mean, my thylacine saw him. Knew what he was."

"How?"

Jackie hesitated. How did she explain this? She didn't fully understand it herself. "The Tasmanian tiger is old. Older than man. Almost as old as Australia. For millions of years, the thylacine's ancestors roamed the body of land known as Gondwana. When Gondwana broke apart, when Australia was born, the thylacine as the world knows it now was also born." She paused, her chest heavy. "The spirit of this country, this land, is entwined with the creatures that live in harmony with it. The creatures born of it and to it."

Marshall cocked his head, his expression serious. "You're talking about the Aboriginal Dreamtime?"

Jackie gave him a slight shrug. "That is one way to describe it." She licked her lips, the dull burn in her throat making her mouth dry. "But I don't know if that is accurate. I've done my best to deny my other existence since I was a teenager, and I had no one to explain it to me growing up." The weight on her chest grew heavier at the banished thought of her early childhood and she closed her eyes. She didn't want to remember those horrific years. Caged, tormented. Alone and abused. Wondering where her parents were. Wondering if they'd survived. She didn't know. Not then, not now.

She let out a ragged sigh, denying the memory before it could claim her. "It's just a...connection...with the land and her spirit," she continued, looking at Marshall. "Whatever it is, when Einar lured me to his...trap...I sensed a disturbance."

Marshall snorted. "In the Force, young Obi-wan?"

She pulled a face at him. "You're a fine one to talk, Pacman. Played any good video games lately?"

He pulled a face back at her, and before Jackie knew what she was doing, the pressure on her chest melted away and she smiled.

How does he do this to you, Huddart? How does this one man with all his secrets make you feel safe? Calm?

Marshall studied her, a small smile curling at the corners of his mouth. "Just how old *are* you, Detective Huddart?"

She laughed, giving him an indignant look. "Surely your mum taught you it was rude to ask a lady that?"

"My mom taught me it was rude to sniff someone else's butt without permission, but she never mentioned anything about asking someone their age." He cocked an eyebrow at her. "Are you avoiding the question?"

Jackie laughed again. "Maybe."

His eyes grew intent. "Why?"

She let out a drawn-out sigh. "Time...moves differently when I am a Tasmanian tiger. A day as a human is like an hour as a thylacine. When I am in my animal form, I don't age as a person."

Marshall's gaze roamed her face. "So you're telling me you could be, what, seventy? Eighty?"

She shrugged, surprised how at ease she felt discussing something so disturbing. "Maybe," she said again.

"How have you kept this a secret?"

Jackie swallowed, looking him straight in the eyes. "Until you came along, I hadn't transformed since I was nineteen."

Marshall drew a quick breath at the confession, his nostrils flaring slightly. He returned her unwavering stare, his hands but a few millimetres from hers. Almost, but not quiet touching her. The seconds of silence dragged and Jackie's pulse thumped in her neck, growing louder, faster, with each beat. Her nipples grew hard, her mouth dry. A low growl rumbled in her chest but whether it was hers or her thylacine's she couldn't tell.

She wanted him to kiss her. She wanted him to take her face in his hands, brush his thumb over her bottom lip and claim her mouth as his. Wanted it so badly the lingering pain in her throat from Einar's knife wound seemed like a fleabite.

Oh, Jackie Huddart, you are insane.

The skin around Marshall's eyes tightened, his jaw bunched and he leant forward.

"So," she burst out, scurrying back on the mattress a little, her heart slamming against her breastbone, "tell me why you didn't know your partner was a dark elf?"

Marshall's smile pulled into a grin, his blue eyes so sharp, his gaze so intense Jackie squirmed. He straightened, giving her a look that clearly said she wasn't fooling him. "Dark elf magick is still a mystery. Even the P.A.C. geek squad admit being unable to comprehend or decipher it."

She frowned, glad to be on a safer subject. That the safer subject was the newly revealed race of her hunter and Delanie's attacker made her want to wriggle her fingers. "How long were you partners?"

"Five years. Long enough for me to have noticed something was amiss. Which I didn't." He turned his head, staring at the curtained window on the far wall. Outside, a neon light flickered, turning the gaudy flowered fabric to a static display of distorted colours. "Long enough for me to have noticed he never seemed to age." He let out a sharp sigh. "I used to think he had a thing for Botox. According to P.A.C. and Einar himself, he was a mage. A lower order one who rarely used his magick."

Jackie studied Marshall's profile. She could see the anger simmering beneath the surface of his sardonic calm, an agitated tension he was trying hard to keep hidden. Or controlled. A part of her—the female part, she was sure—wanted to smooth that tension away with her fingers, her lips. Another part—the cop part? The thylacine part?—wanted to provoke him. Jab at that agitation until he lost his leash on it and divulged the secrets he so tightly guarded. Damn it, she was mated to him for life now, even if he didn't know it. That had to give her some rights, some privileges, didn't it?

She opened her mouth, ready to ask him what he had to do with Einar's "retirement", when he turned to her, the anger gone from his face, his eyes more serious than she'd seen them before. He lifted his hand, touching the tiny gash in her throat with a feather-light caress. "How does your neck feel?"

The change in topic threw her off-guard. She swallowed, the contact of his fingertips sending ripples of anticipation through her body. "Better."

His gaze slid over her face, lingered on her lips and then focused on the base of her throat. "I will kill him for hurting you."

The murmured proclamation stole her breath, and she raised her hand to his, removing his fingers from her skin. "I don't need a knight to right the wrongs done against me, Rourke."

"No, what you need is your mate." He stopped, his eyes growing wide.

Mate.

The word hung between them, charged with crackling heat. There was no mistaking the context behind the word this time. Marshall's expression defined it—his flaring nostrils, his bunched jaw, the searing look in his eyes. Jackie's body defined it—the puckering of her nipples, her quickening breath, the constricting heat in the junction of her thighs.

Mate.

"I don't even know what kind of wolf you are." Even to her own ears, she sounded dazed.

Marshall shook his head. "Does it matter?"

Jackie's eyebrows dipped together. "Yes."

He leant forward, placing his palm against the side of her neck, his fingers threading through the tousled strands of her hair at her nape. "I'm yours, Jackie." He drew her head closer to his with gentle pressure, his whisper kissing her lips. "For life." His lips brushed hers. Soft. Hesitant. Almost nervous.

His warm, hard body melded to hers and a shiver of sheer joy passed through her. They'd fucked like animals twice, rutted like the four-legged beasts they were, but they'd never made love.

Is this what this is now? Love? For life?

Her heart quickened and she let out a shaky breath. She didn't know. But it felt more than good. It felt right.

He brushed his lips over hers, gentle and reverent. "For life," he repeated on a murmur. He kissed her again, lips more fervent, tongue flicking into her mouth to touch the edge of her teeth before he lifted his head and gave her another grin. "And I'm not being sarcastic."

Jackie gazed into his eyes for a long moment. Her head ached with questions, but her heart, her soul, ached with love. The questions, the answers could come later. She threaded her fingers into the silken strands of his messy blonde hair and held him close, feeling the heat of his desire grow harder and longer against her belly. She had no idea where they were, whether Delanie was alive, whether Einar was dead or still hunting her, but Marshall was here, holding her in his arms, his heart beating against hers. And for a selfish, selfish moment *that* was all that mattered.

With a low groan, she pulled his head down to hers,

capturing his willing mouth with open lips. Their tongues met, each fierce and hungry. Wild.

Light-headed, Jackie dragged her hands down Marshall's back, thrilling at the smooth, sculpted curves of his muscles under her palms. A sense of weightlessness came over her, a euphoric giddiness growing stronger with every caress from his tongue, every nip of his teeth on her lips. She curled her fingers over his arse and pulled his hips harder to hers, anchoring herself to his body through a contact that was both burning and taunting. His rigid cock pressed against the sensitive curve of her mons, its powerful need imprisoned by the denim of his jeans. She whimpered, her pussy growing damp. She wanted to feel him inside her. She *needed* to feel him inside her.

She needed his love, his desire. She needed to know they were more than just two animals copulating, more than just two animals under the control of their base instincts. She needed him to take her to pleasures she'd never dreamed possible.

She needed to *be* with him. Connected, joined in every way.

With an impatient growl, she pushed his hips away, moved her hands to his fly and flipped the buttons undone. Before her eager fingers could release his cock however, it sprang free, a long, thick shaft that filled her hands completely and burned her flesh with its pulsating heat.

Marshall sucked in a swift breath, flaring nostrils brushing her cheek, tongue plunging deeper into her mouth. She slid her hand down the length of his cock, cupping his full, heavy balls in her palm before drawing closed fingers back up to his organ's swollen head. A bead of pre-come seeped from the small slit and she captured it with her thumb, smearing the glistening, viscous fluid over the velvet-soft dome. Marshall sucked another sharp breath in through his nose, stabbing his hips forward. His cock pumped into her hand, harder, longer, an urgent need surging through its taut skin.

That need joined Jackie's and she moaned, pulling her mouth free of their kiss. "Please," she whispered on a shallow breath, rolling her thumb across the bulbous head above her fingers. "Please."

"I want to sink into your warmth," he stated, his voice low and shaky, as though he fought with a tremendous force. "I want to feel consumed, taken and owned by you."

"Then do it," she commanded on a gasp. "Don't make me wait any longer."

Ice-blue eyes roamed her face and his body grew still. "Jackie, you need to know…" He shook his head, a frown knotting his eyebrows. "I…I…"

Jackie opened her mouth, but Marshall pressed firm fingers to her lips, stopping her. "Oh, fuck, how do I say this?"

A tight pressure closed around Jackie's heart and she stared into his eyes. "Say what, Pacman?"

That crooked grin returned and he shook his head, running his palm down her torso to squeeze her arse. "That you bring out the animal in me." He leant forward and crushed her lips with his, but not before Jackie saw a sorrowful flicker fill his eyes.

What are you hiding, she wanted to ask, but his mouth moved over hers with such wanton need her head grew giddy and she fell into his embrace, sliding her arms around his neck and giving herself over to their passion.

With a low growl, Marshall pressed her back to the mattress, his lips charting languid paths over her lips, her chin, her jaw and back to her lips again. She whimpered again, wanting more. So much more. "Please."

Without a word, he pulled away from her and, his gaze holding hers, shucked his legs out of his jeans. He stood before her, naked, completely erect and her sex constricted. "Christ, this wasn't…"

He didn't finish. Eyes burning blue fire, he climbed back onto the bed, his hands resting on either side of her head, his knees nudging her thighs apart. His warm flesh pressed to hers and Jackie gasped, a shot of liquid delight flooding into her pussy.

"You're not the only impatient one here, Jackie Huddart." His murmured words caressed her skin. "But I will do my very best to make this last forever." He took possession of her mouth once more, the kiss ravenous and urgent. His tongue dipped into her mouth, charting the edges of her teeth, her lips. He nipped on her bottom lip, sucked on her tongue, flooding her with exquisite heat as his balls rubbed over the flat plane of her belly.

The contact was electric. Bolts of twisting energy scorched a path straight to the gushing dampness between Jackie's thighs. She reached up, wanting to thread her fingers in his hair, to feel the silken strands on her skin, but his strong hands stopped her, catching her wrists and planting them beside her head, holding them still as he continued to ravish her lips.

She arched into him, the heat from his swollen balls seeping into her sex. Calling. Teasing. With a roll of her hips, she drew her sex in line with their heavy weight, grinding her mons against them in slow circles. Marshall groaned low in his chest, the vibrations tickling her nipples. His tongue lashed at hers and he pulled her wrists together, holding them with one hand as the other dragged down her arm to one uplifted breast. He cupped it, pinching its erect nipple between two knuckles until Jackie writhed beneath him, pushing her pussy to his insistent shaft and whimpering in supplication.

A growl rose in his throat and he tore his mouth from hers, scoring it along the line of her jaw, up to her ear. "I've killed paranormal creatures my entire life, but never have I desired one like I desire you. When I saw you…fuck, I desire you more than life. I hadn't planned to, but I do. Nothing will ever change that." Teeth, sharp and even, nipped at her lobe, each stabbing pressure adding to the squirming tension in her pussy. "Nothing."

She moaned and lifted her hips, his words driving her wild, his hands wilder. "Oh, God, Marshall." Her voice fell from her lips in a husky whisper. "If you don't make love to me now, I think I will scream." She pushed her hips harder to his, pressing her heavy, swollen pussy lips to his rigid shaft. "I want you inside me so much. Please…"

His mouth moved over her ear and he chuckled softly. "I want you to scream." His tongue flicked into the shallow shell of her ear before he scorched a path down her neck to her collarbone. He rained her flushed skin with soft bites until she cried out, ramming her sex to his cock, a wordless plea for fulfillment.

But still Marshall continued to deny her. His mouth worked down to her free breast, capturing the taut nipple and suckling deeply. Hot barbs of sensation ricocheted through her, buried into the constricting centre of her sex. "That's so good," she murmured, rolling her head from side to side. "So good."

Marshall's teeth closed around the aching nub, pulling at it in rhythm with his squeezing, fondling hand on her other breast. She arched beneath him, pushing her nipple harder to his mouth, wanting to feel his teeth and tongue raze the sensitive peak more. Her sex contracted, gripping for a cock still so torturously denied her. "I'm aching for you," she said, straining against the hand on her wrists. She wanted to touch him, feel his smooth, warm flesh under her palm.

Instead, Marshall raised his head, blew a fine stream of cool air on her distended nipple and then met her eyes with his. "Do you trust me?"

The question was as serious as the fire in his gaze and Jackie nodded, incapable of forming the word. Yes. She did.

"Don't move your hands." His command whispered over her flesh, his eyes ablaze. "Don't move at all and let me worship your body."

Hot liquid gushed into Jackie's gripping sex as the intent behind his words became clear. Imprisoned by his words alone, by their mounting pleasure, she was his to do with what he would. *Oh, God, Jackie, are you ready for this?*

He palmed her breasts until she whimpered and begged for him to stop. Her sex was so tight and wet she could feel her pleasure dampening her thighs. Lips curled into a lazy smile, he paused long enough for Jackie to drag in breath after ragged breath in an effort to regain control, but not long enough to let the building tension in her body subside.

Just as she began to feel the pressure between her thighs ebb away, Marshall returned his fingers to her nipples, flicking and pinching in quick succession, bringing her to a peak of exquisite bliss again.

"Please," she moaned, pussy flooding with cream, pulse a pounding beat. "Please… Please…" She wrapped her legs around his hips, pulling his jutting organ closer to the sodden centre of her desire. It ground against her clit, parted her folds to push at the tight entry.

She growled, writhing in Marshall's hold in an attempt to impale herself, but he wouldn't let her. He took one nipple into his mouth and rolled the tip between his teeth, nipping and flicking at it with the end of his tongue before moving to the other breast. Jackie moaned and pulled her legs closer to her body, desperate to have his cock stretch her fully. Impatient greed boiled her blood when he straightened away from her body.

"No!" She glared up at him. How could he deny her— himself—any longer?

"Trust me, Jackie," he whispered, piercing blue gaze holding hers. His hands smoothed down her ribcage, over the curve of her hips to her thighs. "Trust." His fingers curled under her arse, squeezed her cheeks. "Trust…" His long fingers spread them wider and she felt a teasing pressure circle the tight, puckered hole of her anus.

"Oh."

Her soft gasp stilled Marshall's hand. Eyes ablaze with raw

passion, he gazed down at her. Slowly, gently, silently, he pushed at her hole a little harder.

A choked cry burst from Jackie's mouth and she clenched her fists, wet electricity surging through her from the delicious contact. She'd never let a living soul touch her in such an intimate way and the unadulterated pleasure consuming her body told her why. This was a sublime experience to be shared only with one in her heart. It was exquisite. It was powerful. It was frightening. Adrenaline heated her blood. She whimpered, wanting to pull away, wanting to impale herself on his hand.

"Trust me," Marshall murmured, somehow sensing the fear in her rapture. "I will never hurt you."

His words caressed her soul. His breath caressed her flesh seconds before Marshall lowered his head between her thighs and plunged his tongue into her pussy.

"Fuck, fuck, fuck!" Jackie cried out, rolling waves of wet heat crashing through her. She bucked into his mouth, whimpering with barely contained pleasure when he drew the tiny tip of her clit between his teeth. Shots of raw pleasure stabbed into her cunt, electrical pulses that made her heart hammer and her juices flow. Marshall lapped at them, the sound of his appreciation, soft moans and low groans filling the light-diffused air.

His tongue laved her spread sex. Tasting and delving between her folds in a mind-blowing pace that made Jackie squirm. She lifted her hips, giving herself to him completely, wanting to be devoured by his mouth.

He feasted on her folds, her clit, pushing her closer, closer to the precipice, until she felt the first wall of concentrated bliss crash through her being.

"Oh, God, I'm coming!"

In a blur of preternatural speed, Marshall rose up from between her thighs and aligned his turgid shaft to her wet, glistening pussy. "Then let me come with you," he said, and plunged his cock into her sex.

Jackie's scream rent the air. A kaleidoscope of blinding colours erupted in her vision, radiating out to infinity like a shockwave.

Marshall thrust into her, his balls slapping her arse cheeks. His free hand palmed her breast, pinched her nipple. His mouth found her neck and sucked.

Another wall crashed through Jackie. Indescribable. Consuming. She clenched her fists, tumbling over the edge as one orgasm after another claimed her. "Yes. Don't stop. God, please don't ever stop."

Marshall's divine rhythm accelerated. He raised his head from her neck and looked down at her with burning eyes, lips parted, chest heaving. "I'm yours, Jackie," he ground out. "Never forget that." His thrusts grew wild, his breathing wilder. "No matter what happens after this, never forget I am yours."

Fresh waves of molten lava welled up in Jackie at his words. Building, building. She looked up into Marshall's face, her mind roaring, her brain fogged with pleasure. She watched him close his eyes as, with a shudder she felt deep in her being, he finally gave himself over to his own orgasm. She watched his nostrils flare as it scorched through his body and pumped into hers.

Two people joined together, their hearts beating in unison, beating against each other. Two people unable to deny what they wanted anymore.

"Trust," Jackie whispered, gazing into Marshall's euphoric face. "Trust."

The single, powerful word resounded in Jackie's mind just as she closed her eyes and surrendered willingly and completely to the power of her orgasm.

And the power of her desire for Marshall Rourke.

CHAPTER ELEVEN

"Why do you wriggle your fingers?"

The question slipped from Marshall before he could stop it, and he bit back a silent curse, smoothing his hand up Jackie's back to hold her closer to his chest just in case she was thinking of pulling away from him.

They lay on the hotel room's sagging bed, their legs entwined, the perspiration from their lovemaking still slicking their skin, their hearts beating in unison. He'd never felt more content. And then he had to go and open his big, Texan mouth.

Smooth, Rourke. Real smooth.

Jackie didn't say a word for a long moment. Her body was still, her hand resting loosely on his chest. He moved his head slightly, trying to see her face without disturbing her position. Two hours of complete and utter bliss and he'd asked a question about something he knew she tried to hide. Damn, he was an idiot.

"It's a control method," Jackie finally answered, the words low and measured. "When I was younger, I had difficulty restraining the transformation into my thylacine form. Stress, anger, almost any negative emotion would push me close to shifting. If I concentrated on the movement of my fingers, how the air flowed around them, how the muscles in each finger flexed and coiled, I could suppress the need to transform."

He ran his hand up and down her back, studying the top of her head. "How often did you shift in front of humans?"

Silence stretched, the hand on his chest remaining motionless, as if Jackie consciously fought to stay calm. "When I was young, very young, often. But only in front of one person. I don't really remember much about my childhood. The earliest thing I can remember is a woman—possibly my mother—telling me to run. Run fast. I don't know what I was running to or from, nor how old I was, but I was little. Very little. Too little for a child to be running through the bush on her own. The next thing I remember is the cage."

Her fingers moved slightly on Marshall's chest, flexing once before she pressed her palm to his chest once more.

"I woke up one day in a cage, in my thylacine form," she continued, voice flat. "I don't know if the farmer caught me in that form, but I can only assume he did. What kind of person cages a little girl who looks barely older than eight?"

Marshall could provide an answer—a sick, perverted, deranged person deserving to be beaten to a bloody pulp—but he didn't. He couldn't. His throat was too thick.

"He kept me caged for a long time. I escaped one day—in human form—and he found me running naked away from his shed. I still think he had no idea the petrified girl on his property was the Tasmanian tiger he'd tormented for so long, until he yelled at me to stop and I transformed mid-stride. He caught me and caged me again. After that, I think he took great delight in seeing how often he could provoke me into shifting. Which, I'm ashamed to say, was often." The fingers on Marshall's chest moved—slightly—and he felt Jackie's heartbeat quicken.

Marshall clenched his jaw, dark anger heating his blood. "Why didn't he turn you in? Tell anyone about you?"

Jackie shook her head, her soft hair tickling underneath his chin. "I wondered that myself for a very long time. There's been a reward for any proven sightings of a Tasmanian tiger since the nineteen-thirties. Every day I waited for people to arrive, to take me away, but they never did." She paused, her fingers moving again. "My first year in the police academy, I ran a complete check on the man. I didn't know his name, but I knew where his farm was. It took me a while, but I discovered everything I could about him. Turns out, he was a wanted criminal. The New South Wales police force had an arrest warrant issued for him. He'd been the main suspect in an assault where the victim, the mayor of Sydney's teenage daughter, had died. Tasmania was the ideal place to hide out, I guess." Her fingers moved again, a soft sigh fanning his chest. "So, he got to play with his little freak of nature undisturbed until she was big enough to..."

Jackie's words faded away, her fingers finally curling into a fist. A hot ball of furious disgust rolled through Marshall and he closed his eyes, thinking of the scared little girl, of the petrified pup. "What happened to him?"

"I escaped the cage one day and killed him."

The simple statement filled him with more joy than it should. He wanted to fold her closer into his body and hold her forever. She didn't say what form she'd been in when the deed was done, nor what transpired to allow her to escape, and it didn't matter to him. Thylacine or human, the farmer got what he deserved.

Marshall pressed his lips to her forehead, breathing her delicate scent into his body. She was a contradiction, Jacqueline Huddart. One part hard-arse cop, one part secretive shapeshifter, one part deeply loyal and emotional friend, one part sensual lover.

She was his life mate and he couldn't be happier.

Then shouldn't you tell her what you've been doing? What you started out doing? Using her as bait?

He closed his eyes, a lump filling his throat. Yes, he should. He had to. It wasn't going to be pretty, but he had to. After everything he'd put her through, he owed her the truth. "Did you ever find your parents?"

The question wasn't what he'd intended to ask, but the truth of what he'd been doing, what he'd initially used her for still refused to come.

Coward.

She shook her head. "If they are alive, I don't know it. It's possible, I guess, with the way time is suspended while trans-formed but I doubt it. The only sighting of a Tasmanian tiger in the last few decades was when I'd foolishly shifted into my thylacine form as a teenager." She shrugged. "But who knows. You've seen the Tassie bush. You know how dense it is. An animal could live forever in that bush and never be seen by a human." Her eyebrows dipped and she paused, a disgusted expression flickering across her face. "A *smart* animal, that is."

He gave her a soft smile. "You are a smart animal, Detective Huddart. You discovered Einar was a dark elf, something all the geeks and suits at P.A.C. hadn't."

She let out a snort, and Marshall suspected his attempt at easing the pain he felt in her heart had failed.

"How did you cure me? If you didn't know Einar was a dark elf, how did you cure me of his dark-elf poison?"

Jackie's unexpected question took Marshall by surprise. He pulled away from her, gazing into her upturned face. "Fae blood."

She frowned. "Fae blood?"

He let his fingers slip from her shoulder to the small wound at the base of Jackie's throat, studying the still-angry, red flesh. His stomach knotted. "The poison of Einar's blade can only be dissolved from the system by fae blood. It's what is being used to treat Del, and Hillerman provided me enough to treat you. Fae blood, particularly virgin fae blood has a multi-tude of reactions on foreign bodies. P.A.C. knows the exact way every non-human being will react to it." He stopped, not sure how to continue.

Jackie tilted her head, her eyes narrowing. "Every non-human being except a shape-shifting thylacine, that is?"

He shifted on the mattress, clenching his jaw. Jesus, how did he go on? "Yes." He nodded, his gaze returning to the hole in her neck for a quick second. "Except a shape-shifting thylacine."

She gave him a level look. "You took a gamble?"

He swallowed, his mouth suddenly dry. "I couldn't lose you."

The raw truth behind Marshall's answer brought a lump to Jackie's throat. "How did I react?" It wasn't the question she wanted to ask, but it was the only one she would allow.

A slight grin pulled at the edges of his mouth, and he ran his hand back over her shoulder and down to the curve of her hip. "You threw up. A lot."

Hot embarrassment flooded Jackie's cheeks and she rolled away from him, pressing her palms to her mouth. She groaned. *Oh, God.*

Scrambling from the bed, she bolted into the bathroom, swinging the door shut behind her. She dropped onto the closed toilet and stared at her feet. How embarrassing.

A soft knock rapped on the door and she looked up, her cheeks burning hotter still. She threw up? She hadn't thrown up since the farmer had electrocuted her non-stop one day until she transformed.

"Jackie?"

She heard the laughter in Marshall's voice and pulled a face. "Did I make much mess?"

"Not a bit," his answer came through the door, muffled by the wood. "For someone all but delusional, you have remarkable aim. It all went in the toilet bowl."

Jackie dropped her gaze to the white toilet seat lid visible between her thighs and groaned again. "How could I..." she faltered, "...if I was..." She bit at her lip, and deep within her thylacine snarled with disgust.

"I held your hair from your face, helped you rinse your mouth after each time and made sure you didn't collapse into the bowl. Getting you to spit out the mouthwash was...interesting I have to say. You seem to be a bit partial to its taste. And when I gave you a toothbrush you seemed to think it was a bone and growled at me when I tried to take it away."

Jackie didn't think she could be more embarrassed. She squeezed her eyes shut, hands pressed to her lips again.

"I would do it again, darlin'."

Marshall's voice reverberated in the small room and Jackie jerked her head up to find him standing in the open doorway. He stared at her, one broad shoulder leaning against the doorjamb, his arms loosely crossed over his chest, that lop-sided grin she knew so well curling one side of his mouth. "All of it, including the rather surreal toothbrush wrestling, and still love everything about you."

Love.

The word slipped through Jackie's mind and she stared at him, unable to say a thing.

Love.

His blue eyes sparkled and his grin stretched wider. "Now I would like to make love to you again, my gorgeous Tasmanian tiger and if you don't leave the bathroom I shall do so right where you sit." He pushed himself straight from the doorjamb. "Never made love to someone on a toilet before, but when it comes to you, Detective Huddart, I'm willing to try anything n—"

She didn't let him finish.

Love.

She leapt from the seat and threw herself against his hard body, silencing his chuckled words with a kiss so deep she felt his growl rumble in his chest. He wrapped his arms around her, lifting her from the floor, his tongue mating with her in fierce hunger.

Love.

Jackie's head swam and she broke the kiss, pulling away from him as far as his arms would allow her. *I love you too.* The declaration formed in her head, its truth potent and undeniable. She did love him, more than she believed possible, but she would not let herself say the words. They were too foreign, too vulnerable. Instead, she said, "Will you shower with me?"

His eyes flared blue desire. "Hmm, let me think about that." Before she could laugh—or slap him—he carried her across the small bathroom, stepped into the bathtub and kicked the mixer on. Icy water spurted from the showerhead and Jackie gasped, the sound becoming a moan when Marshall pressed her against the tiled wall away from the water spray and kissed her until she trembled all over.

His hands cupped her arse, squeezing each cheek as his cock grew long and thick against her belly. Cold drips of water splashed onto her legs and feet, sending little chills through her body, emphasizing the rising heat of her desire. God, she could spend the rest of eternity in the man's arms and never want for anything more.

Marshall's lips dragged from hers, following the line of her jaw, her throat. He growled, squeezing her arse again, and she whimpered, eyelids fluttering closed. "This is not getting us clean."

He chuckled, lifting his mouth from her throat to smile down at her. "I'm rather enjoying getting dirty with you."

Jackie's sex contracted. She rolled her hips against his, the solid length of his enjoyment nudging her mons a testament to his words. "I can tell."

Marshall's eyes flared with desire and he pressed his lips to her temple. "There's a small toiletry kit in my backpack," he murmured. "Let me wash your hair and scrub your back before I dirty you up again."

Jackie's pulse quickened at his request, her breath hitching in her throat. Why did the notion of Marshall washing her hair arouse her so much?

Because it friggen' does, Huddart. Stop trying to find answers in everything and just accept the truth. You've fallen head over heels for the guy and it scares the hell out of you.

It did scare her. And yet it felt wonderful, so damn wonderful at the same time. Her sex contracted again, stronger, more forcefully. Eager. With a simple nod, she stepped from his embrace and climbed from the bathtub.

Marshall's heady gaze raked her naked body and she hurried from the small room, the promise in his eyes making her mouth dry and her thighs wet. The sooner she found his backpack, the sooner she was back in the shower with him.

His cell phone vibrated into silent life on the lamp table and Jackie jumped, shooting the bathroom door behind her a quick look. "Your phone is ringing, Marshall."

"Damn," he called back, voice a touch gargled by water. "It's probably Hillerman."

Del.

Pulse leaping into thumping strength, Jackie crossed the room in two steps, snatching up the phone and pressing it against her ear. "Agent Rourke's phone."

"You stabbed me, Jacqueline." Einar's rasping drawl slid into her ear through the connection and Jackie's throat squeezed shut. "I look forward to returning the favour in kind."

Her grip on Marshall's phone tightened and she stiffened. Red rage prickled behind her eyes. Her heart leapt into her throat. "I am going to hunt you down and kill you, Einar."

A slow tsk tsk clicked on the other end of the line. "Not very police-like behaviour, detective. What would your commander back in Sydney say?"

Jackie grinned, a cold expression of deadly calm she felt all the way to the centre of her being. "I'm not coming after you as a cop. Tasmanian tigers may not be the fastest creatures on the planet, but we are the most tenacious." She let her icy hate flow into every syllable she spoke. "And I'm nowhere near as old as you, elf. I will wear you down until you don't have the energy to run anymore and then tear your throat out."

Silence stretched over the connection, nothing but a faint series of crackles and pops to tell her Einar still held the line open.

"How many times have you fucked the werewolf?"

His voice sounded strained and Jackie grinned again. She wanted him strained. Unsettled. Easier to track prey that way. She shot the bathroom door a quick look, the noises of Marshall showering wafting at her across the distance. She should tell him who was on the phone. She should let him know.

She turned away from the door, lifting the phone's mouthpiece closer to her lips. "Why would I tell you that? I didn't realize you were a pervert as well as a gutless pixie."

Einar hissed and Jackie's grin stretched wider, cold satisfaction threading through her fury. Unsettled and agitated. Good. Very good.

"Is Agent Rourke a good lover?"

A throaty laugh escaped Jackie. "He was *your* partner. Surely you know how thorough he is. How determined to achieve what he sets out to do. Imagine that skilled relentlessness in a sexual partner, and I'm sure you have your answer."

Silence followed her taut, and then Einar said, "You should be more selective about who you mate with, Detective Huddart. It was, after all, Agent Rourke who sent me the information about your existence in the first place."

Numb shock stole over Jackie. She blinked once, her pulse pounding in her neck. Was it true?

No. Why would Marshall do that?

To draw Einar out in the open? What better way to catch a hunter than present him with that which he truly wants: prey.

She blinked again, turning to stare at the open bathroom door. Marshall's tall, lean form moved behind the cloud-blue shower curtain, like a shadow moving through mist. She frowned, her pulse growing faster. Louder.

Bait? He'd used her as bait?

Do you really believe that, Jackie? Do you?

"I look forward to seeing you soon, detective." Einar's smug voice slid into her ear. "Give my regards to the werewolf. It's been a long time since I've seen a dire wolf. I always remembered them being…bigger."

He killed the connection and Jackie stood frozen, Marshall's phone still in her hand. She stared at the Texan's silhouette through the shower curtain, numb disbelief chilling her.

"I'm no threat to you. That's all I can tell you."

"If I could answer those questions I would."

His words came back to her, whispering inside her roaring mind. Answers to her questions that were not answers at all.

She drove her nails into her palms, remembering exactly what he'd said when she'd pressed him about who had Delanie. *"Someone wants something from you. Your friend unfortunately has been caught up in the trap."* And when she'd questioned further all he'd said was, *"It's better I don't answer."*

Ambiguous answer after ambiguous answer, topped off with the most ambiguous of all, *"I'm the man here with you now, not the man holding your friend. Remember that."*

She stared hard at his shrouded form, her breath shallow. He'd never given her a single answer. No matter what she'd asked.

A sick emptiness rolled in Jackie's stomach. He'd used her as bait. He'd set a trap for Einar and Del had been the innocent victim.

Grief—cold and painful and dark—twisted through her

chest. It sank into her stomach. Marshall's phone slipped from her fingers, striking the worn carpet at her feet. She dropped onto the edge of the bed, the musky scent of their earlier lovemaking a faint memory on the air, mocking her. Deep within, her thylacine bristled and even that felt scornful, as if the animal derided her human stupidity.

"Jackie?"

Marshall's voice jerked her stare back to the bathroom door and she found him standing there, looking at her. Water beaded on his smooth skin, a towel wrapped his lean hips and his gaze roamed her face, worry in his sharp blue eyes. "Darlin'?"

Her chest tightened. *Your life mate. The lying bastard.*

Something broke inside her. She frowned, numb still and yet, torn apart with pain unlike any she'd imagined. Empty pain. Like the death of a dream.

He studied her, taking a step forward. "Is Del…?" His eyes widened. "Christ, is Delanie—"

"Did you tell Daeved Einar about my existence?" She cut him off, the question passing her dry lips with calm ease. "Did you use me as bait?"

Marshall stiffened, a barely perceptible tensing of his muscles. He swallowed, his jaw bunching, his gaze locking on her eyes. "I wanted to tell you."

Blistering fury detonated in Jackie's chest. She stared at him. "I hate you." The statement left her in an emotionless monotone.

"Jackie—"

Marshall moved toward her but she shook her head, snapping to her feet and looking around the hotel room. Clothes. She needed clothes.

"Please, let me—"

She leapt at him, slamming him to the floor. Her knees rammed under his armpits, her fingers gripping the tops of his shoulders, digging into his flesh. "You used me as *bait*,

Pacman." She glared at him, her blood roaring in her ears. "And Delanie was hurt because you did. What is there to explain?"

He stared up at her, making no attempt to move. "There was no other way."

She punched him. Hard. Her fist hit his jaw with a dull crack. He took the blow, rolling his head with her punch before turning back to her, his stare seeking her eyes. "I didn't plan on any of this, Jackie. I didn't plan to mate with you. I didn't plan to fall in love with you."

Her chest constricted at his words, but she ignored it. Her thylacine snarled and she closed her eyes, unable to look at him. "You used me."

"There were no other options," he answered simply.

Acrid grief hit her and she scrunched up her face, shaking her head. Mated for life to a lying bastard. Did she kill him? She opened her eyes and stood, giving him a flat stare where he lay between her feet. "There are always options, Agent Rourke."

She stepped away from him, snatching his jeans from the bed as she did so. She needed clothes and his would do. After all, he'd taken everything she had from her. Her best friend, her anonymity. Her heart. It was only fair she took something from him in return.

Marshall straightened to his feet, watching Jackie prowl the room. She yanked on his jeans, the item of clothing ridiculously loose on her tiny frame, the waistline barely touching her slim hips. She hauled his backpack from the floor and upended it, grabbing at his spare white T-shirt before it could finish falling onto the bed. She pulled it over her head. It was too big for her, way too big. She looked lost in its size. Lost and angry.

She has every right to be angry.

A lump filled his throat and he dragged his hands through

his hair, the damp strands a taunting reminder that but a few moments ago they'd been in the shower together, their bodies pressed against each other, their desire tangible. Undeniable.

"Jackie…"

She refused to look at him, dropping instead onto the edge of the bed, her attention locked on the hem of his jeans as she rolled the right leg shorter in savage flicks of her wrists. She was getting ready to leave. He could see it in the strung tension in her body. Leave, or hit him again.

He scrubbed his hands over his face, his gut churning. Shit. What did he do?

"Let me…"

She started rolling up the other leg, her stare fixed on her hands.

He let out a ragged breath, wiping at his mouth. "While Daeved Einar was a P.A.C. agent," he said, keeping his voice level, "he dissected a lycanthrope alive in Virginia who had been using a local old-aged care home as a buffet bar. He tied the man spread-eagle to a bench in the kitchen and proceeded to cut into his stomach—while he was conscious—demanding to know the whereabouts of his pack despite intel telling us there was none.

"In Quebec, Einar proceeded to flay a selkie alive in an attempt to force the creature to reveal the location of his den. We had orders to bring the selkie in for questioning, not because he had harmed anyone, but because he had been linked, albeit tenuously, to a gang who were skinning shape-shifters and selling their coats as mystical aids. In Ireland, he stuffed a banshee's mouth with rotting meat, choking her until she confessed to aiding an attack on a school camping trip. In Tokyo, he beat an Oni until it could no longer stand, because he didn't like the way it looked at him."

He paused for a moment, the memories of his time as Einar's partner turning the saliva in his mouth to bile. "At first, I didn't try to stop the brutality. I'd been appalled, disgusted even, but being partnered with the famous, revered Daeved Einar had blinded me to the wrong being done. P.A.C. had a fierce reputation for bringing to justice any paranormal being stepping out of line. Einar's reputation was fiercer still. As uncomfortable as I was with my new partner's behaviour, I followed the man's lead."

Sour disgust coated Marshall's tongue and he let out a low grunt. "When Einar 'questioned' a succubus suspected of feeding off tourists, I couldn't keep quiet anymore. He called me weak, gutless. He justified his extreme treatment by pointing out how many unwitting victims the demon had sexually devoured in the last year. None of those victims had been killed or physically injured in any way and we could find no residue of any of them in the succubus's *croi*, but that didn't stop his violent attack. It was one atrocity too much. I was forced to subdue him and reported him to the commander as soon as we returned to P.A.C. headquarters."

He stopped. His stomach was a knot of self-contempt. He turned his gaze from Jackie, still bent over her legs with her hands gripping the hem of his jeans, to look out the hotel room's sole window. "Einar's argument at his review consisted of the words *'The world is a better place because of what I do to the perversions of nature.'* Just those words. Nothing more. My report saw him stripped of his record and 'retired', the worst outcome I could imagine. The moment he walked from P.A.C.'s building, any professional restrictions he'd abided by were gone. He was free to hunt any non-human he chose. Free to kill them in any way he saw fit, which he did. And every kill he makes, he sends me a small token of the 'prize'—a talon, a fang, a horn, an eye. Christ, once the genitals of a being I still can't identify—as if to say thank you."

He stopped again, dragging his hands through his hair as he turned back to Jackie. She was looking at him, studying him with unreadable eyes, her expression just as neutral. But looking at him all the same. Not hitting him, not running from him. It was something.

More than what you deserve.

"I have been trying to right a wrong for a long time now, darlin'," he said, meeting her unwavering gaze. "My hands are stained with the blood of every creature Einar has executed since his retirement, whether good or bad—and quite a few before that. More than I care to admit or think about. I set him loose in this world and I have to bring him in. You were the only way I could do so, a target too tempting, too unique to resist. I learned of your existence listening in on the P.A.C. Chatter Squad. An off-handed remark by the werewolf Declan O'Connell in a telephone conversation with his human wife about a shape-shifting cop from Tasmania, and I knew I'd found the perfect bait." He let out another sharp snort. "But it all went wrong from the very moment I saw you in the airport. From the very second your scent filled my nose."

Jackie's chest rose, a swift, silent breath the only reaction to his admission. He shook his head and turned to the window once more, staring at the pale morning beyond the glass and faded curtain. "I didn't mean to mate with you. But the moment I saw you, smelt you, I knew I wanted to. Wanted it so much I could hardly think straight. Knew I didn't have the strength to resist the elemental—shit, the *primitive* desire you awoke in me. I didn't mean to fall in love with you either, but goddamn it, I wouldn't change a thing if it meant that I didn't."

He looked back at her, his chest heavy, his mouth dry. She hadn't moved, and he didn't know if that was a good thing or a bad. But at least she was listening, and he had more to say. "I can't begin to tell you how sorry I am Delanie got caught up in all of this. I will spend the rest of my life, however short or long it is, doing whatever I can to make amends, but if you ask me to apologise for coming into your life, I can't." He took a step closer to her, palms out, stare meeting hers. "Full disclosure, Detective Huddart. I am a two-hundred-and-fourteen-year-old shape-shifting dire wolf, an ancient breed of *canidae canis* thought extinct for over ten millennia and, like you, the very last of my kind. I have killed over two hundred and forty-two 'hostile' non-humans as a P.A.C. agent and am slated for promotion to assistant commander six months from now. I live in Central Park West, New York, in an apartment overlooking the park itself and I will give it all up and move to Australia and become a beach bum or a security guard or a dog walker with just one word from you."

He took another step forward, Jackie's subtle scent lacing into each breath he took, making his head spin and his pulse quicken. She was his life mate. He was bound to her for the rest of his life, and he had no idea if she hated him or not. "I love you. I will love you forever, and I ask you to help me catch Daeved Einar so we can start our lives anew." He paused. Swallowed. "Whether that is together or apart."

Jackie stared at him, silent, her eyes revealing nothing. He waited, his blood roaring in his ears, his heart a sledgehammer in his chest. *Say yes, darlin'. Please, say yes.*

His phone rang, vibrating into sudden life on the floor near the lamp table. Without a word, Jackie leant forward, her hair tumbling over her shoulder in a chestnut cascade he longed to bury his face in. She picked up the vibrating black device and straightened, holding it out to him with a steady hand.

Marshall swallowed again, the urge to take the phone from her fingers and smash it against the wall thick and powerful. He bit back a growl, flicked it open and pressed it to his ear instead. "Rourke."

"This is Hillerman, Agent Rourke," a deep male voice rumbled in his ear and Marshall saw Jackie stiffen, the skin around her eyes growing stretched. She'd heard.

He clenched his jaw, not liking the formal address the undercover P.A.C. agent had used. "What's going on, Hank?"

Silence echoed through the connection for a still moment

and the pit of Marshall's stomach rolled. *Ah, shit. Not good, not good...*

"I'm sorry, Marshall," Hillerman finally said, and Marshall's stare snapped to Jackie's face. "Delanie McKenzie didn't make it."

CHAPTER TWELVE

Jackie's stomach dropped. She stared at Rourke, unable to breathe. Grief choked her. Suffocated her. Took her heart in an icy fist and squeezed until her vision blurred. Del. Del was dead?

The fist of ice crushed her heart again, harder. Slower. She looked at Marshall, a raw cry trapped in her throat. Dead hatred flooded through her and she spun on her heel and ran across the room.

She had to get away from him. She had to go. Before she—

"Jackie!"

Marshall's shout cracked the air, but she ignored him. She had to go. Now.

Yanking open the door, she ran from the room. Grit and stones jabbed into her bare soles as she sprinted across the hotel's car park, tiny shards of pain spearing into her numb grief and empty hatred.

Del...

She ran, the bitumen cool under her feet, the early morning sun stabbing at her eyes. A soft buzzing thrummed against her ears and she sucked in a deep breath, pushing herself harder.

Where are you going?

A shout dusted her back. Marshall. Calling her name. She ran faster, the buzzing in her head growing louder, like a swarm of bees. Angry bees.

Dell was dead.

She pushed herself into a faster sprint, the burn in her muscles beginning to gnaw at the numb fog consuming her, the pain in the soles of her feet spiking into the crushing void.

Del was dead. Her best friend. Her constant.

Her thylacine stalked the edges of her consciousness, angry. Agitated. Seeking release and freedom. Seeking escape. She understood all too easily, but couldn't succumb. Not now. Maybe when all this was over. Maybe losing herself to her Tasmanian tiger was the only way to escape the pain? What else did she have?

The buzz in her head roared, angrier.

Dead. Killed. Killed by…

She surged forward, the muscles in her thighs screaming, a stitch stabbing into her side. She ran faster, aching for more pain. Anything to destroy the numb grief. Anything to silence the buzzing in her head.

Del was dead. Killed by…

The buzzing turned to a deafening roar. The crisp morning air lashed at her, tore into her flesh.

Killed by…

The roar beat at her head, flayed at her mind. Growing hotter, hotter. Louder.

A gut-wrenching sob choking her, she crumpled to the ground. Oh, God, Del was dead. Killed by…

Einar.

The name stabbed into the numb void, pierced the burning roar, a poisoned blade of hatred. She threw back her head, a howl of tortured rage tearing from her soul.

High above her, a flock of galahs screeched, startled by the wild cry. Jackie watched them erupt from the gum trees around her, her tears blurring them into pink and grey smudges. She tracked their flight through the pale sky, envying them their simple existence—no betrayal, no deception, no heartbreak.

Stop thinking about the birds, Jackie, and look at where you are.

Frowning, she lowered her gaze, surprised by what she found.

Dense bush surrounded her, old-growth eucalyptus trees towering over younger melaleuca, acacia and grevillea. Not a building to be seen, not a car horn or human voice to be heard.

Jackie frowned. How had she run so far from St. Helens?

Inside her soul, her thylacine stirred. Jackie frowned deeper. The animal was as confused as she.

She pressed her palm to the ground at her knees, the dew-damp grass soft and cool against her skin. A maelstrom of images surged through her, followed by a connection so profound her heart missed a beat.

She'd been human, but not. Thylacine, but human. Two forms inhabiting the same space at the same time, moving as one. The connection with the land flowed through her, finding her rapid heart. Embracing it. Like a dream embraces time.

Jackie closed her eyes and the connection flowed deeper, filling her with peaceful anger. Calm belonging. Letting her feel the wounds Einar had inflicted on the world and the pain those wounds brought to the time and the dream. She let the pain of every senseless slaughter slip through her. Thread through her grief.

Show her. The wrong being done and the way to end it.

Her thylacine stretched. Preening. Growing stronger. Growing more powerful, even in its inert slumber. Her connection with the ancient spirit of the land fed it. Awakened it. Awakened *her.* Awakened what she'd run from decades ago. What the cold, polluted, industrialized world of Sydney kept from her. A sense of belonging and serene acceptance. The understanding she was a creature of mystical beauty and ancient spirit. A creature of a dream in a time of reality.

She pulled in a long, ragged breath and a sob lodged in her throat. Marshall's distinct scent flowed through her nostrils and she lowered her head, touching her shaking fingers to the clothes she wore. Marshall's clothes.

Hate and grief and utter confusion sank into her chest and she pressed her face into her hands. Even with the surreal unity she now accepted with the Earth, with her thylacine, the smell of Marshall Rourke wrapped around her body and tore her heart apart. What was she doing? God, what should she do?

Go back to the hotel. Beat the shit out of him. Make him hurt like you are hurting now. Make him suffer. Make him pay.

Let him hold you. Let him love you.

She let out a harsh sigh, squeezing her eyes tight. Hold her? Was she a masochist? Stupid?

Would you have done it differently? If you were in Marshall's position? Would you?

She let out another sigh, her stomach a knot of sick tension. Lifting her head from her hands, she looked about herself, staring at the lush bush surrounding her.

The ghost of a memory floated through her head and a wan smile pulled at her lips.

She'd first meet Delanie in the bush. In what felt like a different lifetime ago.

She'd found herself cowering under an ancient cedar wattle tree on the outskirts of a town she didn't recognise. Head buried in her knees, she'd been hungry and scared and covered in dirt and grime, wondering where she was, what she would do now? How long she'd been in her thylacine form, she didn't know, but things were different than the last time she could remember. The cars shooting past her were sleeker, the clothes on the people moving around the streets more brightly coloured. Even the air tasted different—dirtier, as if every particle was coated in filth.

"I'm lost," a squeaky voice had said and she'd jerked her head up, staring at the tall, lanky girl with the bright orange hair smiling at her. "Can you help me?" The girl had extended her skinny arm, holding out a sweater that looked like it was knitted from spun sunlight. "You can wear my jumper, if you like."

After that, Delanie was her best friend, helping her adjust to every new foster family she was dumped with, helping her deal with the strange duel existence she lived, keeping the one secret so big it could have made Delanie a substantial fortune if she'd wanted to tell all. When Jackie had lost control of her thylacine the day after her eighteenth birthday, it was Delanie who found her—four human months later—in a cave high in the hinterlands. Delanie who sat with her in that cold, rocky hollow, never saying a word, a vegemite sandwich—Jackie's favourite lunch—sitting unwrapped on her lap. It was Del who just let the animal Jackie had been grow accustomed to her calm presence until the human Jackie was re-emerged, scared and confused and more than a little flea bitten.

For years, she and Delanie were never far apart. Not until Jackie had moved to Sydney to escape the all-too potent pull of her thylacine.

A tear slipped down Jackie's cheek, cool on her flushed skin. "Oh, Del. I'm sorry."

Don't just be sorry, Huddart. Do something about it.

An image of Daeved Einar rose through the dark fog of her grief, smile smug, silver blade glinting in the waning moonlight, and her chest constricted.

Do something about it.

She swiped at the tear on her cheek, black anger twisting through her sorrow. If the hunter wanted her that badly, she'd let him have her. All of her, not just the thylacine shape-shifter. If he wanted her, he'd get the whole lot: the Tasmanian tiger, the cop, the woman whose best friend he'd killed with a poisoned knife. The creature from an ancient time of ancient dreams. Four very dangerous creatures all in one small package.

She cast the dense bushland a steady look, letting its peaceful beauty and the memory of Delanie ebb through her for one calm moment before turning around and breaking into a dead sprint. Back the way she had come. Back to the hotel and Marshall Rourke. She would deal with her life mate's deception later, with the hollow void he'd created in her heart, but for now she needed him.

She was going hunting.

The rising sun's soft light beat at her back, heating her skin and the ground beneath her feet as she ran to the hotel. A few people—some dressed for work, some for jogging, some walking their dogs—watched her sprint past them, their expressions startled. She didn't wonder—a five-foot-three female running barefooted at break-neck speed wearing men's clothing would make anyone suspicious. She pulled a shallow breath, trying not to take Marshall's scent into her lungs. She didn't know what waited for them both at the end of this. She didn't know if she could ever forgive him. Hell, she didn't know if she *wanted* to forgive him, but she needed him right at this present. No matter how angry she was, no matter how good a cop she was—and she *was* good—no matter how tenacious her thylacine spirit was, she couldn't take Einar out without him.

Her heart squeezed at the thought and she bit back a frustrated growl. The first thing she would do when face-to-face with the man was hit him. Hard. After that…

The hotel loomed before her and she increased her pace, her stare locked on the open door. For the first time since leaving him, Jackie wondered why Marshall had not come after her. She remembered him calling her name as she ran across the car park, but that was it.

He may be a deceiving bastard, Jackie, but he's not an idiot.

Coming after you would have been the worst thing he could have done at that point and you know it.

And so, it seemed, did Marshall.

Because he is your life mate?

Her stomach tightened into a knot at the question. Mated to an extinct werewolf from a secret American organisation, who used her as bait and was willing to become a dog-walker to be with her. God, if Delanie were here, she'd laugh her skinny arse off.

Tight pain stabbed into Jackie's chest and she faltered, her feet slowing beneath her. She stared hard at the open hotel door, her mouth dry, her pulse thumping in her neck.

Deal with Einar first, Jackie. Then you can figure out the rest of your life.

She nodded once and jumped the small garden strip, curling her hands into fists to stop her fingers from wriggling. God, when did her life become so bloody complicated?

Crossing the threshold, she took two steps into the hotel room and stopped. Marshall wasn't there.

"Pacman?"

Silence answered her call and she frowned. Her stare moved to the closed bathroom door. She walked to it and gave it a gentle push.

Empty.

Maybe he came after you, after all?

Turning on the spot, she studied the small hotel room, an uneasy sensation squirming in her belly. Nothing about the room looked out of place, but it felt... "Wrong."

The whispered word sounded like a gunshot in the silence and she frowned again, balling her hands into tighter fists. Her thylacine snarled, its agitated energy razing her spine. The hair on the back of her neck prickled and she clenched her fists harder.

Wrong. It felt wrong.

Why? Surely he came after you and you missed each other?

Surely that's all it is?

Jackie flicked her gaze around the room, the urge to wriggle her fingers a constant itch in her nerve endings. Two things about the situation put her on edge. One, Marshall's sense of smell was phenomenal. He'd detected faint traces of Delanie on the air when Jackie could only smell the night. If he'd followed her scent he wouldn't have deviated from the path she took, no matter how fast she ran. And two, he had no clothes. She'd taken off in the only clothes he had, and she doubted he'd fit into the jeans and shirt he'd packed for her.

Why didn't you put them on before you fled, Huddart? Hmmm? Even when you were so angry with Marshall you wanted to shoot him yourself, you still covered your body in his clothes, his scent. There's something a touch Freudian about that little fact, don't you think?

"Shut up." She snapped her hands back into fists before her fingers could begin to dance. "Focus on the situation, detective, not your goddamn pathetic state of mind."

She paced the room, studying the minimal furniture, the rumples on the sofa cushions, the folds in crumpled bed sheets. Everything looked the way it had before she ran. Nothing was different. Even his phone was still—

Jackie's mouth went dry.

His phone. Why was Marshall's phone on the floor? He'd had it in his hand when she left. Why would it be on the floor now? Almost hidden under the bed?

As if kicked there?

She hurried over to the phone and scooped it up, a heavy pressure wrapping around her chest. Why would Marshall go away without his phone, unless he went somewhere in his wolf form?

Or was taken against his will.

Flicking it open, she looked at its display. Three missed calls, all from a blocked number. She scrolled through the phone's functions, looking for the list of Marshall's contacts.

Maybe Hillerman could tell her what was going on? The walking office block had to know something, right?

Growling, she snapped it shut and threw it onto the bed. She couldn't access any function on his phone, not even the list of the last calls he dialed. Not without a PIN and she had no idea what those four numbers were. Not at all.

"Damnit."

Walking back to the doorway, she stared out at the quiet car park. His scent still lingered on the clothes she wore, still slipped into every breath she pulled. Not only teasing her, but haunting her. She'd lost Delanie this morning and now it seemed she'd lost Marshall too.

The thought sent a shard of something dark and bleak into her soul and her thylacine whined. She narrowed her eyes, glaring at the long shadows stretching across the car park. What did she do now? She couldn't call the only connection to P.A.C. she knew of. She didn't know Hillerman's number, nor could she call P.A.C. itself—Hello, Operator. Can I have the Paranormal Anti-Crime Unit's head office, please? Umm, somewhere in America, I think? She couldn't call the local cops —Hello, this is Detective Huddart from Sydney City Command. My best friend's been killed by an elf and my lover's gone missing. By the way, he's an agent for an American agency dealing with paranormal crime and a werewolf, so can you send out Animal Control while you're at it, please? The only soul living she knew who may be able to comprehend her situation was Declan O'Connell, and the Irish werewolf would be of no help more than one thousand five hundred kilometres north of where she was.

What about Detective Peter Thomas? O'Connell's brother-in-law? He knows of the existence of shape-shifters. His partner and suspected lover was a werewolf.

Jackie chewed on her bottom lip. What did she say to him? Heya, Detective Thomas. This is Detective Huddart. You probably don't remember me, but I spoke to you briefly a year or so ago in a Sydney mansion. I'm actually a shape-shifting Tasmanian tiger and I think the dark elf currently hunting me down here in Tasmania is responsible for killing your old partner. Can you help me find my two-hundred-and-fourteen-year-old life mate werewolf please, so I can stop the elf before he kills us too?

No, no matter which way she looked at it, she couldn't call for backup. The only man who could help her was Marshall, and he was nowhere to be found. Which worried her to no end.

What if he's hurt?

She scrubbed at her face with her hands, her stomach rolling. Damn it, what if Einar had taken him? What if the elf had killed him?

"Stop it, Jackie. You're getting yourself in a state."

She pulled in a slow, deep breath, tuning out the distinct scent of Marshall on the air. She needed to be calm. She had to work her way through the situation. If she didn't, all the finger wiggling in the world wouldn't stop her transforming into her thylacine form, and despite the newfound connection she shared with her inner animal and the ancient land in which it existed, she wasn't ready to be lost to the creature. Not yet.

She released her breath in a long, measured sigh, pressing her hands flat to the sides of her thighs as she studied the pale morning sky. She had to find him. Track him if need be. Her sense of smell wasn't as good as his, but she would find him. She couldn't be without him. He was her mate for life and she…

Her heart clenched and she bit back a guttural groan. She loved him. "Even if he's a lying, sarcastic pain in the arse."

Lifting her nose to the slight breeze flowing across the car park, she drew in another deep breath.

And let it out in a gasp when Marshall's phone rang behind her.

She dove back into the room, snatching the phone from

the bed, flicking it open and pressing it against her ear all in one fluid action. "Yes?"

"Isn't it ironic that the man who once used you as bait to catch me," Einar's croon scratched at Jackie's ear through the connection, "is now the very thing that will bring *you* to me?"

Jackie's thylacine snarled, the creature's fury roaring through her. She gripped the phone, staring through the open bathroom doorway at her reflection in the small mirror on the wall. Eyes the colour of burnt toffee looked back at her—her animal's eyes. Not hers. Steady and primitive and wild.

Hunt, track, kill.

"You didn't need to go to so much effort, Einar," she said, her voice barely a murmur. "If you'd waited but a few minutes I would have come to you anyway."

Einar's laugh wheezed over the connection, making her smile. A cold, dead smile. "Ah, but where would the fun be in that, detective. True, you were the initial target of my hunt, but since discovering my ex-partner is a dire werewolf I've amended my plans." He paused, and Jackie heard her inner animal growl in the brief silence. "My only question now is who watches who die?"

She bared her teeth, her smile growing colder. "I know the answer to that." The eyes of her thylacine gazed back at her from her face. "I'll tell you when I get there, shall I?"

Marshall lifted his head and studied the room around him, ignoring the dull ache in the back of his head and the sharp pain at the base of his spine. He was in what looked like a teenage girl's bedroom. The walls were covered in posters of actors and singers all in various stages of undress, all male, all from the late nineties.

He sat up, the pain in the small of his back a drilling scream of burning ice. Continuing his inspection of the room, he noted the pristine condition of the bed, the collection of soft toy animals in the corner, the ballet slippers hanging on the back of the closed door and the fine film of dust on the candy-pink bookshelf dressing table. Definitely a teenage girl's bedroom.

Whose bedroom, Marshall? Shouldn't you be asking that question? Whose bedroom and whose house? Einar's dumped you here alone and he wouldn't have done that if he didn't think it was secure. What's he done with the original occupants?

A foreboding sense of unease coursed through him. He pressed his hands to his knees and pushed himself to his feet. The unexpected feel of course material under his palms drew his attention to his legs. Someone had dressed him, no doubt Einar himself, in black combat trousers. The type worn by P.A.C. agents on field missions.

Marshall narrowed his eyes, pushing his hand into the right hip pocket. His fingers brushed something thin and hard and, letting out a snort, he withdrew the small object, knowing what it was before he even looked at it.

A message.

He flipped the flat rectangle piece of plastic over on his palm and looked at it, dark contempt unfurling in his gut.

Einar's P.A.C. ID card.

The man was taunting him.

Closing his fist around the card, he pushed it back into the pocket of the trousers he wore. It wouldn't surprise him in the least if they were, in fact, his trousers. His ex-partner always took great delight in the little details of an interrogation. Dressing Marshall in his P.A.C. uniform when they both knew he wasn't on an official mission held all the trademarks of Daeved Einar.

The dull ache in the back of his neck flared to a hot throb and Marshall swiped at it with gentle pressure before taking a quick look at his fingers. Blood smeared them, bright red and slightly tacky to the touch. Whatever Einar had hit him with back at the hotel, it had done the job.

A growl rumbled in his chest and he rubbed at his neck again. Damn it. If he'd followed Jackie when she'd fled from him, like his gut wanted him to, he wouldn't be in this ridiculous situation. Instead, for the first time in not only his P.A.C. career, but his *life*, he'd listened to his heart, his head, and let her go. He'd known there'd be no talking to her in her current state of mind, and he didn't blame her. Time was what she'd needed. Time to think about what he'd said to her, what she felt. If she came back and told him she never wanted to see him again he'd understand. Hell, he deserved it. His heart would break, but he'd understand. So, even though every molecule in his body wanted to go after her, beg her to forgive him, he'd stayed put in the open doorway and watched her run as fast as she could away from him. And when he couldn't see her anymore, he'd walked back into his own room.

He had no memory of anything after glimpsing Einar's reflection in the bathroom's tiny mirror as he bent to pick up his cell phone from the end of the bed. One minute he'd been aching for his life mate, the next, he was standing in a bedroom, blood oozing from the back of his head, the base of his spine killing him, dressed by a psychotic dark elf with revenge issues.

Another growl vibrated low in his chest, his beast less than impressed with the situation. "Time to finish this, Rourke. You've fucked everything else up so far, time to bring the whole thing to an end."

He took a step toward the door and collapsed to his knees, white-hot pain slicing into his lower back. Arcing up his spine. Into his chest.

Gritting his teeth, he pushed himself upright and reached behind his back with one shaking hand, the pain exploding into blistering heat. His fingers skimmed the base of his spine, something wet slicking their tips before another arc of excruciating agony shot through him.

The fucker's stabbed you, Marshall. Right at the base of your spine. You're lucky he didn't sever your spinal cord.

The chilling thought turned Marshall's mouth dry. He pulled in a slow breath, forcing the pain from his mind. It wasn't the wound that affected him. Einar's blade had missed anything too important. He suspected what was causing his grief was the very thing that had killed Delanie McKenzie and almost killed Jackie. Poison.

How long can you fight it, Marshall, before it takes you out?

Long enough to neutralize the pointy-eared bastard and find Jackie. Wherever she was, she wasn't dead. He could feel it in his soul. Einar may have gotten the jump on him, but Jackie was still out there alive. Possibly still pissed at him.

Maybe that's for the best? You've done nothing but bring her pain and death. The farther she is from you, the better.

He let out a low sigh and forced himself to his feet again. Fresh pain rolled through him at the thought of a life without the tiny Sydney detective. Hot and tearing pain made his heart feel like it was being compressed, but he shut his mind to it. It would serve him no purpose but to weaken him. Until he'd dealt with Einar, nothing else mattered.

To his surprise, the door swung open when he turned the knob, a long and cheery hallway stretching away from the bedroom. Eyes narrowing, he stepped from the room, the worn carpet under his bare feet keeping his footfalls silent. Framed images of a family studied him from the sky-blue walls. A man in his fifties and a woman possibly only a few years younger rested their hands on the shoulders of a smiling young girl dressed all in pink with braces on her teeth. Marshall's stomach tightened at the contented love in the photo. The occupants of the house. He clenched his fists, cold anger twisting through his focused calm. If Einar had killed them, or harmed them in anyway…

He turned his mind from the humans, continuing to move through the house. Every muscle in his body coiled, expecting Einar to leap at him any given moment. Yet each room he came to sat empty and disused. Nothing undisturbed, no sign of a struggle or violence.

He drew a deep breath, tasting the air. The salty odor of human lingered on the air, the walls and floor and furniture infused with the family's presence. And something else. An emptiness that made his nerve-endings tingle.

You should have known Einar was something other than a mage. How many times had you wondered why he gave off no scent? It wasn't that he didn't give off a scent. It was that the damn dark elf removed it from the very air.

Pulse quickening, he tuned his senses in to the sounds of the house instead. His inner beast snarled with the need to be released but he kept the dire wolf in check. Now was not the time to shift. The massive creature was a formidable force, one even a psychotic dark elf would have trouble defeating, but he still did not know if Einar knew what he was. Nor, for that matter, what affect the poison from Einar's blade would have on his other form. In all the tests run by the P.A.C. science guys on how non-humans reacted to elvish magick, none had been conducted to see what would happen to a dire wolf. Why would they when as far as they were concerned, the dire wolf shifter was extinct.

That kinda intel would've come in handy about now, wouldn't it, Marshall. Kinda fucked up there, didn't you?

He suppressed an angry grunt. He'd fucked everything up about this mission. So much for being the agency's newest golden boy.

Approaching the last room of the house, he dropped into a low crouch, his stare locked on the open doorway. The air hung heavy with emptiness—a sure indicator his ex-partner was on the other side. And yet, this time something else seemed to cut the surreal void. A smell of mouldy loam and rotten moss.

Jesus, is that what he really smells like? Thank God he kept it hidden all these years.

Hot pain shot up Marshall's spine, reminding him he was wounded, but he remained motionless. How did he do this?

"Do you still take sugar in your coffee, Agent Rourke?"

Marshall scrunched his face and dipped his head, letting out a humourless snort. Fuck. He straightened to his full height and rounded the corner, the stab wound in the base of his spine a blistering ball of pain.

Einar stood at the far kitchen bench, his back to the door, appearing—to all intents and purposes—to be making a cup of coffee. "I never took sugar in my coffee, Einar." He stopped two steps into the bright, airy room, his nerve endings firing, his back a world of agony. "In my tea, yes. Coffee, no." The cloying stench of blood and decomposing meat filled his nostrils and he flicked a quick inspection over the spotless kitchen. "Where are the occupants of this house?"

Einar turned and gave him a small smile, and Marshall tensed. The man hadn't changed since he'd seen him last, two years ago standing in the P.A.C. commander's office. He still stood like a conceited aristocrat. He still oozed deadly promise. His skin still looked like tanned leather. His eyes still burned with empty malice.

Without uttering a word, Einar placed two mugs on the table between them, smiled at him through the wispy white steam rising from each one, and then walked to a closed door to his left.

Marshall narrowed his eyes. Einar was limping. Only slightly and he was doing his best to conceal it, but a limp all the same. Interesting.

"I see your fondness for humans hasn't changed." Einar tsked with condescending distaste, the sound all too familiar to Marshall's ears. "A weakness you have not learnt to control." He pressed his palm flat on the door and pushed.

It swung open, revealing a small laundry room shrouded in dim shadows. And three people lying stiff on the floor. A man, a woman and a teenage girl.

"They are not dead," Einar spoke. Marshall jerked his stare back to his ex-partner, struggling to keep his wolf in check. "Their death would serve no purpose." Einar grinned, flashing teeth much more pointed than before. "At least, not until now."

Marshall's beast snarled, surging for release. He stood motionless, jaw clenched, face composed. He knew this game. Einar played it very well. Antagonise the enemy until their control cracked. "How did you know I sent you the intel on the thylacine?" he asked, changing the subject. Deflecting Einar's strike.

Einar let the door to the laundry swing closed, his eyes glinting with smug delight. "Who else would? Who else had a reason to put me in a specific place?" He moved back to the table and Marshall noted how his ex-partner favoured his right leg. How the material of his trousers seemed to be stretched over something high on his thigh. Something like a bandage wrapped around an injury? "Who else but my noble partner trying to flush me out so he could right his own foolish wrong?" He picked up one of the steaming cups of coffee and raised it in a salute. "How pathetic it is you totally failed in your objective."

Marshall shrugged, ignoring the sharp shard of pain the action sent stabbing into his neck. "Wouldn't say that, Einar. After all, the thylacine is still alive, and you're here in Australia. Exactly where I wanted you to be."

Einar laughed, a rising chortle that made the hair on the back of Marshall's neck stand on end. There was nothing sane in that laugh. Nothing joyful or humourous either. "The thylacine will be here very soon, Rourke. And the moment she walks through the front door, I win. I get to kill the last Tasmanian-tiger shape-shifter in existence before I butcher the last dire werewolf alive. By the way, Agent Rourke, very clever of you to keep your true form from me. It would have made our working relationship rather…tense."

Marshall smiled. "Well, you know me. Always thinking of others before myself."

Einar studied him, the corners of his mouth twitching. "Hmmm. Tell me, was fucking Jacqueline Huddart part of your plan to catch me, or was it an added bonus?"

Marshall's blood ran cold, his pulse leaping into furious flight. "Didn't realize you were a peeping Tom as well as a psychotic killer, Einar. Did you put that on your P.A.C. job application?"

Einar grinned, pointed teeth flashing again. "Watching you mount her from behind like the filthy animal you are was quite an education. And rather arousing, I admit. I've never been more excited at the thought of ridding the She-God's world of two abominations as when I witnessed you copulate." He raised one eyebrow and took a sip of coffee. "I must say however, the thylacine looks to be a very energetic sexual partner, and quiet noisy too. The sounds she made when you stuck your dick in her—"

Marshall rammed the table into Einar's gut, folding the man in half. The untouched cup of hot coffee splashed over Marshall's arms and stomach but he didn't care. Fury ripped through him. Cold and absolute. He shoved the table again, driving his ex-partner backward, a growl bursting from deep within his throat.

Einar snapped up his head, eyes burning blue hate. He let out a wild cry, the sound high and piercing, flung the table aside and lunged straight at Marshall. He struck him in the chest, slamming him to the linoleum floor, his hands wrapped around his throat. "You think you can kill me, wolf?" His fingers sank harder into Marshall's neck. "With the poison from my blade pumping through your blood?"

Searing pain detonated in the base of Marshall's spine, up his back into his head and chest. He grabbed at Einar's legs, black stars bursting in his vision, and drove his fingers into the wound high on the man's right thigh. Something hot and wet flowed over his hand and Einar threw back his head, wailing in that same high-pitched cry.

Marshall bunched his fists together and smashed them against Einar's chest, punching him backward. The pain in his lower-back erupted in excruciating fire and he bit back a sharp hiss, his muscles cramping. He rolled onto his stomach and snapped to his feet, spinning to face his ex-partner a mere second before Einar could recover his. He struck out with his foot, driving his heel into the man's gut. Einar's back crashed into the edge of the kitchen bench, the impact making the cupboards shudder. Doors flung open, crockery tumbled from the shelves and smashed into pieces on the floor around Marshall's bare feet. He threw himself at the dark elf, his inner beast slathering for control. His hands wrapped around Einar's throat. "You think elf poison can slow down a dire wolf?"

He slammed his fist into the man's nose, again, again. Ink black blood burst from each nostril and smeared his knuckles, but he didn't stop. The pain in his back turned to ripping agony, but he didn't stop. The blood in his veins felt like boiling acid, surging for his heart, but he didn't stop. He smashed his fist into Einar's nose again, his pulse pounding in his ears. Einar bucked beneath him, and before Marshall knew what was happening, his ex-partner reared backward, using the bench as a pivot-point, and shoved his feet into Marshall's stomach.

The room turned to a blur of beige as he reeled backward, hideous black blotches blooming in his vision. His gut cramped, followed by his chest. His knees buckled and he crumpled onto all fours, head swimming, heart racing. Faster. Faster.

"Of course, I think elf poison can slow a dire wolf down." Einar's feet appeared in his sight, the left one painted with Einar's own blood. Marshall lifted his head just in time to see the man's fist punching down at his face. White pain detonated in his nose, up into his eyes.

"Why wouldn't it?"

Einar grabbed Marshall's hair and yanked him off the floor. The dark elf's knee smashed up into his chin, driving him back farther. Blood gushed from his nose, down his throat, choking him, drowning him.

"A dire wolf is just an old dog who didn't know when to die."

Einar's foot slammed into Marshall's crotch and he bowed into a stiff arc, blistering pain lacerating his mind.

Jackie.

Einar moved to stand over him, a long silver knife gripped in his left hand. He smiled down at Marshall, his normally blue eyes glowing an iridescent red, his pointed teeth glistening with saliva. "And as you know, I'm very, very good at putting old dogs out of their misery." He crouched down beside Marshall, head tilted to the side, elbows resting on his bent knees, knife dangling above Marshall's gut with arrogant nonchalance. "When the time is right."

The cloying stench of rotting moss filtered into Marshall's blood-clotted nose and he slipped his blurred, black-fogged gaze to the man's thigh, a weak laugh bubbling up through his throat. "She made you bleed…" He smiled, his face screaming in pain at the movement of its muscles. "How's it feel?"

Einar hissed, a venomous sound, and he slammed the hilt of his knife close to Marshall's nose. "You're but an hour away from death, wolf," he sneered, his spittle burning Marshall's cheek. "Just long enough to watch me gut the thylacine bitch before I skin you a—"

A snarling streak of russet-gold smashed into Einar's ribs, barreling him sideways. His knife skidded across the linoleum and his head smacked the floor with a dull crack. Marshall stared—blood and pain blurring his vision—at the large animal standing on Einar's chest, pinning him to the floor, its long, sharp teeth bared a mere inch from the man's stunned face.

Jackie, no.

The thylacine's ears pricked, but it didn't move. Its muzzle wrinkled as it snarled again, its front paws pressing harder on Einar's shoulders, its stiff tail a motionless whip extending from its straight spine.

Jackie. Marshall's gut clenched, his breath growing rapid, shallow. He tried to move, but couldn't, his body engulfed in agonizing pain. *No. Run. Get away.*

A black shimmer of light rippled over Einar's flesh, his iridescent eyes burning brighter. "Hello, detective," he murmured, grinning up at the animal on his chest. "Glad you could—"

The thylacine didn't let him finish. Or rather, Jackie didn't. She transformed, her Tasmanian-tiger form rending into her human in the space of a heartbeat. Her elbow smashed into Einar's throat with brutal force and speed.

A wet glurk burst from the man's lips. His legs and arms flopped on the floor, a spasm as violent as the blow Jackie delivered to his throat claiming him. And still she didn't move, her knees gripping his hips, her stare trained on his face. Unwavering, unrelenting. Inescapable. "I told you I wasn't coming after you as a cop," she whispered.

She slammed her elbow into his throat again, followed by the back of her fist to his temple. He flopped beneath her, eyes bulging, a keening cry tearing from his throat. His hand flapped at the floor, seeking his knife, and Jackie smashed the side of her right fist down on his wrist, her face expressionless as the sound of shattering bone filled the room.

"Bitch!" Einar roared, skin rippling black light again.

"Jackie," Marshall called. Dread pooled in his gut. He tried to move again, to get up, to go to her, to help her, but his body refused to obey. Pain devoured him. It burnt him alive from the inside out. "Get away. He's changing."

Einar's leathery flesh shimmered black once more. He wailed, still reaching for his knife, his hand flopping on the end of his arm like a dead squid. Blood flowed from his nose, his thigh. His eyes flared with red hatred. "Fucking kill you, you cunt!"

His scream stabbed straight into Marshall's core. He'd heard that banshee tone before. Einar was at the edge and nothing would stop him now.

Jackie narrowed her eyes, her naked body covered in sweat, her muscles coiled to taut steel. "I'm pretty certain I'm the one on top." Her shoulder's bunched and she smashed her left fist into his jaw. Blood and teeth spewed from his mouth.

He screamed again, a high squeal unlike any Marshall had heard and, limp fingers slapping at the blade of his knife, he vanished.

Jackie was on her feet and beside Marshall before he could blink, her grim expression hardly changing, as if Einar's sudden disappearance was commonplace. She crouched down beside him, scooping one arm under his back and hauling him upward. "We got to get you out of here." Her words caressed his pain like a gentle kiss and he gazed up at her, barely able to see her through the black fog taking him. "I don't think he'll be gone for long."

"Run," he wheezed, trying to lift his hand to touch her face. One touch. "Get away."

She chuckled, shaking her head as she jerked him to his feet. She slung his arm around her shoulders, her tiny frame taking his weight even as he tried to pull away from her. "You're a complete moron, you know that."

He laughed, the sound a liquid gargle. "I've been told so."

For a split second, her gaze held his, her clear amber eyes shining with a clarity, a strength not there before. Her nostrils flared and she pressed her lips to his, the kiss quick and harsh and more wonderful than he could fathom. "C'mon, Pacman," she muttered, heaving him closer to her body. "Time to run away from the ghost."

CHAPTER THIRTEEN

Jackie dragged Marshall from the kitchen, past numerous doors, each one opening to a room silent and wafting with the sickening scent of Einar's blood. It was an odor she'd never forget or mistake—the smell of hidden shadows and rotting roots. She pulled Marshall closer to her body, holding him tight as she shuffled along a hallway festooned with framed pictures of a smiling family. He weighed a ton, his hard body like a long sack stuffed full of burning rocks. The heat radiating from him told her all too easily what she feared. She didn't need to look at the wound oozing blood low on his back to know Einar had stabbed him.

She ground her teeth, fury and fear eating at her. If Marshall died...

"At least I still got my skin," he slurred, his feet tripping over each other as she moved them through the house. "Gotta be somethin', right?"

She laughed, surprised by the wry humour she heard in the short sound. "Shut up, Rourke."

Einar would be back. Wherever the pointy-eared bastard went when he did his poof-there-he-goes trick, he wouldn't stay there long. Not when he knew he had an easy target to hunt, and at the moment, she and Marshall were a very easy target.

Then hurry the hell up, Jackie. You know where you're going. Get there. Fast.

Easier said than done, what with a semi-catatonic, some-what-delirious werewolf in tow. She gripped Marshall's hand and pulled his arm tighter around her shoulder, drawing him closer still as she jerked open the back door—the very one she'd slipped through as a Tasmanian tiger not ten minutes ago. She wouldn't let him go. If it meant dying, she wouldn't let him go.

"You shouldn't have…you should…"

His voice faded to a garbled mumble and then silenced altogether, his arm turning limp around her shoulders. Jackie gave him a sharp shake, relief flooding through her at his low and decisively annoyed grunt. He was alive. That was the main thing at the moment. Stopping at the back gate, she snatched Marshall's backpack where she'd hidden it in the leafy fronds of the garden and hooked it over her elbow. It was extra weight, but there were things inside she'd need later. Things Marshall needed.

She hurried faster away from the house. Thank God, Einar had selected a place based on its secluded position. The small brick single-story sat nestled amongst the lush bush on the outskirts of St. Helens—the perfect spot, no doubt, to butcher paranormal creatures without being disturbed.

A weak snort buzzed in her ear and she felt Marshall swing his face toward hers. "Dire wolves mate for life, Jackie." The words were slurred so much they were almost incomprehensible, but Jackie's breath caught all the same. "Once we mark our mate we are bonded until death takes us." A wet chuckle gurgled up his throat and he seemed to burn hotter. "Didn't think it'd be this quick though." He let out a low groan, the noise vibrating through his scorching body into hers. "I wanted to…"

"You're not dying, Rourke," she murmured, keeping her voice calm. "You're too bloody annoying to die."

He wheezed out a weak chuckle. "Love you, detective," he slurred on a rasping breath.

Her throat felt thick and she squeezed her eyes shut for a second, shutting out the dense scrub around her, the clear blue sky overhead. She swallowed, Marshall's proclamation rocking her more than it should. Being mated for life to him was one thing, him being mated to her however...

A calm flow of energy rolled through her—ancient, timeless and dreamlike. She increased her pace, opening her eyes to stare at the slight hill rising up from the bush before her. The spirit of the land had a warped sense of humour if it thought a Tasmanian tiger and a bloody dire wolf were a match deserving of calm and approval. Someone should have told it the two were—

Made for each other. Both ancient spirits, both the last of your kind, both unable to resist the undeniable desire you feel for each other. Now stop carrying on like a ten-year-old and get to where you have to be.

She hitched him higher against her body, doing her best to avoid tripping over the rocks, fallen tree branches and wombat burrows covering the ground. The terrain wasn't making her task easy, but then, the Australian bush had never been easy to move through as a human, even here in Tasmania. The land devoured foolish, arrogant, ignorant humans and left the bones for the animals to chew. The Aboriginals knew that. Jackie's ancestors knew that. The ancient country was never meant for human population. Survival of the fittest took on a whole new meaning when it came to traversing its savage interior, and in the case of her ancestors, survival meant transforming.

But you can't do that now. Not until you have Marshall safe.

"The very second I saw you, I knew you were going to be trouble," she muttered, dragging him over a massive fallen tree trunk. Her bare foot slipped on the moist green moss and she

SAVAGE TRANSFORMATION | 217

stumbled, her teeth clicking shut. She threw Marshall's backpack over the log, needing both arms to help him over.

"Didn't mean to…"

She laughed, once again surprised by the warm mirth in the sound. What's the best way to know you're in love with a guy? Be able to laugh with him when you're both on the run from a murderous dark elf. She slipped her arm under his armpit and held him close, scooping up his backpack before hurrying into a stumbling jog again. "Shut up, Pacman. It's my turn to talk now."

Marshall chuckled, a shallow hiccup of breath, but a chuckle all the same. His arm tightened around her shoulder, his feet moving with more purpose. "Yes, ma'am."

She shook her head, her heart tight, a small smile playing on her lips. "I've fought what I am my entire adult life," she went on, each word a gasping pant—damn, he was heavy. "I've tried to deny it. I ran from it. I cursed it and hated it." She fixed her stare on the rise before her. Closer. They were getting closer.

Hurry.

"But until you came along," she puffed, sweat stinging her eyes, the branches of a low bush scratching at her bare legs, "I've never really understood it."

She felt Marshall's gaze on her profile but chose not to look at him. She needed to keep her focus on her target. If she looked into his eyes and saw Einar's poison devouring him, it would undo her. "You bring out the animal in me, Marshall," she said instead, pushing past a clump of jasmine-choked acacia. "I can't believe I've said something so bloody corny, but you do."

Her foot fell into a wombat burrow and she careened sideways. Sharp pain ignited in her ankle, shooting up her leg. She bit back a growl and struggled to straighten up. Damn it, they were so close. So close. Only a few feet left to go.

A growl rumbled low in her chest, an irritated gnarr that

set her nerve-endings on edge. Angry. Her thylacine was angry. More than angry.

Jackie snorted. Impatient bitch. She stopped, her ankle a world of ache, her lungs burning. She closed her eyes, a frustrated sigh bursting from her. "Whose stupid idea was this?" she muttered. What had she been thinking? Running up into the bush, seeking a place she didn't know? A place her newfound connection with the land told her was there, calling her? "This isn't a plan, this is lunacy."

Marshall's lips pressed to her temple, warm and soft, and she started, swiveling her head to look at him. "You bring out the human in me, Detective Huddart," he whispered, his eyes clearer than she'd seen them since dragging him from the house. Blood still flowed from his shattered nose, sweat still ran from his forehead, but his eyes held hers and spoke a truth she could never doubt. "And my human trusts you as strongly as my wolf." He brushed her lips with his again, the salty taste of his blood and sweat stirring the animal deep within her being. "Now, tell me you love me so we can get our asses to wherever it is we need to be."

Jackie couldn't help herself. She laughed. Shaking her head at the half-dead Texan draped around her shoulders, she pressed her lips to his. "I love you, P.A.C. Agent Marshall Rourke."

He wheezed out a chuckle, his arm tightening around her shoulders with weak pressure, holding her closer to him as he returned her kiss. "Of course you do."

Warm joy washed through Jackie. She gazed into his eyes, every molecule in her body tingling. She'd said it. Aloud. She'd said it and it felt good. No, not just good. Powerful.

Right.

Fresh strength surged through her muscles. She hitched Marshall higher up her body and began walking again. The spirit of the land called her, a wordless song deep in her soul that she heard with her entire existence.

The inhospitable terrain gave way to soft grass, softer ferns. Silken leaves stroked her legs, her hips. Cool caresses that sent little ripples over her flushed skin. She moved faster, a tingling thrum stirring in her core. Tugging her. Pulling her. Her thylacine groaned, the sound wholly and completely one of contented calm. A sense of belonging flowed through her. She frowned, the surreal potency of the sensation disarming her even as she welcomed it. She'd fought *this* her whole life?

The grass beneath her feet became velvet, the drops of morning dew resting on each blade slicking her soles. She moved faster, the call on her being growing stronger. Deeper. Ancient and new all at once. Strange and familiar. Marshall seemed to grow lighter on her shoulders, although she knew that was an impossibility. And yet he was no burden to carry. No load to bear.

The trees seemed to part before her, the clean scent of eucalypt slipping into her every breath, nourishing her. She looked around for the rock formation she'd never seen before but knew was there all the same. Four rocks resting together, an outcrop of granite older than the trees and soil around her. Four rocks forming an alcove in which Marshall could wait. Protected. Safe. Unseen. Four rocks to keep him from Einar until she could finish what the hunter had started.

She looked around the landscape—her home, her place—and saw the rocks. The tingle in her soul grew stronger and her breath caught in her chest. She knew this place. She remembered it. She had been here before. A lifetime ago. The memory of her family, her mother, her father, rolling through the torment of her past. She'd been born here, safe in the protection of the rocks. Her mother's arms her world, these rocks her home until the men with the dogs and guns came. The men stinking of liquid death—swilling it from cans gripped in their large hands. The dogs stinking of human violence, straining at the end of chains, saliva spattering from their snapping muzzles, dripping from their gnashing teeth. The men and the dogs finding them, a family of three. Finding them, tormenting them. Chasing them. Chasing them until her father shifted into his animal form and her mother yelled at her to run away. And then the guns began to…

The memory faded and Jackie stared at the rocks, her heart pounding, the pain in her heart as strong as the love she remembered all so well. She'd returned home. And her thylacine howled with grief and joy.

"This place feels…" Marshall's mumble drew her attention from the rocks and she turned her head, looking at him. He studied the outcrop, a frown pulling at his sweat-slicked forehead. "Right," he finished.

Jackie smiled, pulling him closer to her body. "It is right."

She crossed the short distance to the formation, hunching into a semi-crouch as she helped Marshall into the dark cave the four rocks made. Velvet-soft moss covered the ground, thick and spongy. She lowered him to it, making sure he lay on his side before tugging open his backpack. Inside, wrapped in the cotton T-shirt he'd packed for her who knows how long ago, was a small glass vial. If what was in that vial—a luminous violet liquid—was what she thought it was…

"Marshall," she whispered, turning back to her life mate. His chest rose and fell in rapid, shallow jerks, his body twitching. "Marshall, I need you to look at this."

His eyelids fluttered open and Jackie choked back a raw groan. His eyes were glassy, unfocussed. She took his right hand and placed the vial against his palm, closing his fingers around its slim shape. "Marshall," she whispered again, lowering her head closer to his. "I need you to tell me what this is."

His lips parted, his tongue scraping over their dry, split surface. "Blood."

Jackie let out a silent sigh. She drew her head closer to Marshall's. The heat baking from his body was like an open furnace. "Is this what you gave me? How do I give it to you?"

His lips moved, soundless words she couldn't understand.

"Marshall." She lowered her head until her ear hung above his mouth. "Marshall, how do I give it to you?"

Nothing.

She pulled away, staring at him. His eyes were closed again, his breath shallower still. And slower. Too slow. She shook her head. No. This wasn't the way it was meant to happen. This wasn't the plan.

"Not…enough."

Marshall's croaked whisper tore a sob from her throat and she shook her head again. "Yes, there is, Pacman." She closed her fingers around his hand, the vial enclosed within his fist taunting her. "Stop being a bloody wuss."

He chuckled, blood bubbling past his lips with the weak laugh. "Didn't mean…to mess up your life."

She closed her eyes, refusing to let the angry tears welling in their corners fall. "Stop being a dickhead, Rourke."

"Okay." The word was barely more than a breath.

A bitter laugh gouged at her chest and she rolled her eyes, turning back to Marshall's backpack to riffle through its contents, searching for Marshall's phone. If she could call Hillerman, someone from P.A.C., anyone, maybe they could tell her what to do. She couldn't lose him. She couldn't. Not when she'd finally accepted who she was. Not when she'd finally admitted that she loved him. She couldn't. Life couldn't be that unfair. Hands fumbling with Marshall's phone, she sucked in a shaking breath, and froze.

The sickly-sweet stench of Einar's blood slid into her nostrils, like the putrid vapor from decaying mulch.

She snapped her stare to the opening of the rocky alcove, scanning the narrow slither of bush she could see beyond as she pulled another breath. Shit.

He wasn't there yet, but he was close. Close enough to taint the air with his poisoned existence.

Shit. She wasn't ready.

She closed her eyes and wriggled her fingers, forcing her frantic heart rate to slow. *Settle, Jackie. Settle.* She'd lured the hunter here for a reason. She had to remember what it was.

Throat tight, chest heavy, she bent at the waist and laid her lips against Marshall's feverish forehead. "If you die on me while I'm gone, Pacman, I will track you down on the other side and give you a damn good beating, understand?"

She didn't wait for his response, if there even was one. She didn't have a second to spare. Straightening to her feet, she slipped through the narrow opening and scaled the rock formation, standing motionless on the highest point. She held her arms slightly out from her body, legs spread wide enough to let the gentle breeze swirling down the hillside stream between her thighs. Over her sex. Her hair lifted at the nape, tousled by the tugging wind caressing her cheeks and lips. Her nipples puckered tight, a chill of calm anticipation rippling through her. She lifted her chin and, letting her thylacine surge to the surface, threw back her head and howled.

She transformed mid-call.

Einar moved through the bush, every sense he possessed narrowed onto the thylacine's scent. She'd dragged the werewolf with her. Rourke's odor threaded through hers in weak ropes of decay, making Einar smile. His ex-partner was almost dead. Almost. Which meant he still had the chance to string the werewolf up by his ankles and gut him alive.

A tree branch snagged at Einar's shirtsleeve, tearing the fabric. He hissed, jerking his arm free. He hated this place, this land. The spirits of this place denied the supremacy of the fae, refused to kowtow to their right to rule all that was natural. As soon as the thylacine and the dire wolf were gutted and skinned, he would leave the place for good. There may be other creatures here worthy of the kill—yowies, bunyips and the elusive Lungkata—but he would not hunt them. He'd had enough of Australia to last him another five centuries, maybe more.

The gentle breeze that had been playing over his skin picked up, blowing harder into his face and he grinned. Jacqueline Huddart's perspiration drenched the air. He could taste her sweat in his mouth. Saliva coated his tongue as he tasted something else, something far more potent and musky. She was not only close, but naked and still in human form.

Perfect. What better way to torture Rourke than to sample the delights of his lover before killing her.

Hurrying his step, he pressed his right hand to the still-seeping wound high on his thigh. His spit-bath had not had the result he'd hoped for. The poison of his blade still lingered in his blood, weakening him. The werewolf would not have been able to take him by surprise, beaten him so badly, if he'd been free of its lethal magick. The thylacine bitch definitely would not have driven him to the floor if he'd been successful in cleansing it from his system. He narrowed his eyes and continued walking up the slow rise, heading for the slight hill directly in his path. He would stab Detective Huddart in the leg first, sinking his blade into the muscle surrounding her thigh bone, slicing into it with slow relish. She would buck and thrash beneath him, but he would hold her down and watch her face and revel in the pain and defiant hate he saw there.

His heart pumped faster at the intoxicating thought and he moved quicker, lifting his nose to the wind, sucking her scent into his lungs. Around him, the trees creaked and groaned, their branches swaying in the rising wind, their leaves rustling against each other in an increasing roar. A wild, raucous laugh shattered the air, each loud note punching at his ears. He snarled, glaring up into the closest tree at a large grey and brown bird. A kookaburra. A perversion of nature almost as vile as the very creatures he hunted. What kind of spirit gave birth to a bird that laughed?

As if aware of his stare, the kookaburra ceased its infernal noise and swung its head toward him, studying him from the safety of its branch. If he didn't hunt larger prey, he would pluck it from its perch and wring its neck.

The kookaburra threw back its head and laughed again, the sound rising above the roar of the trees.

Einar gripped the hilt of his knife harder, turning away from the galling bird. Perhaps he would stay a moment longer in this backward, perverse country. Long enough to kill at least one laughing bird. After that, he would deny the proclamation of the Im'oisian elders and return to the realm of the fae, find a virgin and bleed her dry, dissolve the poison in his blood and then resume his existence in the human world. He'd heard of a pod of selkie in the Scottish Highlands. Perhaps, after ending Rourke's life, he'd head north. The humid heat of Australia really wasn't pleasant. A change of climate would do him good.

But first, the thylacine.

A gust of wind slammed into him and he stumbled back a step. The very air was ripe with Detective Huddart's scent. She was so close. He could smell her fear in her sweat, taste her adrenaline in her exhaled breath. His dick stiffened, the thrill of the hunt flooding it with hot blood. This was why he did what he did—yes, the existence of such creatures offended him in every way, but it was the hunt he lived for. The epic battle for life between two beings of strength and purpose. A battle he won every time. A battle finishing in the sweetest way with the loser's life force seeping from its body, its heart slowing, slowing until the organ pumped blood no more.

Einar's mouth filled with fresh saliva and he slipped his way through a clump of prickly bushes. Jacqueline Huddart was in his nose and on his tongue. His grip on his knife tightened. The hilt thrummed against his palm, almost a living thing, forged in the pits below the realm of the Im'oisian to perform one duty and one duty only—butchering all he hunted. An extension of his arm.

Twigs and branches snagging on his clothes, the wind lashing at his face and hair, he stopped at the edge of the scrub and cast his gaze around the clearing before him. The thylacine was here. Somewhere. He slid his stare to the large outcrop of craggy rocks to his left. He narrowed his eyes, studying the formation. Was she hiding there? He pulled in a breath, but the wind whipped around him in a wild maelstrom, confusing his sense of smell. Dropping into a loose crouch, he studied the ground, looking for any signs of her progression.

The wind gusted at him, blowing topsoil, leaves, twigs and dead grass across the empty stretch before him, lashing around his ankles, whipping him with tiny particles of dirt. He squinted as dust scratched at his eyes. There were many tracks on the ground, but none of them made sense. Animal tracks, to be sure, but what kind? And where did they go? It was as if a cursed zoo had crossed this very way but a few moments ago.

He squinted, scraping his thumb pad over the bottom edge of his knife. He hated this country. "I know you're here, Jacqueline," he murmured, returning his attention to the four granite rocks before him. "But are you where I think you are, or is that just what you want me to believe?"

He stared hard at the rocks, pressing his fingers to the ground. Feeling the earth beneath him, seeking vibrations, seeking—

Something bit him. He jerked to his feet, glaring first at the tip of his middle finger and then at the ground where he'd placed his hand. An ant larger than any he'd seen scurried toward his foot, rust red in colour with pincers large enough to see clearly from a standing position. He raised his foot and twisted the ball of his boot against the ground, mashing the ant into the soil. "Fucker."

Lifting his head, he watched the rocky outcrop and stepped back deeper into the scrub. Every nerve in his body told him Jacqueline Huddart was in the dark alcove, most likely nursing the dying werewolf in her arms. He could draw her out, wait her out or—

An animal padded out from the bushes to his left, its sleek golden-brown coat glossy in the pale morning sun. The dark stripes on its back and tail were like bands of wet ink painted on its fur.

Einar froze, watching the thylacine raise its head and sniff the air. He drew the essence of his presence back into his body, holding it to him. Erasing his existence from the very world around him. The creature would have no knowledge he was here, even if the cursed wind blew at his back. Until he chose otherwise, Jacqueline Huddart was unaware she was being watched.

His lips curled into a slow smile. Perfect.

Caressing the blade of his knife with his thumb again, he redistributed his weight further onto the balls of his feet. She could not outrun him. He'd tested her speed earlier. She may hit like a lightning bolt, but she wasn't as fast as one. And with the wind blasting at him from behind her, she would not hear him coming at her. As soon as she lowered her head or turned away, he would be on her, his knife ready to sink into her back leg, severing her cruciate ligament, returning the wound she'd given him in kind. Just as he promised he would.

His smile stretched wider. After that, he'd track down his deceptive, secretive ex-partner, suspend him from the nearest tree and begin the fun. His cock grew stiffer.

The end of a hunt was sweet. The kill, sweeter. And this hunt, this kill, was the sweetest of all.

The thylacine lowered its head to the ground, sniffing the dirt near its front paws, tail wagging in lazy swipes.

Einar adjusted his grip on his knife and grinned. Now.

He shot from the bushes in a silent sprint, stare locked on the unsuspecting creature, knife raised. Elated rapture surged through his veins.

He screamed in furious disbelief when the thylacine lifted its head and transformed into Jacqueline Huddart, a cold smile curling her lips.

Jackie leapt at him. Crashing into his chest, driving him backward. He snatched at her hair, swinging his knife at her side, his eyes wide and burning with shocked contempt. She threw herself sideways, taking him with her, blocking his strike with her elbow as she rolled them both across the ground. She'd taken him by surprise. She was at her strongest, her animal and human soul as one for the first time. The spirit of the land, her land, her home flowed through her. If she was ever going to beat him, to make him suffer for what he'd done to Delanie, what he'd done to Marshall, it was now.

The wind lashed at them both, the trees roared, the sound growing wilder, louder. He writhed on the ground beneath her, fighting for his feet, the wicked silver of his knife blurring in deadly arcs in the corner of her eye. She ducked a savage swipe, smashing her forehead into his nose. She didn't have much time. He would disappear on her soon. Turn tail and vanish the second he believed she was bettering him.

She had to finish this. Now.

She smashed her forehead into his nose again, his blood wetting her face, stinging her eyes. She growled, the sound purely her thylacine, and struck him again, forehead to nose. Again. Again. Again. He bucked beneath her, thrashing against her body. Wailing. Screeching.

And then, blood gushing from his nose, he grabbed at her neck and drove his thumb into the small wound at its base. She snapped into a violent arc, agony spearing into her chest, down into her heart.

"Every prey has a weak spot, Detective Huddart," he snarled, driving his thumb in deeper, scraping at her flesh from within. "I thought yours was the human cunt and the were-wolf, but I was wrong." He pushed her backward, thumb gouging at the wound his knife had caused but a few hours earlier, teeth flashing at her in an insane grin. "You just. Don't. Like. Pain."

He thrust his body upward and slammed her back into the ground, gouging his thumb deeper into her throat. Choking her. Suffocating her.

Killing her.

He lowered his face to hers, his lips pressing to the side of her face. "But here's the thing," he whispered, voice bloated with triumph. "There's going to be a lot more pain, and no amount of subterfuge will stop it."

"Oh, I wouldn't say that."

Einar snapped his stare to the left, staring at the naked man standing but a few feet away. "No!"

"Looks like you've been fooled once again," Marshall drawled, just as Jackie shoved her knees up to her chest, planted her feet on Einar's chest and shoved him high into the air.

Marshall leapt—transforming mid-arc into a black wolf the size of a grizzly bear—and smashed into Einar, muzzle snapping shut around his neck. He drove him to the ground and pinned him there, front paws rammed against his shoulders, teeth buried in his flesh.

"No!" Einar screeched, thrashing underneath the wolf. Blood gushed from his neck in glistening rivulets, spurting onto the wolf's black muzzle. "No!" He writhed and bucked, arms flailing. "No!"

Jackie climbed to her feet, staring at the wolf, her thylacine howling, growling with ancient rapture. She stood motionless, the wind slipping around her like a fading caress, watching the wolf sink its teeth deeper into Einar's throat.

And then a sudden downward blast hit her and she looked

straight up, squinting at the sleek black helicopter hanging above her. A helicopter she recognized all too well.

Hillerman.

The wolf raised its head, looking down at the gibbering man. Blood dripped from its whiskers onto Einar's chest. The glaring morning sun turned each drop into a glinting onyx bead. With a shudder of its body, the wolf was Marshall once more, his fists pinning Einar to the ground, his face etched into disgusted contempt. "You don't deserve to live, Einar," he snarled. "But you don't deserve an easy death either."

He straightened to his feet, glaring at Einar still lying on the ground. "Don't bother translocating, elf. P.A.C. have a lock on your true DNA now." He stepped back, closer to Jackie, bending at the waist to reach for Einar's knife. "Your hunting days are over."

Einar hissed. "Not yet, they're not." He threw himself forward, straight at them both, his skin turning pitch-black, his eyes glowing red. He struck Marshall first, human façade gone. Large black hands wrapped around Marshall's throat, choking him, strangling him, talon-tipped fingers sinking into his throat.

And then Einar froze, his eyes growing wide, his mouth falling open.

Marshall's nostrils flared, his stare locked on Einar's face. "I beg to differ," he said, seconds before Einar crumpled to the ground with the hilt of his knife jutting from his armpit, blood oozing from the entry wound in a steady flow. "But what do I know? I'm just an old dog, aren't I?" He stared down at Einar, his expression impassive as the elf's body shuddered with one spasm, two, three, before going limp. Still. "Or is that a weak, gutless fool? I never can tell?"

Jackie let out a harsh breath and, before Marshall could raise his stare from Einar's lifeless form, she stepped up behind him and slapped him on the shoulder. "I told you not to move."

He turned, arms protecting his head, a wide grin on his lips. "No, you told me not to die. There's a difference."

She swiped at him again, and he laughed, snatching her wrists and tugging her closer to him. "In fact, I think you threatened to follow me to the—what did you call it, other side?—and beat me senseless if I did." He folded his arms around her, and she let him, pressing herself to his lean, hard body, resting her cheek against his heart. It beat with a steady pace, strong and sure and she smiled, burrowing closer still.

"How...?" She let the question hang, knowing she didn't need to finish it.

Marshall smoothed his arms up her back, threaded his fingers into her hair to tilt her head back. He gazed down into her eyes, that lopsided grin she loved so much curling one side of his mouth. "Maybe there was enough left in the vial." He touched his lips to her forehead in a lingering kiss that sent a ripple of joyous excitement down her spine. "Or maybe dire wolves are immune to elf poison." He grinned, his hands skimming to her arse, cupping each cheek in a firm hold. "I am pretty tough, you know."

Jackie grinned back at him. "There you go again with the sarcastic quips, Pacman."

He laughed. "Hey, you don't think you fell in love with me for my looks, do you?" A contemplative frown crossed his face and he tugged her hips harder to his. "Oh, wait, that's right. You think I'm goddamn sexy."

Jackie groaned, her heart—no, her very soul aglow with happiness.

Marshall nudged her forehead with his, his hands squeezing her butt. "Speaking of sexy," he murmured. "We're both buck-naked and Hillerman is just about to land that helicopter of his. You didn't think to pack us some clothes before you so insanely rescued me?"

Jackie laughed, smiling up at him. She opened her mouth, ready to tell him what she thought of the idea of him and clothes at this point in time and stopped. Frowning, she turned to study the small, bright yellow phone that suddenly dropped to the ground beside their feet.

Marshall looked at it, his arms not moving from her body one little bit. "Huh, wonder why Hillerman is throwing his phone at us?"

Jackie frowned at him and wriggled a little from his embrace to scoop the phone up. She pressed it to her ear, a sudden lump in her throat. "This is Detective Huddart."

"I've been trying to call you for the last ten minutes."

The weak croak in Jackie's ear stole her breath and she snapped straight, staring at Marshall. "Del?"

"Who else would it be?" Del's voice—barely more than a rasping whisper—sounded down the connection.

"But you're dead," Jackie burst out. "I heard Hillerman tell Marshall you didn't make it."

Del laughed, a weak cackle that filled Jackie's eyes with stinging tears. "Yeah, well I didn't for a bit. But these P.A.C. guys are pretty bloody clever for Yanks." There was a pause. "And cute."

Jackie pressed her hand to her mouth, biting on her lower lip. *Oh, God, Del. She's alive.*

"Just out of interest," Del went on in that rasping breath, "what have you two been doing? Playing fetch?"

"I see dying hasn't made a difference to your sense of humour." Jackie grinned, dragging her fingers through her hair as she held the phone to her ear. She wanted to cry. No, laugh. No, both.

"No," Del croaked, "but it's been hell on my wardrobe. Do you know how hard it is to get blood out of silk?"

Jackie laughed, her heart swelling with joy. Delanie was alive. And her same old self. "Stop your complaining, McKenzie. You got to ride in a helicopter. Wasn't that on your list of things to do?"

Her friend chuckled, the sound like a hitching wheeze.

"Talking of things to do, have you seen Agent Hillerman?" She paused, chuckling again. "I'd do *that* in a—"

"You definitely are better," Jackie cut Delanie off, shaking her head. "And why do I get the feeling you're not joking?"

"Because you know me so well," Delanie answered. "Now tell me, how long have I got to plan your bachelorette party?"

EPILOGUE

Four days later.
Launceston, Tasmania. The bottom of Australia.

Jackie Huddart rolled onto her side on the massive king-size bed and smiled. She watched Marshall stalk toward her across the hotel room's lushly carpeted floor, the sight of the man completely and utterly naked doing wonderfully strange things to her tummy. Her tummy, her heart. Her soul.

Damn it. How was she going to tell him she was leaving tomorrow?

They'd spent four days sequestered away in the most luxurious hotel room she'd ever seen, laughing, joking, relaxing. Four days of losing themselves in each other's bodies anytime and every time they wanted. Four days of discovering what it meant to be together, completely together without fear of impending death or dismemberment.

It was kind of nice.

She grinned at the understatement. "Kind of nice" didn't come close to describing it. In fact, Jackie was pretty certain there wasn't a word *to* describe it. Not just the sex—which was unbelievable—but the deep sense of everything being what it should be every time Marshall looked at her, every time he touched her. The undeniable contentment she felt at the sound of his voice, the sheer happiness she couldn't ignore.

Nor want to exist without. Ever.

And she had to leave tomorrow.

Don't think about that yet. That's still twenty-four hours away.

Stopping at the foot of the bed, Marshall gave her a slow grin. "So, room service ordered." He dropped onto the mattress and moved toward her on all fours, his gaze locked firmly on her face. "What pray tell, do you want to do while we wait for breakfast, Detective Huddart?"

Jackie's belly flip-flopped, her body telling her exactly what it wanted to do. Wrap her arms around his neck, pull him down on top of her and kiss him senseless. To begin with. After that—

Marshall's phone rang, the unmistakable sound of Duran Duran's "Hungry Like the Wolf" filling the room.

"You've got to be kidding me?" He glared at the offending device over his shoulder. "Talk about bad timing."

Jackie laughed. It was P.A.C. calling. The head of the agency had spoken at length with Marshall since Hillerman returned them both to civilization, each conversation growing shorter, until the last one—occurring less than an hour ago—had lasted less than ten minutes.

Marshall had taken all the calls on the hotel room's balcony, returning every time with an expression on his face Jackie couldn't decipher. She'd asked him the last time if everything was okay, and he'd dropped her a wink and a drawled, "Don't worry about it, darlin'."

Before she could question him again—she was still a cop, after all—he'd climbed onto the bed and buried his head between her thighs, effectively ending any thought except how amazingly talented his tongue was.

Now, with Duran Duran emanating from his phone so soon, Jackie couldn't help but suspect the amazing tongue fucking Marshall had given her may have been a diversionary tactic. He was, after all, a field agent from a secret US agency.

She lifted an eyebrow at him. "Are you going to get that?"

For a short moment, she thought he wasn't. He looked down at her, that same unreadable expression on his face that he'd worn before, his eyes holding hers. And then, with a lopsided grin, he climbed off the bed and snatched up his phone from the side table.

"Rourke here," he said, giving her a quick glance before snatching up his robe and crossing the room to step out onto the balcony again.

Jackie's chest tightened and she slumped back on the bed. She didn't know what unsettled her the most, that Marshall seemed to be keeping something from her, or that she was keeping something from him?

She had to return to Sydney tomorrow. Her commander expected her back on the job. She had cases to close and paperwork to complete. She *was* a cop. A Sydney cop. And she had to go back. Life—real life, not the wonderful existence she'd been living the last four days—didn't stop because she'd fallen in love.

So, when are you going to tell Marshall?

"You know," Marshall commented from the balcony doorway and Jackie jumped, her pulse quickening. Had she thought the ten-minute phone call short? This one must have only lasted sixty seconds. "I used to think you would be a mean poker player, but your face is telling me all sorts of things at the moment."

For some reason, Jackie's pulse beat faster. Maybe it was the laconic tone to his voice, maybe it was the way he threw his robe aside, revealing the naked strength of his body. Maybe it was the rigid length of his cock jutting upward from the junction of his thighs. "And what is my face telling you?" she asked, pushing herself into an upright position and fixing him with a level gaze.

He chuckled, straightened from the doorjamb and crossed to the bed. "That you have something to tell me."

He placed his hand on her shoulder and, with barely any resistance from her, pushed her backward, covering her body with his in a slow, fluid slide.

Jackie's pussy flooded with damp tension and she sucked in a shaking breath, smoothing her hands up his back as she met his eyes with hers. Damn it, she didn't want to go. Not now. Not ever.

"But before you do tell me," he murmured, grazing his lips along the line of her jaw until he nuzzled at the little dip beneath her ear, "there's something I have to ask you."

Jackie stilled, her breath catching in her throat.

Please don't ask me to move to America.

The unexpected thought whispered through her head, bringing with it the sudden realization she wasn't going anywhere, not even back to Sydney. She was home. Where she was meant to be. Tasmania was her home. It was in her heart and blood.

Just as Marshall was.

And she couldn't live without either, God help her.

Lifting his head, Marshall studied her, his expression once again unreadable. He cupped her face with one hand and brushed his thumb over her bottom lip. "Fancy transferring to the Tasmanian police force?"

Jackie placed her palms on his hard bare chest and pushed him away, her pulse pounding in her neck. She fixed him with a level look, her throat squeezing tighter still. "Why?"

He grinned. "You know all those phone calls I've been making this morning? Well, the last one was the director of P.A.C. officially accepting my resignation. Albeit, quite reluctantly and with a few choice words."

Jackie's heart leapt into her oh-so-tight throat. "Resignation? Why…?"

Cocking one eyebrow, he lowered his head back to hers.

"Would I resign?" He chuckled softly, the deep sound vibrating through his body into hers. "Might have something to do with the dog-walking business I bought here in Launceston a couple of hours ago."

Jackie's eyes widened. He'd bought a dog-walking business? Here in…

Launceston, Jackie. Your home.

He caught her gasp of surprised joy with his smiling mouth, his mouth slanting over hers. His tongue traced her lips and she wrapped her arms around his neck and pulled him hard against her body, deepening the kiss with wicked abandonment.

It seemed her heart and blood was right. She *wasn't* going anywhere. She was exactly where she was meant to be.

With Marshall. In Tasmania.

Deep within her soul, her thylacine growled. Contented and utterly at peace.

And downright horny.

SAVAGE RETRIBUTION

SAVAGE AUSTRALIS, BOOK 1

LEXXIE COUPER

PREVIEW: SAVAGE RETRIBUTION

SAVAGE AUSTRALIS, BOOK ONE

An animal rights activist is about to get a crash course in werewolves. One she may not survive.

Savage Retribution
(*Savage Australis*, Book One)

Dublin—Four Months Ago

The stink of sex, sin and death seeped into Declan O'Connell's nostrils, overripe and acrid all at once. His lips curled into a silent snarl and he stepped deeper into the dank, dim building, the hair on his nape prickling.

This is not right.

The thought sent a ripple of tension through his already tight muscles. It *wasn't* right. The whole night hadn't been right; the anonymous tip about his sister's killer, the insistence he be here—at this place—at this time, the derelict, abandoned condition of the building. It didn't add up.

McCoy's not here, Dec. Shit, he's never been here. You can't even smell him on the air. Face it—this was a set up. And you've just walked right into it.

The snarl on his lips turned into a low growl and he felt the muscles in his body begin to coil tighter. Stretch. Grow.

Change.

Teeth grinding, Declan forced back the beast, denying it control of his body. He didn't know who had brought him here under false pretence—more than one person wanted him dead, and not all of them knew what he truly was. Better to walk out of the situation, not lope out on all fours.

A soft sound—barely louder than the snap of a dry blade of grass—shattered the silence of the derelict brothel and Declan froze.

He *wasn't* alone. Someone was—

The dark blur hit him from the left. Hard.

Something large and heavy crashed him to the ground. Teeth, long, sharp and slick with saliva, snapped at his face. He was barreled across the debris-strewn floor, chunks of concrete and shards of broken glass grinding into his knees and elbows, biting into his flesh even through the leather of his jacket. His favorite Levi's tore but he didn't give a rat's ass. Not with a fucking huge, black wolf trying to tear his throat out.

The animal lashed out, razor-sharp teeth missing his neck by a hair's width. Declan felt hot saliva splatter his cheek. He struggled on his back, pinned to the crap-covered floor by the wolf's writhing, savage weight. The stench of urine attacked his breath, invaded his senses with the mark of an animal Declan had tasted before.

His eyes snapped wide open, locked on the burning, iridescent gold stare of the wolf attacking him.

You!

The word formed in Declan's head. Cold. Furious.

Seconds before the beast in his own blood roared into existence and he changed. Human muscle into canine. Man into wolf.

He bucked the animal off him, snapping at its soft underbelly as it flipped and twisted to the side. Warm, coppery blood filled his mouth and throat. He leapt onto all fours, staring at the black *loup garou*, smelling apprehension and pain leech from it in thick, sickly waves.

Baring his teeth, he held its gold stare, his growl low. *You've fucked with the wrong wolf, asshole.*

"Gotcha."

The voice—low, smug and female—sounded to Declan's left at the exact second something sharp, pointed and icy sank into his neck, right at the spot where vein became jugular. Intense cold, like the breath of Death itself, consumed him. His muscles contracted, his heart seemed to swell and, wracked in pain, he collapsed to the floor.

Incapable of movement.

Trapped. And utterly vulnerable.

MORE ROMANCE FROM LEXXIE
COUPER...

Fire Mates Series

Sera's Dragon
How to Love Your Dragon
Tigress and the Dragon
Scorched Desire

The Always Series

Unconditional
Unforgettable
Undeniable

The Outback Skies Series

Bound to You
Breathless for You
Burn for You
Bare for You
Better with You

The Heart of Fame Series

Love's Rhythm
Muscle for Hire

Guarded Desires
Steady Beat
Lead Me On
Blame it on the Bass
Getting Played
Blackthorne

See the full book list at www.lexxiecouper.com

ABOUT LEXXIE COUPER

Lexxie Couper started writing when she was six and hasn't stopped since. She's not a deviant, but she does have a deviant's imagination and a desire to entertain readers with her words. Add the two together and you get erotic romances that can make you laugh, cry, shake with fear or tremble with desire. Sometimes all at once.

When she's not submerged in the worlds she creates, Lexxie's life revolves around her family, a husband who thinks she's insane, an indoor cat who likes to stalk shadows, and her daughters, who both utterly captured her heart and changed her life forever.

Lexxie lives by two simple rules – measure your success not by how much money you have, but by how often you laugh, and always try everything at least once. As a consequence, she's laughed her way through many an eyebrow raising adventure. You can find details of her writing at www.LexxieCouper.com

CPSIA information can be obtained
at www.ICGtesting.com
Printed in the USA
BVHW030143060320
574226BV00001B/10

9 780648 653295